Praise for *Shadow of Light*

"*Shadow of Light* is a heady mix of metaphysics and astrophysics, theology and quantum science, end-of-the-world apocalypse and madcap comic romance, all served up in a great bouillabaisse that is part thriller, part science fiction, part mystery, but mostly good old-fashioned story telling. Mr. Power is aptly named: he casts a potent spell from the first page, and doesn't break it until well past the last one."

—MARK BUCHANAN, BESTSELLING AUTHOR OF
Your God Is too Safe AND *Spiritual Rhythm*

"After reading Rodney Christian Power's book, I recognised that he is not only a master story teller, but a gifted craftsman who intuitively knows how to entertain and hold the reader's attention from beginning to end. What a great read from an imaginative, talented writer. *Shadow of Light* will make a great movie."

—SARAH NICHOLS, HOLLYWOOD SCREEN WRITER
AND AUTHOR OF *One Step at a Time*

"*Shadow of Light* is a terrific story, one I will read again just for the joy of it."

—GORDON PINSENT, AWARD-WINNING AUTHOR,
ACTOR, AND PLAYWRIGHT

"The work of an emerging master who is sure to be soon hailed by all readers, *Shadow of Light* is rich with insight, challenge and texture. A rewarding read, no matter your literary tastes."

—ROBERT MACDONALD, AUTHOR AND PUBLISHER

❧

ACKNOWLEDGMENTS

I wish to acknowledge the invaluable assistance of Kenneth Tapping, Ph.D., Astrophysics, M.Sc., Space Physics, B.Sc., Mathematics and Physics, astronomer at the Dominion Radio Astrophysical Observatory in British Columbia. Dr. Tapping was kind enough to review the manuscript and provide me with details on how the universe is unfolding. However . . . this being a work of fiction, there are places where I chose to wander off into the great unknown. So if you happen to come across something not quite kosher, please do not hold Ken responsible. To misquote Rudyard Kipling: Science is science and miracles are miracles, and ne'er the twain shall meet.

My thanks also to Queenie Huling, Director of Public Affairs for Kings Country Hospital in Brooklyn, for taking time to show me around this magnificent building.

RODNEY CHRISTIAN POWER

SHADOW
OF LIGHT

Charlotte, Tennessee 37036

❧

This book is dedicated to the
memory of our daughter Jo-Ann,
who didn't want to leave early,
but had to go anyway.

As if you could kill time without injuring eternity.

Henry David Thoreau

MONDAY

0725 HRS

∽

The reason Brooks Hennessey found himself in church that morning was because he'd missed Sunday Mass. If he had missed Mass because he was sick or traveling or something like that, he would not have bothered. But the third commandment was sacred to him. The sixth commandment, the reason for his absence, he had learned to accommodate ages ago.

Brooks had spent the entire weekend with his new mistress, Annie. Annie was twenty-two, Brooks forty-four, but the age difference presented no problem, at least not in this early stage of their relationship. A passionate lover, the big man had no license to display his talents at home, which left him little choice but to seek consolation elsewhere. As for Rachael, she didn't seem to care one way or another what Brooks did. They still maintained a cordial relationship but hadn't shared the same bedroom for eight years.

So come Monday, Brooks was up at six sharp to make certain he caught early Mass before work. Brooks did not aspire to being a *good* Christian—his lifestyle prohibited such a lofty goal—but being brought up in an Irish Catholic family had superimposed a certain structure on his life. Going to church was part of it. Although, true enough, as a result of his affairs he could not receive Holy Communion, and it was this self-imposed separation from God that weighed so heavily upon him.

He raised his head to take another quick peek at the Gang of Five, as they were known in his younger years: five great frescos laid out in a semicircle behind the magnificent marble alcove that housed the crucified Christ. All the main players were there: Moses, David, Jesus, John

3

the Baptist, and Paul. For some reason this morning Brooks felt as if those cold painted eyes were bearing down on him. He had the distinct impression that John the Baptist in particular was annoyed about something.

When the church door creaked open halfway through Mass to allow old Mrs. Kelly to enter, Brooks had no way of knowing his nefarious lifestyle was about to suffer a fatal blow. He could hear the labored breathing as she made her way up the long church aisle, her cane tapping away on the tiled floor. Brooks was kneeling on the outside of the tenth row, immediately right of the center aisle.

The old lady struggled by him, heading for her usual spot in the front pew. Brooks knew her well enough, had spoken to her a few times at the church socials, the bake sales. He recalled her keen sense of humor. "Don't forget, Brooksie," she'd once said to him, "God gave us laughter to keep us sane." But the old gal had a sharp tongue in her head and could tell you off at the drop of a hat if need be. Only a few weeks ago Brooks had listened to her lay into some kid for wearing his baseball cap in church.

Then, suddenly, she was down. Flat out, just like that.

The basilica of St. Andrew's was less than one-tenth filled, and Kathleen Kelly quickly became the center of attention. Brooks reached her first. As he was helping the old lady to her feet, he was shocked to discover that she had just taken a good beating: glasses askew, bright blood dripping from her nose, her upper lip torn open, one puffed eye bruised and closed.

"Good Lord! We'd better get you over to a doctor right away."

Mrs. Kelly righted her glasses and fixed her one good eye on Brooks Hennessey as she pushed his hands away. Her would-be benefactor could smell the blood mixed in with the sharp tang of mothballs wafting up from the green velour dress she wore. Up close like that her body odor easily overpowered the lingering echoes of yesterday's burned incense.

The old lady wiped the blood away with the back of her left hand, took a good grip on her cane, then continued toward the front of the church. Brooks had no choice but to follow awkwardly behind, a kind of overgrown guardian angel, his two huge hands hovering beside the frail shoulders ready to catch her if she went down again.

To his surprise, Mrs. Kelly lumbered past the front pew and began to make her way up the altar steps. Part way through the Consecration,

Father Harry Flynn paused with the chalice in midair to take a quick look at the strange entourage climbing his steps.

Father Harry was seventy-four, eight years younger than Kathleen Kelly. He just cleared the five-three mark, and his ample girth brought to mind nobody more than Friar Tuck of Sherwood Forest fame, or at least the way the movies portrayed him. Beneath his shining dome was a round, cherubic face easily given to mirth.

Being pastor at St. Andrew's Parish, located bang smack in the middle of lower west side Brooklyn, gave him, if not the ultimate pragmatic outlook on life, then one close to it. Many of his parishioners believed if the devil himself popped up beside him, Harry Flynn wouldn't bat an eye.

Nevertheless, he could read danger in the one cold blue eye now bearing down on him. He frowned and gave a short jerk of his head, a clear signal to Brooks to get this battered creature off his altar.

The big Irishman took a firm hold of her shoulders and whispered, "Come on now, let's go have a seat and I'll take a look at you."

But Kathleen Kelly had not come to church that particular morning to attend Mass. She had an entirely different purpose in mind. "You take your frigging meat-hooks off me, Brooks Hennessey. I got something to say, and neither you nor his Royal Highness here—" she cast a mean, squinty look in the priest's direction "—is going to stop me."

Mrs. Kelly might be a diminutive little thing, just parchment stretched over a few old bones, but she owned a voice as shrill as a banshee. Harry Flynn took a deep breath. He had not yet spoken the words that would change the wine into the blood of Christ. He lowered the chalice to the altar.

Everyone in church was intent on the unfolding drama.

Reaching under his vestments to switch off his microphone, Father Harry glided around the altar to put an end to this nonsense. Two red-soutaned altar boys hastened to back out of his way.

In a whispered but firm voice he said, "Now see here, Kathleen, you get yourself off of my altar this instant and let Brooks run you over to Lutheran."

Harry Flynn's face froze when the old lady slapped her cane down on the altar, hard. Before he or Brooks could move a muscle, she swept it across the marble surface in one swift motion, scattering the filled chalice and the ciborium with its sacred hosts across the sanctuary. Blood-red wine sloshed over the tiles while the communion wafers drifted down through the air like tiny wingless angels.

Turning to face the assembly, Mrs. Kelly shouted, "It's all a big farce—that's what it is! Where is Jesus Christ? Do you see him? No, because he's not here, that's why!"

The startled priest clamped his hand over her mouth while Brooks pinned down the old lady's arms. False teeth or not, they bit Father Harry's finger clean through to the bone. He uttered something unrelated to the service and jerked his hand away.

"Four times in four months—the cowardly little friggers! Take my purse, shove me around, beat me up—and me a poor old widow! I come up here and pray. I ask for help. Just get them to leave me alone, I ask. I'm an old woman. I never carry more than twenty bucks. This morning I only had five. So they beat me bad. I called out to Jesus Christ . . . "

She paused then, as if the strain had become too much. Brooks saw the tears falling away from her one good eye. There was no question of removing her now. Brooks knew it, and Father Harry knew it. He looked at Brooks and shook his head.

"I didn't want a whole lot out of life, just to be left alone. But they won't leave me alone, because I'm old and weak. If God was real, like we been told, He would never allow such going's on. He would never—"

Her mouth sprang open and a loud gasp fell out. She dropped the offending cane and made a grab for the nearest corner of the altar. Brooks still had his arm around her shoulders, but he was too slow to prevent her collapse to the floor. The two men knelt beside her and watched as the frail bones began to shake violently.

Brooks raised her head with one hand while Father Harry picked up one of the hosts and placed it on her tongue. She spit it out.

At that moment Brooks became aware of a tearing sound, a sudden wild rush of air, a pressure on his lungs. He thought this unnatural, but quickly forgot about it when he noticed one startling blue eye staring up at him with such vehemence that it made him cringe.

"You're a fool, Brooks Hennessey," she managed to croak. "Get away from all this while you can. Don't waste your life like I did. It's all a big lie . . . "

He could see that she was fading fast.

"And Jesus Christ—" she twisted her bleeding lips into a sneer "—*is the biggest lie of all!*"

Kathleen Kelly's final condemnation echoed across the church's hushed interior and seemed to hang in the air. Eileen Cantwell, a nurse over at St. Paul's, appeared beside them. She pushed the men aside and placed her finger on the old woman's carotid artery. Unable to find a pulse, she pressed her ear against the woman's chest.

Nothing!

Pale, she looked up into the priest's eyes. "May the saints preserve her, Father. She's gone, she is. Just like that, the poor darling."

Father Harry whispered, "Are you certain, Eileen? She had a lot of fight in her only a moment ago. Can't you do something to . . . " But his voice died away with Mrs. Cantwell's stern look and vigorous shaking of her head.

The whole episode had taken but a few minutes, which caused Brooks to wonder if Kathleen Kelly hadn't just been struck down from on High.

Father Harry rose to his feet, switched on his throat mike, then turned toward his anxious congregation. "Dear friends in Christ, it is a sad and terrible event we just witnessed here this morning. This poor woman, overwrought as she was, mocked the power of Almighty God and has now paid the price. I want all of you to come up and gather around the altar so we can say a prayer for the soul of Kathleen Kelly. I fear at this moment she is in desperate need of our help."

0740 HRS

⚜

There had always been some concern about Sarius. He was an independent spirit, and independent spirits provided ample reason for concern. Belonging to the lowest of all angelic orders, the Ophanim to be precise, he was headstrong and mischievous to the point of driving his fellow angels to distraction. His recent requests to become a human guardian were rejected as a matter of policy.

As angels are wont to do from time to time, Sarius had merely been seeking a process that would lend purpose to his existence; but alas, no member of the Ophanim or even of the three levels above them, had ever been accorded such high privilege. The Chief Guardian, Saraqael, along with other notables of the realm, held a firm belief that the lower orders were entirely unsuitable. They were all too prone to creating mischief, which is why their movements throughout the universe were closely monitored by the big boss, Metatron, who on numerous occasions had found reason to voice his concern to the Master. But God usually allowed His firstborn to do what they wanted, within reason. Both Saraqael and Metatron were of the opinion that God derived a certain degree of enjoyment from their unbridled activities, not unlike a doting father with a house full of exuberant children.

Of late, due to the close of another earth millennium, curiosity had prompted Sarius to once again tune in on the human experiment. The last time he had visited earth was to watch Moses lead the Israelites out of Egypt. This time around, the angel had been observing for some fifty years, a mere pinprick of eternity. Although he regularly covered the entire globe, Sarius tended to spend much of his time in America,

9

where on occasion he was known to succumb to the urge to intervene in the activities of human affairs where he was not allowed. Direct interference by the Guardians was considered a normal part of their mandate, but not for other angels, at least not without permission.

New York City, Brooklyn in particular, intrigued this particular visitor because he found it to be a true microcosm of all the earth's peoples. More races and colors and religions were squeezed together in Brooklyn than in any other place on the planet.

So it was that Sarius, hovering beside Brooks Hennessey's right shoulder at the very moment of Kathleen Kelly's unfortunate demise, made the abrupt and completely unauthorized decision to take over her body.

Brooks held Mrs. Kelly's tiny head tenderly in the palm of one hand, his eyes closed, while members of the congregation shuffled into place at the foot of the altar, all craning their necks to get a better look at the poor dear.

"*Blessed Mother of God!*" exclaimed Mrs. Cantwell.

Brooks opened his eyes to find that Mrs. Kelly's good eye had also popped open, and a broad smile, more like a smirk, was planted across her face. Amazed, he withdrew his hand from behind her head.

Father Harry had already begun the prayer, but stopped, looked down, then took a step back when Mrs. Kelly suddenly sat up without the use of her hands, just sprang forward as if an unseen force had pushed her.

The cause of all the furor finally stood up and stared at the wine-soaked altar, at the tiny communion wafers scattered around the floor. She touched her puffed-up eye as a mystified look crept over her battered face.

After a moment or two she turned and smiled shyly at her would-be mourners. "It's a terrible thing I've done for sure, but my poor old head was rattled from the beating I'd just taken."

She took up her little blue walking cane, patted Mrs. Cantwell's hand affectionately, then departed the altar without visible effort.

The crowd parted in astonished silence to let her through, but she'd taken only a few steps when she turned around and called out in an authoritative voice, "You, Brooks Hennessey, you'd better come along with me." In a dry tone she added, "Perhaps you might pick up something useful for that foolish thing you publish."

Brooks was owner and editor of the weekly neighborhood paper, the *Village Review,* mostly advertising with local gossip added for color. He hesitated, but Father Harry whispered in his ear, "I don't care if you have to carry her, but get her over to Lutheran Medical Center for an examination. It's obvious that beating she took has addled her brains."

Brooks was six-six, two hundred and seventy pounds, a gentle giant. Mrs. Kelly was four-eleven, eighty-three pounds. One could scour the entire borough, from Bay Ridge to Spring Creek, from Greenpoint to Coney Island, and never find a more mismatched couple.

Outside, high up on the church steps, the newly-overhauled Kathleen Sarius Kelly, in full possession of the old woman's retained consciousness, including her arthritis, decided right off to shed those memories associated with pain. The angel had successfully mapped out human physiology when he first took an interest in them, and simply by taking in a few gulps of polluted Brooklyn air, successfully replaced most of the atoms in Mrs. Kelly's bloodstream. Next he forcibly expunged those cellular memories he did not wish to retain, allowing their defective molecules to float free in the environment, perhaps to settle in on some other unsuspecting and perhaps undeserving person.

Sarius was fully aware that he had far exceeded the limits of non-interference, and puzzled though he was by this sudden uncontrollable urge to become directly involved in human affairs, he did not see any reason why he should hobble around in pain as Kathleen Kelly had done. As an afterthought he removed her twisted glasses and tossed them in a nearby refuse container. The angel would not be needing them.

It was mid October, the weather clear and still warm, but the big old elms on either side of the church steps were already sprouting clusters of gold and a few smatterings of red. The visitor saw, with new eyes, that the buildings across the road were a clutch of four-story brownstones, although their actual colors were cream and brick and tan, with the lower level a series of little shops: a flower shop, a grocery store, hair stylist, an animal clinic, and Mario's Unisex, which gave Sarius reason to pause, not being fully acquainted with the term *unisex.* Myriad odors assaulted the angel's reclaimed nose, the most pleasing by far coming from an Italian bakery in the next block.

Brooks was puzzled. If he didn't know better, he would have sworn old Mrs. Kelly was viewing the area for the first time. As he waited, he considered that even though the new millennium was well underway, a whole lot of people, in New York, in America, everywhere in the world, were still fidgety about the notion that God was going to pull the plug. Certainly, with the current economic woes and the usual worldwide rumblings of war, natural disasters, and famine, a fair swath of quirky religious groups were quick to jump on the Mayan calendar bandwagon and beat their drums, but he suspected most folks were fed-up with hearing this drivel day after day.

As they made their way down the granite steps, Mrs. Kelly glanced up at her huge companion. "Annie," she said, forming her swiftly-healing bruised face into a wry smile.

Brooks took a sudden coughing fit, covering up his shock as best he could. "How's that, Mrs. Kelly?"

She banged her cane against his ankle. "Now don't go being foolish with me, Brooks Hennessey. I know for a fact that you misbehaved yourself eleven times in the space of forty hours. There's a whole lot of randy teenagers around who can't keep up that pace. Little wonder that young woman has gone crazy over you."

Inwardly Brooks cried out, *I don't believe this!* He and Annie had driven thirty miles north to a nondescript little motel on the outskirts of White Plains. How could Mrs. Kelly possibly know about their weekend?

Monday morning commercial traffic along Fifth Avenue was brisk. An '88 Dodge pickup truck full of pumpkins eased by them, its rusted cab crammed with dirty-faced children twisting their necks in all directions. Angry drivers screamed obscenities as they pulled out around the truck. Seven little Chinese girls holding hands scurried across the street in the smoky wake of a city bus, their identical bright blue costumes making them appear like giant beads of lapis.

"Yes," Mrs. Kelly said reflectively, "too bad it's all over with. Give her a call, why don't you; break the news as gently as you can." She tucked her little rouged cheeks into a sudden grin as if her suggestion was the funniest thing she'd heard in ages, then glanced up at Brooks, clicking her false teeth a few times before adding, "Tell her you found a more experienced woman. That ought to do it."

Brooks knew Father Harry was right. Old Mrs. Kelly was definitely screwy in the head. As they crossed Fifth Avenue with the light, he realized they were heading south, away from Lutheran. "Listen here, my love, I was just ordered to get you over to the hospital for a check. Why, at your age you never know what the damage might be. Then you should have a talk with the police, give them descriptions of the dirty devils who beat you up."

They were at that moment passing beneath a faded red awning that advertised Spanish-American cuisine, and still heading south. Next to the restaurant was the narrow entrance to a private residence with a big gray garbage container parked beside the door.

A warm childhood memory came charging into the angel's consciousness.

Mrs. Kelly stopped, rolled up the sleeve of her dress. "Tell you what, Brooksie, how about you and me twist wrists." Smiling, she added, "That's how me old dad used to settle his affairs. If you win, off we go to the hospital. I win, then it's on we go as I command. That fair enough?"

At this point Brooks was only humoring the victim. *If this is what it takes to get her out of my hair,* he thought, *it's a small price to pay.*

Mrs. Kelly rested her elbow on the lid, the meatless arm with its spindly wrist ready for action. The big man knew he'd have to be real careful or he might hurt her, but setting his paw up against her tiny hand was a sight good for a laugh any day, and he could not resist a quiet chuckle.

"You ready now?" Brooks asked his miniature opponent.

"Indeed I am, and don't go getting too surprised if I happen to beat you, okay?"

Three black kids, preteens, paused to catch the action. They said nothing, just stared at the odd couple. The bigger kid was toting a ghetto blaster that spewed forth rap music so loud it made the walls of a nearby building vibrate. The kids soon realized they were watching some kind of playacting. Why, or for whose benefit, they didn't know.

Bang! The big man's knuckles slammed hard against the steel lid. "I warned you. Want to go again?"

Brooks, his knuckles raw and bleeding, gritted his teeth, crushed her hand in his, and pulled. Mrs. Kelly held his hand steady, turned her head toward the boys and said, "Mr. Allmand is real tired of you children hassling him. You stay away from him now, or I'll come after you and whale the daylights out of the three of you. That's a promise."

Then she drove Brooks's hand so hard into the steel lid that he thought all his bones were broken. *"Jesus Christ!"* he cried out in pain.

"Not allowed, Brooks! Definitely not allowed. You use the Man's name once more, I'll scour your mouth with bleach."

Brooks had tears in his eyes. The three kids shrugged. They knew a sham when they saw one. Moving off, the one with the noisemaker called out, "Screw you, Granny."

Granny studied the kid for a few seconds, then reached out with her cane and jerked him back by the neck. The fact that the kid was twenty feet away did not escape Brooks.

The youth was a foot taller than Mrs. Kelly. He took a good swing, but she caught his hand and held it. At the same instant, the blaster's twin speakers went silent.

After a moment of scowling intensity she lightened up and said, "This is your lucky day, Darryl. You don't deserve it, but I've decided to let you go." She released her hold on the scared youth, then cracked him on the elbow with her cane. "But mark my words: I'll give you a good thrashing if you don't behave yourself. Well?"

Darryl's eyes flared so wide they were more white than black. He nodded vigorously.

"Can't hear you, Darryl."

"Yes, ma'am—I mean, no, ma'am. We gonna stay away from Allmand's Grocery. Promise."

Mrs. Kelly rubbed her bruised eye open and gave the boy a warm, motherly smile. When the CD reactivated itself, she declared in rap-like verse: *"Hey, Darryl, rap is crap. Ain't no one ever tell you 'dat?"*

Brooks had his damaged hand jammed tight under his left armpit to help squelch the pain. He was half-sitting back against the garbage container, deeply in shock. He had just seen things happen that were not possible.

A bewildered Greek hairdresser and his young wife stood in the doorway of their nearby shop, watching the action. Mrs. Kelly reached up and extracted Brooks's hand. The moment she touched it, the pain vanished.

"A little penance wouldn't go astray, lover boy."

Brooks was not real surprised to see that his hand looked good as new. In a fervent whisper he said, "Listen here, Mrs. Kelly, you want to tell me what the hell's going on?"

Donning a strange, half-twisted smile, she replied, "Hell is one thing that is definitely not going on. Why don't you tell me, Brooks Hennessey? Go ahead, give it your best shot."

The big Irishman sensed the new vitality, noticed that the puffed eye was almost completely healed, the bruises already withdrawn. He was very aware that he had just witnessed a miraculous event. Three or four, more likely.

Thoughtfully, but with his heart racing a lot faster than it should, he said, "We figured you were a goner in church. Mrs. Cantwell was sure of it. Then you popped up off the floor like Lazarus, walked down the steps without any problem, flattened my hand like it was a baby's. And you just pulled that kid back from twenty feet away with a two-foot cane. Now I see your face is nearly fixed up. Something happened in there, didn't it?"

Smiling vaguely, her newly rejuvenated eyes continuing to register the activity along the street, she replied, "Go on."

Aside from his weakness for the opposite sex, over the years the editor of the *Village Review* had come to adopt a relatively devout lifestyle: heavily involved with church functions, personal friends with half a dozen priests, on a first-name basis with Bishop O'Rourke. He read his Bible, said a few prayers most days, contributed more than his share in the collection, and regularly shelled out a few bucks to the local bums.

Above all, Brooks Hennessey was a believer. He knew that something very wonderful and very remarkable had just taken place right under his nose. And whatever it was, he was part of it.

He stared down at her: eighty-two-year-old Kathleen Kelly. A tiny, frail-looking creature with a narrow, triangular face covered with patchy brown age spots and inundated with wrinkles. Sunken cheeks, a pointed nose, dentures stained brown from all the tea she drank. Her hair was white and without body, done up in an odd-looking bun piled on top of her head. The only saving grace were her eyes, clear and blue as a summer's sky, and it was those eyes that dominated Mrs. Kelly's appearance.

Brooks shrugged his great stooped shoulders. "You were real mad up on the altar, yelling out that everything was a big farce. Then you dropped deader than a Thanksgiving turkey. A few minutes later you came back to life all full of piss and vinegar and began doing impossible things. I believe . . . well, even though you were being disrespectful, I think God answered your prayers, gave you all this strength—to do what, I can't guess. Scary, it is."

She caught his arm, urging him off the trash container and south along the sidewalk. "No doubt about it, God does work in mysterious ways. Even a bit of a mystery to me, to tell the truth. Anyway, I have a little matter to attend to, then we'll go by my place, pick up a few things. You suppose Rachael would mind if I moved in with you?"

This caught Brooks off guard. But he wasn't about to question what was taking place. "Boy . . . do you know Rachael?"

"Never met her, but, well, let's say I heard about her. Ice water in her veins. I admit it might take a bit of doing: you bringing home this pathetic old granny, one foot in the grave, threatening her lifestyle. Umm . . . what if you told her God asked you to look after me. Think she'd buy that?"

"Not a chance. But . . . " Brooks grinned at the idea racing through his oversized skull. "Rachael works out, keeps in real good shape. If you were to pull the same wrist stunt on her, that'd knock her down a peg or two."

"Bang on the money, Brooksie." Mrs. Kelly smiled, stuck her nose in the air, sucked in another lungful of atoms, did a major reshuffling of the trillions she already had, then proceeded to spin her cane around and around in her left hand with all the finesse of a professional baton twirler.

0810 HRS

❧

For sure, Mildred Manuel was a dowdy old thing, short and plump, without a look to bless herself. Even on a good day she looked befrazzled. Wild gray hair, and the cheap makeup she plastered onto her broad, flat face, usually in a hurry, often looked like the aftermath of a small battle. She had wide-spaced, poppy brown eyes, without any lashes to speak of. Her eyebrows, plucked to death at an early age, were only pencil lines, and smudged at that. But Millie had a heart as big as a football field, a smile that would melt a banker's heart, and one glance into those big doe eyes oozing with compassion, you knew right away that God had sent her into the world for the specific purpose of taking care of His less fortunate.

Since she lived only two doors away from Mrs. Kelly in an old but respectable brownstone just three blocks east of St. Andrew's, Millie knew absolutely everything that went on in the older woman's life. And there had certainly not been the slightest hint of any involvement with the editor of the *Village Review*. Having spotted the unlikely smile on her friend's face from half a block away, the one frail arm intimately linked into Brooks Hennessey's, the cane twirling away, Millie reacted to this peculiar sight by plunking herself in their path.

"Where are your glasses?" she demanded to know.

"Threw 'em away."

"That a fact? I happen to know, my dear, that you're blind as a bat without them."

"Not anymore," answered Mrs. Kelly with a proper tilt to her chin.

"Hmph! And what about your face?"

"Fell out of bed. But not to worry, because it so happens that this lovely young man has been kind enough to invite me to move in with him. Doesn't that just blow the air out of your drawers?"

Millie was twenty years younger than Mrs. Kelly, but looked more like ten years younger. Their friendship went back fifty years, and even though they loved and cared for each other without reserve, they often teased each other mercilessly. Her usual flippancy dulled for the moment at this news, Millie's face paled at the thought of Rachael Hennessey looking after her friend. How many days before the push over the staircase or a quick shove into the pool?

"God love us all, Kathy. I hope Brooks don't take offense, but Rachael Hennessey can't take care of a cat. How is she going to look after the likes of you?"

Brooks did not see the necessity of joining in the discussion, and therefore kept quiet, even if it was his wife they were badmouthing. The two women chatted away while Brooks tried real hard to figure out the purpose of the exercise. Did Mrs. Kelly really die? Had God allowed her to come back with some special powers? If so, why?

The discussion ended with a promise to meet later in the day. Moving along the sidewalk, Mrs. Kelly surprised Brooks again when she abruptly swung right into a dark alley.

"What now?"

With tiny feet moving so fast Brooks had to stretch out to keep up, she replied, "We're going to drop in on some old friends."

Seconds later Brooks spotted three young men propped up against a crumbling brick wall at the rear of Harry Shuster's restaurant smoking some cheap pot. Mrs. Kelly stopped when the trio came into view.

"You stay here, Brooksie. Watch the fireworks if you want. Little friggers will scamper away for sure if they catch sight of the likes of you keeping me company."

The three were not at all little, but long, skinny Puerto Rican dudes, early twenties, squinty eyes, scruffy beards, ponytails, silver rings dangling for one ear lobe, orange leather skull and crossbones vests—real meanies. Deafening rap music reverberated off the brick walls surrounding them. Hugging the wall so he would not be seen, Brooks knew instinctively that these were the ones who had earlier pounded the hell out of Mrs. Kelly. For some inexplicable reason, he felt sorry for them.

"Well now," drawled the leader, one Juan Guzman, as he slowly straightened up, "if it isn't that ugly hag again."

His cronies grinned at each other, automatically spreading out to surround the old woman. Each man registered the fact that their victim's face looked as good as new, better even, which was strange, considering they had knocked her about barely an hour earlier. Although this registered a note or two of confusion, it quickly became lost inside their squishy brains.

Mrs. Kelly walked right up to Guzman, tapped her cane lightly against his forehead, smiled, and said sweetly, "Time's up, Juan."

The boss man grabbed at the cane, missed, then made a vicious swipe at the old lady, who moved beyond his reach faster than the eye could follow.

"Twenty-seven years old, with the last ten spent wreaking havoc in this neighborhood. You're a real bad one, Juan—a complete waste of a life. You got nothing at all going for you. Nothing."

Mrs. Kelly's eyes grew as cold as cold can be. "Never picked a fight with a grown man, have you? Raped that nine-year-old Virginia Walters over at the old Mason warehouse last month. Girl's a real mess now, her mind all broken into little pieces. In fact, Juan, you might be interested to know that you have the distinction of being the lowest scumbag in the entire lower west side, and that's saying something. I see no reason why you should be allowed to continue preying on the old, the weak, people who can't protect themselves."

The other two remained still, awaiting orders. The little old woman turned to them and said quietly, "Better don your asbestos suits, boys. The party's over."

Brooks never did figure out what happened next. In essence, the three hoodlums vanished before his eyes. After waiting a minute or so to make certain his vision wasn't playing tricks on him, he walked over and stood beside a very serious Kathleen Kelley.

He took a cautious look around, saw no sign of the Puerto Ricans, then reached down to shut off the ghetto blaster. "Where did they get to?"

Mrs. Kelly didn't answer for a few moments, seemingly deep in thought. She finally looked up at him, her forehead etched with concern. "I wasn't sure how that would go down with the chief."

She shook her head several times, her tidy little hair bun flopping back and forth. More to herself than to Brooks she added, "I think they're losing interest. Not a good sign, Brooksie, not good at all."

Then Brooks noticed a small pile of white ash at his feet. A tiny pyramid. He had nearly stepped on it. A thin wisp of smoke rose from the ash. Although his sense of logic rejected the swift and terrible conclusion he reached, this same sense of logic was completely shattered when, upon glancing around, he spotted two more identical pyramids.

When Brooks looked hard into the old woman's sky-blue eyes, his heart jumped into his mouth. In a croaking voice, he said, "You're not Mrs. Kelly, are you?"

Sarius was giving serious consideration to the potential fallout from his provocative actions. A few moments went by before the angel replied, "Do I look like Betty Grable, maybe?"

"I'm out of here!" Brooks declared in a louder voice than he had intended, then turned around and took off down the alley.

1430 HRS

❧

Rachael Hennessey's husband made his real money on the stock exchange, the newspaper thing being partly a hobby and partly the fulfillment of a boyhood dream. Most weeks it brought in barely enough cash to pay the sixteen people who ran the operation.

While Rachael was heavy into creating a certain lifestyle for herself, that is to say hobnobbing with the rich and famous, or at least as far up that ladder as she could climb, Brooks's insistence on keeping his pathetic little weekly going was a constant source of embarrassment in her life. At the many social functions she attended, her name was often linked to the *Village Review,* and more often than not the discovery of this relationship was a cause for mockery among the group. She'd gladly leave the man, except for two major reasons: Brooks gave his wife all the cash she wanted to play the kind of games she thought were important to her and, while she harbored little respect for her husband, she still cared for him. Brooks Hennessey was one of those rare individuals who had managed to get through life without offending a single person. It was impossible to dislike the big buffoon. If only he would show some tolerance toward her artistic friends and at least try to see things from her point of view, they could be so much closer.

Rachael swung her 550SL off Ridge Boulevard into the circular driveway. She was returning from a tough round of tennis. Thirty-nine years of age and dreading the big Four-0 just seven months away, Rachael pushed herself harder and harder as that time drew closer.

She was pleased to see that Mr. Algundo, the Spanish gardener who came three times a week, had already cleaned up the leaves around the perimeter of their rambling white stone mansion.

Reginald, the Hennesseys' so-called guard dog, was a vast, over-weight St. Bernard that might have been Brooks's kid brother, they were so much alike. Reggie loved everyone, although his affectionate deep barks of greeting had scared away more than a few unwanted vis-itors over the years. Racing out to the Mercedes, his long tongue dan-gling and ready to apply to Rachael's face if she let him, the dog came to a sliding halt at the sight of her tennis racket poised to whack him on the nose.

"Behave yourself, Reggie," she warned. "And stay away from my car!"

He flopped down in disappointment and watched his mistress run up the steps into the house. A few minutes later, bored with sitting in the sun, he took a moment to lift his leg and sprinkle the left front wheel of the red Mercedes before ambling back to his usual spot beneath the big oak tree at the rear of the house.

There Reginald found a curious sight—a small but very old human, seated on a bench beside the fish pond. The dog quickened his pace somewhat, puzzled at how the intruder had managed to get inside the grounds without his knowing about it.

The old woman turned at the St. Bernard's approach, reached out with one frail hand and rubbed his nose. The big dog knew right away that he had found a friend and plunked himself down on the ground at her feet. The visitor took off her shoes, stuck her toes in the thick fur, and moved her tiny feet back and forth. Reggie sighed in contentment.

This pleasant state of affairs lasted about twenty minutes.

"Who the hell are you?" a shrill female voice called out from an open window near the top of her four-story dwelling.

Mrs. Kelly swung around, smiled up at the window, then said to the dog, "Big trouble coming, Reggie. Better get ready."

Barely a minute later Rachael Hennessey appeared dressed in a deep blue terrycloth bathrobe, feet bare, blond hair all wet. She marched right up to the two and gave the dog a hard look before asking, "How did you get in here?"

Mrs. Kelly pulled her shoes back on before answering. "Brooks loaned me his gate opener."

Beautiful though she was, Rachael Hennessey owned a pair of pale green eyes that almost never warmed. Right at that moment they were the color of glacier water. "That's crap. Now get your unwelcome ass off my property before I toss you out."

Mrs. Kelly was also dressed in green, a long, horrible thing with more than a hint of olive, a color that would make some people puke. Her shriveled features, to Rachael, were downright vile.

Smiling her very best smile, the old woman said, "Too late for that, sweetie. My things are already in your south guest room. Your husband, bless his soul, invited me to come and stay here in your lovely home. Isn't that grand?"

Impatient, Rachael grabbed hold of the intruder's arm. "I asked you to leave politely. So don't hold me responsible if you get hurt."

But Rachael was unable to move the old lady. Reggie watched in apparent amazement as his mistress tugged and tugged, but the arm never budged an inch. He let out an involuntary woof of encouragement in support of his new friend.

"Your husband happens to be a very dear friend. You might even say he is the oldest friend I have." She chuckled. "Seven full hours now."

The hideous cackle, combined with the offensive body odor coming her way, forced the younger woman to back off. Rachael realized some kind of trick was being played on her, but nevertheless felt intimidated by what had just taken place.

Mrs. Kelly placed one blue-veined hand on Rachael's arm. "I know it's difficult, dearie, a decrepit old thing like me falling into your life from out of nowhere, but believe me, it won't hurt a bit."

Her initial shock worn off, Rachael began to assert herself again. "Take your hands off me, you old bat." Backing away, she snarled, "If Brooks Hennessey is responsible for this, I swear to God he'll pay for it!"

She stomped up to the patio, grabbed the phone, and punched in numbers. "Put my husband on—now!" she snapped.

Brooks was inside his modest little office working on Friday's editorial, but he wasn't getting too far because his mind kept wandering. A knock on the glass partition made him look up.

Marsha Brown pointed at the receiver pressed to her bosom, screwed up her face, and shouted, "Trouble, boss. Your wife."

Brooks took up the telephone, closed his eyes, and touched line one. "Rachael?"

"Listen to me, you big tub of lard. I have a stinking old granny in my back garden who claims you invited her to come and stay with us. What the bloody hell is going on?"

He swallowed a few times. His worst fear had just become real.

"Uh . . . I can explain. Has she . . . what is she doing?"

"Nothing, just sitting out by the fish pond. Look, this person is a real weirdo—and she scares the hell out of me. Either you come home right this minute and remove her, or I will get the police to do it. You hear me?"

"I'm on my way. Don't do anything. Just stay away from her."

"You had better be able to explain this, or I promise you will be sorry."

Brooks replaced the receiver, aware of beads of sweat forming on his forehead. He didn't believe for one moment when he ran away this morning that he had seen the last of old Mrs. Kelly—if, indeed, this person *was* Kathleen Kelly.

The ride from Flatbush to Bay Ridge usually took him fifteen minutes along the Parkway. Brooks took the long way home on purpose, down Fourteenth Avenue through heavy traffic and back up Seventieth Street, to allow him some time to think. All kinds of irrational thoughts and ideas presented themselves, but the editor of the *Village Review* knew he had to face up to reality: A supernatural event had occurred that morning in church.

Rachael was pacing back and forth in front of the house when the steel-plated gate finally swung open and Brooks steered his blue hybrid Chrysler LHS into the circular driveway, easing to a halt in front of the four-columned entrance. Twenty-six minutes had elapsed since she called him.

She jerked the door open. "Damnit, Brooks, where have you been? She's gone into the house now, making herself at home. I order her out, she just shows me all those rotten teeth in a big dumb grin. She's unpacking her clothes, if you can believe it, and not only that—she smells!"

Brooks stepped out of his car and touched Rachael on the shoulder, something he rarely did anymore. "Calm down, honey. I'll go talk to her."

"Are you out of your mind? I don't want you to *talk* to her—I want her *out!*"

His wife was so fired up that she was almost frothing at the mouth. Since Rachael Hennessey was the original Ms. Cool, Brooks found all the fire and energy rather appealing, even a bit sexy.

He was part-way up the front steps when Reggie came tearing out of the house and smashed into him. Someone with a lesser mass than Brooks would have gone flying.

"And your bloody animal went on my car again! I swear to God I'll cut his balls off if he does it one more time."

Rats! thought Brooks. It had taken him a full month of clandestine instruction to teach Reggie to go up against the left front wheel of the Mercedes. Be a real chore to unteach him.

With the St. Bernard panting excitedly against his hip, he made his way through the open foyer, past Rachael's Yamaha grand piano that played itself, between her two life-sized, five-armed Indonesian dancers, past her array of exuberantly colored canvases that showed, near as Brooks could tell, nothing but exuberant colors. It was usually the fireplace that stopped visitors in their tracks, for this stunning creation had been constructed entirely from handpicked rose quartz rock. Thirty feet wide and five stories high, it extended all the way up to the eight oval skylights that gave the foyer its year-round brightness. The fireplace was two-way on the main floor, serving both the foyer and the living room behind it.

He dumped his jacket on a chair as he turned down the hallway, following the scent as true as any bloodhound. She was in the guest room Rachael had done up all frilly-like for her out-of-town girlfriends, the one with the best view into their spacious backyard with the piano-shaped pool and fish pond.

He peered hesitantly through the partly-open door.

"Come on in, Brooksie, my love. I'm having a little visit with your friends."

The overweight St. Bernard astonished his overweight master by leaping onto the bed and plunking his great head down in Mrs. Kelly's lap. Reggie was not even allowed in the house, much less on the furniture. Worse still, Arcturus had somehow gotten loose, and was now hopping around on the ledge of a bay window. When he saw Brooks, the old one-eyed African Gray screeched, *"Fatso! Fatso! Fatso!"*

This was a recent addition to the parrot's vocabulary, one that seemed to apply equally to Reggie or Brooks. Where it had come from, Brooks did not know, but he suspected the housekeeper, Mrs. Ortez, because the word had a distinctive Mexican twang.

"*Friggin' in the riggin'*" the bird declared, doing pushups on one leg, showing off for the company.

"Arcturus shouldn't be loose in the house. He tends to rip things apart." Especially fingers and Rachael's sheer curtains, which he was now eyeing gleefully.

The angel allowed Mrs. Kelly's sea of ancient wrinkles to fall into a look of dejection. "Is that any way to greet a friend? You are my friend, aren't you?"

"Not sure about that. Maybe. Ah . . . you plan on staying long?"

"God knows."

Brooks didn't like the sound of that. He took a few cautious steps toward the parrot. "We're talking days here, or weeks?"

"Not too long, 'cause I'd get into trouble for sure."

He grabbed for Arcturus, but the wily bird was too fast and shimmied up the inside of the sheers, its big claws ripping into the delicate material. Brooks cringed.

"Trouble? Who with?"

She looked up from scratching Reggie's neck. "My boss. Truth is, I'm a little surprised he allowed me to do this in the first place."

Jesus! Now she had him wondering about aliens.

"Warned you about that, Brooks Hennessey. I don't even want you to *think* the Man's name—unless you're praying, of course. It's all right then." Her eyebrows did a funny little dance as she added, "And I am most certainly not an alien, at least not in the sense that I beamed down from a UFO."

Brooks had no choice but to forget about the bird and seek out the big Queen Anne chair Rachael had bought at an auction. Once seated, his heart pumping like crazy and his face several shades paler than when he came in, he said, "*You just read my mind!*"

Sarius gave a little shrug. "Your thought impulses are hardly subtle. I can read Reggie's too. Right now he's thinking, *Don't stop, don't stop.* You got one neglected animal here, Brooksie. Big dogs like this need lots of love and attention, just like women. Both Rachael and Reggie seem to be lacking in that department. You're out there with sweet little Annie showing off in the sex department, while your two closest friends are going through a dry spell. Seems to me like your lifestyle could use a little realignment."

Not without some trepidation, Brooks leaned forward. "You're not Mrs. Kelly, are you?"

It was a beautiful October day, and the mid-afternoon sun leeching through lemon-colored sheers covering the two picture windows cast a fine golden glow across the room. Arcturus had happily settled into the top of one of them. Outside, autumn's industry was in full bloom, evident by the activities of a thousand small creatures preparing for winter. These were clearly heard by the angelic visitor as he filtered through the vast number of derivatives implicit in the question.

When she didn't answer, Brooks persisted, "What happened to the Puerto Ricans?"

Without taking her attention away from Reggie's drooling lips, Mrs. Kelly replied, "Those boys have gone to an unhappy place, Brooksie. A most unhappy place. Believe me, you don't want to know about it."

As Brooks choked back the horrible thoughts racing across his imagination, she looked him directly in the eye. "This is none of my business, but you might be interested in knowing that the main reason Rachael seems so cold all the time is due to outright frustration. Your wife happens to be an intelligent woman with a fine, analytical mind. If she fails to find a meaningful outlet for it real soon, you are going to have serious trouble on your hands. I'll tell you something else, Brooksie— in the eight years you two have slept in separate rooms, that girl has remained faithful to you. And believe me, she's had more offers to hop into the sack than Imelda Marcos has shoes."

Watching Brooks's jaw drop prompted a light chuckle. "Thought you'd like to know. So don't leave it too long. Now if you don't mind, Reggie and Arcturus and me will wander outside to enjoy your lovely fall air. I must say, feeling it all around me and actually breathing it is different than I thought it would be. Kind of pleasant."

She looked over at the bird and said, "Come on, baby. Momma's going for a little walk."

To Brooks's amazement, the parrot immediately took flight and landed noisily on the old lady's shoulder. A distinctive ripping sound preceded his flight. Once hunkered down, Arcturus squinted his one good eye at Brooks and declared, *"Off with his head!"* This was followed by a raucous cackle that he assumed was laughter.

Just before leaving the bedroom, Brooks took a quick glance at the sheers, knowing there would be hell to pay the minute Rachael spotted the damage. Watching the strange ensemble make their way down the hallway, he wondered how the bird had escaped in the first place. Its permanent home was in Brooks's study up on the top floor, because Rachael did not want the filthy creature anywhere near her friends. Brooks had picked up Arcturus from a drunken Aussie sailor six months back for fifty bucks and only later found out that the bird knew more bad language than he did. Not only that, but the little devil seemed to get immense enjoyment from ripping pieces of flesh from fingers. Brooks was suspicious about the sudden personality switch.

"By the way," Mrs. Kelly said just before she vanished from sight, "Millie will be dropping by around six. Nice if we could all have supper together."

He considered telling her that she should really discuss that with Rachael, but didn't think it was such a good idea under the circumstances. Setting aside the shock of his wife's innocence—which he fully accepted as gospel—he scrambled around inside his head for some innovative way of telling Rachael that not only was Mrs. Kelly not leaving, but yet another old gal was on her way over for supper.

1545 HRS

⁊

"Dammit, Brooks, this house is not a geriatric ward! I'm calling the cops right this minute."

He extracted the portable phone from her hand. "Whoa now, honey, it's not that simple."

They were in the kitchen, which Rachael had just redone for the fifth time, this time in earth tones. New metallic wallpaper, slate flooring, custom fixtures and appliances. The price tag was a cool quarter million. "Didn't you notice there was something odd about her?"

Rachael was five-ten and slim as a reed. She had changed into a gorgeous raspberry lounging outfit. From her seated position on one of the bar stools facing the lunch counter she looked up into her husband's face. Brooks owned a perverse sense of humor, so she could not always be certain when he was being serious. But she had the distinct impression that right now he was really uncomfortable.

"Spit it out, Brooks. What is going on?"

He laid the phone down beyond her reach, then jerked his tie loose and opened the collar of his shirt. "Listen, if you don't want to cook something, I'll run down to the deli. And yeah, you're right—something is going on, but I haven't a clue what it might be. That's the honest to God truth."

Rachael studied her husband of eighteen years. "So this stinking old biddy calls the shots—is that it? Damn it all, Brooks, she has absolutely no right to be inside this house, and I want her out of it—now!"

Brooks grasped his wife by both shoulders. "Listen to me. Kathleen Kelly died this morning in church—right up on the altar in the middle of the Consecration! At least I think she did."

29

Rachael stood up, her forehead coming within inches of his quivering Adam's apple, and asked the obvious question: "If that isn't Mrs. Kelly, then who is in my guest room?"

"Jes—oops! That's what I've been trying to tell you. *I don't know!*"

Rachael sank back down on the stool, not knowing what to believe. But she was definitely shaken. Behind her the descending sun streamed in through four south-facing picture windows overlooking the Verrazano-Narrows Bridge.

"I just hope this is not another one of your sick jokes."

He went on to tell her the whole story, right down to the three piles of ash. She grew quite distraught. Rachael had been raised a Catholic, but other than weddings, funerals, and midnight Mass at Christmas, she had not entered a church for a good many years.

Finally she whispered, "What are we going to do?"

Brooks took the stool beside her, placed his arm around her shoulders, and drew her close until her head rested on his chest. "There's something else. She can read my mind. Reggie's too. So you'd better be careful what you say, and think."

Rachael's shudder prompted Brooks to search around for something comforting to add. "It looks like you and I were . . . well, kind of chosen, I suppose. We're just going to have to play along with her, do what she says, within reason."

"But shouldn't we notify the police or something? I mean, what is she—an alien, an unhappy spirit, what? In the garden I was unable to budge her arm—it was like trying to move a steel pole, and if she banged your hand down like that, well . . . "

Brooks could think of nothing more useful to say, but he was somewhat amazed at the way his heart was reacting to his wife's lovely head being pressed against him. Knowing that she had remained faithful to him all these years summoned up a charge of emotion he had difficulty controlling. Carefully, so as not to break the spell, he leaned down and kissed her hair. Rachael sighed and trembled some more.

She had arrived in Brooklyn with her parents in the fall of that wonderful year, and the first time Brooks caught sight of her at St. Andrew's he was bowled over. Even in a city crammed with gorgeous women, Rachael Kalevala's cool Scandinavian looks sparkled. He fell in love with her on the spot. But it took three months before she would even speak to him, six months before she agreed to date him, and three years of intense courting before she agreed to marry him.

The marriage had been successful. Rachael soon fell in love with her cuddly teddy bear of a husband, and their life really was quite wonderful. This went on for about five years. To this day Brooks could not put his finger on the exact moment when things began to go sour. Although Rachael possessed everything he ever wanted in a woman, she was not exactly hot-blooded, her immediate family being one generation removed from Finland; a country, Brooks assumed, where sex came in low on the priority list.

He admitted that it might have started out with his spending so much time getting the *Village Review* up and running. And faithful though he was up to that point, his flirtatious nature probably contributed to it. Or it might have been the discovery that they were unable to have children, a result of Brooks's defective prostate.

Whatever the cause, there was little Brooks could do to halt the erosion of intimacy in their marriage and the eventual settlement into a routine of mere coexistence. Dullness and mediocrity became the order of the day, and Rachael frequently exhibited her loss of respect for her husband through snippy little remarks that were at times downright caustic. Brooks needed affection. He craved sex. With Rachael shut down in both departments, he took the next natural step in the process. The act of taking a mistress clashed with his staunch Catholic upbringing, but it was the only avenue left open for him.

Brooks himself was the third son of a drunken, on-the-take, beat-his-wife-and-never-miss-Sunday-Mass Irish cop. In his later years, the old man had so much alcohol in his veins that his nose lit up in the dark. He managed to make it to retirement only because in his younger days on the force he had stumbled across the kidnapped daughter of an influential state politician and was awarded the medal of bravery for being stupid enough to jump in front of the kid and catch a bullet intended for her. The old man lasted seventeen months in that blessed state of being able to guzzle booze both day and night before his liver self-destructed. No tears were shed for Paddy Hennessey.

Brooks's mother, God bless her, was a saint. She'd spent forty-seven years married to that cruel monster, a sentence more punishing than anything ever meted out by any court. She'd endured a mere three months into Paddy's retirement, couldn't stand the sight and the smell of him twenty-four hours a day, and gave up the ghost. A whole lot of tears followed Mary Hennessey's death.

Brooks was the only one of three brothers to stay on in Brooklyn, and he visited her grave for forty days straight, a kind of vigil, and prayed for her constantly. His old man never once had the benefit of any prayers from Brooks; nor, Brooks was reasonably certain, from any of his family. Wherever Paddy Hennessey had gone, Brooks did not want to follow, hence his renewed enthusiasm for Holy Mother Church following his father's death.

Brooks had sad eyes, big brown bloopers like Reggie. He stooped slightly, a carryover from earlier times when he stood head and shoulders above his classmates. As a kid he was big and soft, a perfect target for the bullies. And they had their way with him. That is, until one day the Irish cop told his son that he was bloody well going to stand up and fight like a man or get the hell out of his house. Brooks chose the lesser of two evils and began to fight back at school, which fortunately took only two minor scuffles before word got out that he had retired as the class punching bag.

Like his overweight carcass, Brooks's face carried too much flesh. But strip off a layer or two of fat and a Gregory Peck nose and a Gary Cooper jaw line would pop out at you. His football tackle size and generous mouth helped, but the main reason for his success with women was because Brooks was polite, never pushy, always listened intently, and was always gentle. Above all, he was understanding—the very attributes that had drawn Rachael to him in the first place. Rachael knew of his escapades, decided she could live with it. She soon realized that missing out on sex was not the end of the world.

From his earliest days, Brooks had liked to play with numbers. Mathematics fascinated him. Ten years old, he'd sit up in bed at night, long after mandatory lights out, and shine his flashlight on the pages of an algebra textbook. Then at age thirteen, right on schedule, the sudden emergence of dozens of budding little bosoms in the classroom began to distract him. He longed to touch one. His longing became so intense that he would often lie awake and think of ways to get his hands on one or two. What he did, in his shy bumbling way, was promise the dumbest girl in class, who wasn't all that pretty, that he would do her homework for a full month if she would let him fondle her breasts.

Years later he realized that Denise Abbott wasn't nearly as dumb as she let on. It was just that she had little interest in school or in the learning process as a whole. She took the big Irish kid's offer to heart, saved herself a lot of work, and they settled into a routine of regular love-making every Thursday afternoon at four in a darkened corner of the old Bremmer warehouse over on First Avenue. Brooks got much more than he asked for, came to the conclusion that sex was the greatest invention in the entire history of the human race, and never looked back.

Fortunately, by the time he and Rachael were married, he had discovered that his talent for numbers could be put to work in the marketplace. With the help of a friendly banker and more than a little nerve, the big Irishman quickly began to amass a fair chunk of wealth, which went a long way toward improving his image to both Rachael and her concerned parents. Although, true enough, he derived no real satisfaction from making oodles of money on the stock market. It was just something he did. He had a gift for it. His real job was running the *Village Review*. Seeing his little weekly hit the streets every Friday morning with his name riding the masthead as editor and publisher never ceased to instill in him a sense of pride and accomplishment.

Looking down at Rachael now, at the pure gold in her hair, remembering that first indescribable surge of love during their early days together, Brooks was overcome with a deep sense of shame for having betrayed her. At the same time, he had to admit that unless his wife went through a big-time metamorphosis, he could not foresee the possibility of those days ever returning.

Sarius, Reggie, and Arcturus had returned to the bench by the fish pond. The setting was pretty as could be, with butterflies fluttering about and goldfish glittering like diamonds in the sunlight. There was only a hint of coolness in the air.

Bare feet once again resting on the dog's back while the parrot happily chased after butterflies, the angel was only halfheartedly monitoring the activity in the kitchen. His new role—part human and part angel—was not nearly as simple as he thought it would be. In fact, the abrupt change had left Sarius feeling decidedly ill at ease, which in turn prompted his angelic instinct to question the reason for this sudden and unnatural desire to take on human form.

The angel set about reviewing what he knew of past cultures in this particular galaxy. Natural disasters notwithstanding, most had successfully reached the threshold of the atomic age, the first major hurdle on the road to civilized behavior. But for the great majority, the journey ended soon after mercenary forces let loose their weapons of mass destruction. Indeed, this had become such a common occurrence as to be considered a natural termination point in the evolutionary process.

Still, eleven great civilizations had managed to escape unscathed from the more primitive electromagnetic energy level and enter the next plateau of development: the understanding and harnessing of gravitational forces. It was truly unfortunate that only one of those highly advanced cultures was still around, and many within the Kingdom fervently hoped that one day they too would be able to take that final step, where the quantum replaces the particle, when the body finally sheds its physical attributes and dissolves into pure energy and intelligence.

As for the earlier ones, Sarius recalled moments of great excitement, the intense yearning for the aggression curve to flatten out before it was too late. Yet all ten had failed. Time after time after time after time, their valiant efforts decimated and lost forever amid the terrible hydrogen wars that engulfed them.

Earth was different. A painful experiment, yes, but one that gave humanity the means to resist the Evil One who resided in the Lower Kingdom, the One who mocked Creation and worked so hard to destroy it. Unfettered by time, Sarius could at a whim relive that most dramatic of all moments when the very heavens resounded in battle. He had been there. If he wished, he could be there again.

In the Twelfth Dimension there was no past, no future, only the present, in which all creations, old and new, resided together in great overlapping loops of time. Nothing died. Not a single image had been struck from the record. It was all there, all things in their created and evolved forms. Sarius had only to slip through whatever doorway he wished to view eternity. This he did now, seeking answers.

1900 HRS

❧

Millie, as might be expected, was all dolled up when she pushed the red button on the outer gate. She'd truly had no idea that Kathy was on such good terms with the Hennesseys, who were considered upper echelon within the tiny Irish enclave that still maintained a foothold in Brooklyn's lower west side, and she was anxious about dining with such exalted company.

Brooks glanced at the video screen and said into the speaker, "Come on in, Mildred. Don't pay any attention to our dog if he shows up. Reggie likes to bark, but he wouldn't hurt a fly."

He gave Rachael a quick wink. "I'm going out to meet her. Everything okay?"

"I suppose so."

Cooking came in last on Rachael's list of priorities, so a wonderful Greek woman usually stopped in to prepare the meals whenever they had company, but Elena required a day's notice. Brooks had earlier thawed four T-bone steaks in the microwave that were now being done on the broiler. He had peeled the vegetables, whipped up the salad, and extracted a couple of bottles of decent Bordeaux from the wine cellar.

Millie wore a rose-colored dress and a cream-colored woolen pullover with tiny wild roses woven into it. She had worked real hard at her makeup and the end result wasn't all that bad. Reggie finally showed up to sniff out the new visitor. He lingered long enough to see that everything was in order, then ambled back to the south guest room. Brooks shook his head. This was not the Reggie he knew.

Brooks took Millie into the kitchen. Rachael wiped her hands and came to meet her. Like the dog, Rachael had also undergone a change over the last two hours. She had grown really quiet. The last few times she spoke to Brooks her tone was mild, bordering on friendly.

"Hello, Millie. I've seen you down at the Safeway store a few times, and of course Brooks is always mentioning you in the paper."

Widowed at an early age, Millie had gone on to become a member of so many community groups that she sometimes lost count. Her entire purpose in life was to help others. She said nervously, "I'm real pleased to meetcha, Mrs. Hennessey."

Rachael's smile widened. "Enough of that. I'm Rachael. And I insist that you make yourself at home. Can Brooks get you a cocktail?"

Wide-eyed, Brooks thought to himself, *Wow, this is just like old times.* He took Millie by the arm again, directing her toward the living room. Reggie met them in the hall, and behind him came his newest friend.

It was not the same woman Brooks had earlier left in the guest room. This woman wore a three-quarter length off-the-shoulder dress in a vivid midnight blue, a gown really. However she had applied her makeup seemed to make the wrinkles vanish, and her pure white hair was done in swirls that fell to her left shoulder. An elegantly designed sapphire necklace caught his attention, as did the matching earrings. On her left ring finger she wore a large pearl-like ring, except the cloudy blue color gave out far too much light to be a pearl.

Mildred could only stare in dumfounded silence. Brooks gulped a few times, then said over his shoulder, "Rachael, you'd better come out here."

Rachael's astonished appraisal left her with the distinct impression that she was viewing royalty. Having enjoyed his little surprise, Sarius said, "You think I look good? Come in here, and I will show you something far more interesting."

Mrs. Kelly went on into the living room. When Millie caught up she whispered in her friend's ear, "How did you do it?"

Mrs. Kelly smiled and replied, "Nothing but pure talent, my love."

Inside the spacious and well-appointed room furnished with fine rosewood furniture and a dozen vibrant oil paintings, Sarius asked Millie to go and stand beside the fireplace. Her outfit blended perfectly with the rose quartz. Then the angel directed Brooks and his wife to the opposite side of the room and stepped between them. The three were now looking directly at a rather perplexed Millie.

"Are you ready?" Sarius asked his hosts.

Rachael was beginning to think the whole episode was some kind of a dream, but she had lost her fear of Mrs. Kelly and after a quizzical glance at her husband, replied in the affirmative.

Sarius took Rachael's hand in his left hand and Brooks's in his right, then said to Rachael, "Don't get upset now, my dear. The light will be bright at first, but it won't hurt your eyes."

Then, upon that final word, the room exploded in light. Not white light but warm, gentle light that vibrated and danced around its origin: Mildred Manuel. All colors in their natural state blended with one another and radiated from the core of goodness this wonderful woman had become. Sarius had felt the urge—although he had to admit it might well have been Mrs. Kelly's own urge—to show them how this very special person appeared to him.

As swiftly as it had come, the light vanished. Still holding Mrs. Kelly's hand, Rachael muttered in amazement, "She's an angel."

Sarius thought this a nice conclusion. "Not yet, but someday."

"It comes from giving," Brooks added, after letting out his breath.

Sarius gave his arm a squeeze. "Bang on the money, Brooksie."

Millie eased away from the mantelpiece and walked over to Mrs. Kelly. Brooks and Rachael excused themselves and returned to the kitchen.

Millie stared at her old friend for a moment or two and finally shook her head. "Good Lord, Kathy, is it really you?"

Sarius placed a comforting hand on her arm and led her to a Greek-style malachite-green divan with sculptured rosewood arms. After both were seated, Mrs. Kelly said casually, "Am I that different?"

Millie rolled her eyes and fingered a piece of the silky blue material. "Just look at you; you're the Queen of Sheba for heaven's sake. I have never seen a more beautiful gown. And that glorious sapphire necklace. Surely it's not real?"

" 'Tis so."

"My goodness! And your ring—it seems to create its own light. What is it?"

Mrs. Kelly raised her left hand slightly. "Not from around this neck of the woods, love. Comes from far, far away."

"I guess Mrs.—uh, Rachael lent you all this."

"Not quite."

Brooks appeared with a tray and two small glasses of Baileys Irish Cream. Each of the old ladies took a glass, and Brooks watched Mrs. Kelly carefully place the glass to her lips and taste the liqueur. He had somehow expected her to refuse it. She nodded approvingly and downed the whole thing in one gulp.

"This tastes nice, Brooksie. Too bad so much grief comes from it."

"From Baileys?"

"You know what I mean."

Brooks knew. He also knew that Mrs. Kelly had shed a lot of years since entering the church that morning. "When are you going to tell us?"

Millie gave her friend a hard look. "Tell us what?"

Mrs. Kelly replaced her empty glass on a hardwood coffee table covered with tiny porcelain birds. "Oh, something we spoke of earlier."

But when she glanced up at her large host, Brooks was surprised to see that her sky-blue eyes were tinged with uncertainty.

2130 HRS

❦

The atmosphere at dinner was amazingly light, considering that a real live miracle was unfolding before their eyes—two miracles, in fact, because this unique state of affairs had come about as a direct result of a newly renovated, upbeat Rachael Hennessey.

For reasons Brooks did not understand, she had decided to accept their unusual company with a certain uncommon zest. Her eyes twinkled, and her conversation sparkled. Notwithstanding his misgivings about Mrs. Kelly, Brooks found the two old ladies a delightful change from the self-centered artsy types Rachael usually invited to dinner, and he was content to sit back in mild enthrallment and listen to his wife regale them with humorous accounts of her chance encounters with certain celebrities at the prestigious Southcott Golf and Country Club.

But much of Rachael's prattle had been to cover up her own anxiety. Whatever about Millie, a truly harmless old soul, she already knew Mrs. Kelly was anything but harmless. After dinner, while Brooks was pouring each of them a glass of Burmester vintage port, Rachael's gaze wandered back to the unusual ring Mrs. Kelly wore: a hemispheric light blue stone, but so bright that it seemed unnatural. This, too, made her uneasy.

Rachael finally summoned the courage to ask the question that had been tormenting her all evening. She sat up straight, took a deep breath, and said to the stately person in the blue gown, "A decrepit old woman came into my garden today. What happened to her?"

Mrs. Kelly drummed her fingers on the table top as if she were considering the question.

Millie, seated beside her, added in a sardonic tone of voice, "Yeah, why don't you let us in on your little secret."

Sarius had inherited Kathleen Kelly's entire life. Her every thought and deed, her joys and fears, her full scale of emotions, were now his. The visitor realized there was a real possibility that his own thought processes could be affected by these human characteristics. This, he admitted, could lead to complications.

With a face more solemn than he had affected all evening, the angel said, "At the moment my biological clock is two months into my seventy-sixth year. By the end of the week it will be at sixty-eight."

Millie let out a coarse chuckle and said, "Don't you just wish?" She assumed her friend had hung a fair chunk of her brains over the yardarm. Either that, or the goodly amount of booze Kathy had lowered into her miniature frame had done its job.

Brooks gave Rachael a tight-lipped glance and jumped into the conversation with both feet. "You reversed the aging process!"

Sarius shrugged. "Simple enough, once you know how."

"Why?" whispered Rachael, believing, but not understanding.

"I should think the better question is—why not?"

Millie began to show real signs of distress, so much so that Mrs. Kelly took her friend's quivering hand in her own and squeezed. Smiling at her, Sarius said, "Now get a tight grip on yourself, Mildred, because what I have to say is guaranteed to knock your socks off."

Of course, Sarius was able to exert his will and thereby effectively calm Millie. That being done, he stood up and eased away from the table to lean back against a display cabinet crammed with expensive Murano crystal. Looking directly at Brooks, he said in a low voice, "Let me begin by telling you that my name is Sarius. I am here because . . . well, I suppose it was because the opportunity arose when Mrs. Kelly expired rather unexpectedly."

Millie's right hand flew to her mouth. Her left hand clutched her heart.

Brooks swallowed a few times as he became aware of his own heart pounding like crazy. "You mean, like, you're not supposed to be here?"

Sarius gave the question some thought before replying. "Probably not."

Least affected by this declaration was Rachael. After all, she already knew her dinner guest was not Mrs. Kelly. "Sarius . . . " she said, rolling the name around as if she were tasting it. "And where does Sarius come from?"

The heavenly intruder was carefully assessing all their reactions. This kind of confrontation was not what he had in mind when he assumed human form. "The Final Dimension, my dear. None other, I assure you."

"You live in another dimension?"

Sarius smiled. "Live? I think not. Pass through, more likely."

"Are you really an angel?"

"You already know the answer to that."

Brooks whispered, "Wow!" under his breath.

Rachael's eyes widened in triumph, "And you are a woman!"

"Am I?"

"You look like one. You sound like one."

"Means nothing, my love, nothing at all. Outward appearances, you know."

"Then what sex are you?"

Sarius had seen this coming. "For goodness sakes—not everyone, or everything, has reason to procreate. Sex has a specific function: to create life, which obviously has no meaning to us."

At that moment Reggie, who had somehow managed to wiggle underneath the table to be at the feet of his new mistress, forgot where he was and stood up. Dishes and glasses went flying into the air and smashed into each other with a terrible clamor. The aftermath caused Brooks to close his eyes in horror. He could visualize the gun being held to Reggie's head.

True, under normal circumstances, Rachael would have gone ballistic, but now she merely glanced at the disaster before turning back to her unearthly guest. "So you are truly asexual."

Sarius shook his head in mild dismay. He had never quite grasped the human fascination with sex. In a more authoritative voice he said, "My dear lady, you say that as if it were the end of the world. Far from it. You may be interested to know that I have observed a great variety of creatures evolve well beyond random propagation of species. Sex was left in the dust. I can assure you those particular life forms didn't miss it one little bit. Just one less cause for dissension."

"Other creatures," muttered Brooks excitedly. Millie was speechless, her open mouth arching up and down like a fish out of water.

Sarius twirled Mrs. Kelly's right hand disdainfully. "Did you really think the universe was created for you? My goodness, the whole thing was done for us—the firstborn, if you will. Amusement, variety, entertainment. We never lack for fresh worlds to explore. Indeed, that so many of you believe you are alone in the cosmos might well be classified as the ultimate denial of reality. Look into the night sky, and see for yourself. Every single star has its own solar system, and it should be painfully obvious to anyone with even the slightest glimmer of intelligence that a good percentage of those planets must contain the necessary elements for life to evolve."

The angel paused for a moment, recalling some of the stranger species he had encountered in his travels. A smile spread across the old woman's face. "True, not always life as you know it. But yes, I can assure you that Creation truly is an endless process: so vast, so wonderful, so rich in diversity that I observed this planet in detail for only the second time just a few years ago—during the Cuban missile crisis, to be precise. And I came then just to watch the fireworks."

"Which did not materialize," Rachael commented, her pretty blonde head tilted and her green eyes rather distant.

"Fooled us completely."

A sudden surge in Millie's pulse worried Sarius. He walked back to the table and placed Kathleen Kelly's hands on the stricken woman's shoulders. "Yes, Millie, it's bad news, I know, but your dear friend did pass away this morning. You'll have to forgive me for doing this to you, but when the time comes for me to leave, you three will need to attest to Kathleen's second death, as it were."

Brooks Hennessey's mind overflowed with possibilities. But even with his natural curiosity racing in all directions, one overriding question stood out above all others. In a voice charged with intensity, he said, "Tell us about God. Where is He? What does He look like?"

Sarius placed a soothing hand on Millie's cheek, projecting just enough energy to act as a mild sedative. Once he was certain Mrs. Kelly's dearest friend was under control, the angel sat down again.

The table was large enough to seat sixteen, but the four were clumped together at one end with Rachael at the head beneath a large Salvador Dali original full of colorful clocks drooping over a marble

SHADOW OF LIGHT ✒ 43

railing with an azure blue ocean in the background. This particular oil happened to be the most expensive item in the house. Brooks was seated to her left, the two women on her right.

Sarius stared long and hard at his host before responding. "Wise men have acknowledged that if one cannot find God in the petals of a flower, He is not to be found anywhere."

"Yes, of course, no argument," Brooks said impatiently. "But God— the real and true essence of God. Tell us about that."

Ignoring the interruption, Sarius continued. "And another, Augustine, said that God is more truly imagined than expressed, and exists more truly than He is imagined. A clever man, Augustine, well ahead of his time."

Rachael, too, was growing impatient. "But *you* know, don't you?"

Sarius noticed the painting for the first time and found Dali's notion of killing off time rather interesting. Then the angel cleared away a few pieces of broken glass and placed Mrs. Kelly's right hand flat on the table, palm down. "Go ahead, you do the same," he said.

Their special visitor realized he would be able to take them only so far, because no creature living on this planet was capable of grasping the nature of the One who created All.

"I'll have to leave Kathleen Kelly's manner of speech behind for this little jaunt. The poor dear would have found the dynamics of time and eternity tough slogging for sure."

Brooks shot Rachael a wide-eyed look of trepidation as he flattened his right hand on the table. Millie sighed deeply, uncertain of anything, but feeling quite good about it. Rachael's entire body tingled with anticipation.

Sarius began by telling his tiny audience to focus their attention on the backs of their hands. "What you see is very familiar: flesh, a part of the elastic surface that protects your bones and muscles and organs. Scratch it and blood will dribble forth. Now lean closer and study the folds in your skin. Here, deep inside the pores, you will encounter the living cells that make up your flesh. These cells are nothing more than tiny liquid sacks of proteins, each containing several strings of molecules. Inside this molecular structure are the various atoms: oxygen, carbon, hydrogen, helium, argon, and so on."

The angel glanced up at Brooks. "Interpreting the true makeup of the atom is still centuries away, but this is where I must take you because it is the only way I know to answer your question and have you understand it."

The angel's voice had taken on a pleasant hypnotic overtone that left the three little choice but to follow along as he entered the very heart of the atom. Unknowingly, Brooks Hennessey, his wife, and Millie were embarking upon a journey where no human had gone before.

"At this subatomic level, trails of light can still be seen, but far, far away, like meteors shooting across the sky. Can you see them?"

Immersed in the darkness of the atom, and being the tiny points of infinity that they were, the three looked around in wonder at the heavens that are contained within the nucleus of every atom in the entire universe. Sarius remained silent for a full minute, allowing them time to absorb this last of the known frontiers of present-day science. He would be taking them much deeper.

"What you see now is mainly space—a flickering shadow here, a trail of light there. Those might represent a spinning electron, perhaps a vibrating neutron or proton. It could be one of the many kinds of bosons and leptons darting about, or even one of a great number of elementary particles yet to be discovered. And yet, the distances are so great that you see little except darkness. As we go deeper still into this vast emptiness we may encounter certain space-time events—some scientists call them particles; others call them waves. Neither description is apt, as this is just one of many realities yet to be determined.

"Here is where we must leave behind the world as you know it and cross the frontier between matter and energy. Deeper and deeper we go, smaller and smaller we become, until the nearest particle wave inside the atom is a thousand light years away from us. But we can no longer see it because we have entered a secret place where time has no meaning, where all reference planes cease to exist. Down here there is no before or after, no sense of proportion. There is only darkness, and we are part of it."

Not a heartbeat could be heard in the room, because the three mortals were no longer in the room. They had broken through the quantum barrier and entered the unknown.

"Yes," Sarius intoned in his compelling asexual voice, "down here you quickly come to realize that the atom, like the universe itself, is made up almost entirely of space. One is exactly proportional to the other. But what is not apparent, even at this level, is that there really is no such thing as empty space. The darkness you observe, my earthly friends, is *full* and *alive*. It is full of energy, and it is alive with intelligence. Humanity will need several thousand years of research before you can hope to penetrate this final barrier—because this is where Truth resides.

"Here, within the darkness of quantum gravity, where pure intelligence and pure energy have identical properties, lies the answer to eternal life. We call it the Divine Darkness. And this, Brooks Hennessey, is the home of your Maker. Here the universe, the atom, and the One who created All, are fully indivisible. At this primordial level of existence, all of Creation, including you three, are joined together in one great sweep of eternity as surely as your fingers are joined to your hand."

The angel allowed his audience time to assimilate, then continued. "You might well wonder how this vast empty space inside the atom can truly be God, since the particular atoms we are discussing are part of your own living cells. There is nothing new here, I assure you. Mankind first became aware of this mystery when God revealed to the prophets of old that He resided within them. Many of the saints, like Paul, told you outright that the Spirit of God dwells inside you. Indeed, this greatest of all gifts is what places humanity above all other creations: You are the first God-creature that has come into existence."

Sarius considered what he was about, then abruptly decided to reveal the final chapter, unpleasant though it was. "And, you will be the last. Even holding the infinite power of the Creator within your primitive life forms, you have failed. He dared to make you part of Him, to His own image and likeness, as I have just explained, a supreme act of love that was intended to be your guarantee of life eternal. By it your creation was given the power to resist the forces of evil.

"*You, and you alone,* have something no other creation has ever been given: *Every single human being born into this world can aspire to Perfection!* Yes, for those who successfully navigate this passage, death marks the beginning of a truly incredible journey. Sadly, you chose not to embrace this greatest of all gifts. You chose instead ignorance and depravity!

"No, not all of you—not you three. But a great many have."

Once again the angel considered the apparent lack of interest in his recent activities and added softly, "Perhaps too many."

2015 HRS

❦

Dan Copeland's breath came away in thick vapors as he reached up to check a bushing on the homemade adapter fitted to the top of the University of Hawaii's 88-inch telescope. The adapter was used to hook on a charge-coupled device, commonly referred to as a CCD, which would allow the instrument to detect light photons from the farthest reaches of the cosmos. A contingent of Japanese astronomers was to arrive within the hour, and they would expect everything to be ready. Copeland's job was to ensure that the big telescope was fully operational, calibrated, and ready for action.

"Evening, Professor," a voice from down below called out. "Nice to see you on the hill again."

This was old Ern, one of two permanent caretakers who lived on site. "Evening, Ernie. How's the family?"

"First class, thanks. More Japs, I hear."

"Yeah."

"How's she look?"

A few clouds still floated about, but these were held close to the valley floor by a generally constant inversion layer. Only two hours ago a sharp easterly wind had succeeded in clearing the air and lowering the humidity. This boded well for the Japanese, who were anxious to get started on their five-night program. Every hour of darkness was precious to them. Up here, at the 14,000 foot summit of Mauna Kea, viewing conditions were now optimum.

"I'd say she looks perfect, Ern."

Before climbing back down into the huge cylindrical dome with its distinctive hornlike projection, Copeland rotated his head to do a slow

47

scan of the heavens. Venus was bright on the western horizon, brighter here than anywhere else on earth. Mars, the red planet, was clear in the southeast, within the constellation Aquarius. High in the northwest was the constellation Lyra, with Vega at its apex. Even though he did not really believe in God, the velvety background of stars, bright and clear and alive, always filled the astronomer with deep feelings of reverence and awe.

Yet tonight was not a normal night. Something unusual was going on, something that, for reasons he could not quite grasp, Copeland found rather disturbing. Meteors were a common enough sight, except he had never before seen them occur in bunches. One, two, three, all within the space of a heartbeat. Most unusual. He also found it odd that this activity was confined to a single location: the southeast quadrant, the same sector where a number of new comets had recently been seen. Could all this have meaning?

A passage from Shakespeare's Julius Caesar came to mind: *When beggars die there are no comets to be seen, but the heavens themselves blaze forth the death of princes.*

If this prediction held true, the astronomer considered as he descended the ladder, then someone important had just moved on.

Copeland went through the startup routine with the kind of intimate knowledge that came from being around the 88 for close to twenty years. Yet this was not his regular job. He was a teacher, one of the best in the business. Ron Hamada, the regular telescope operator, had gone off to Kenya for a three-week vacation, and Copeland did not mind in the slightest filling in for him. He loved the old 88, and if given a choice, would trade jobs with Hamada any day.

A muffled screech in the far corner of the control room made him turn his head. This was Fika, the resident spider monkey, one of few animals that did not seem to mind the high altitude.

"Evening, Fika."

The monkey did several exuberant bounces off the sides of her cage before settling down. Copeland had mixed reactions whenever he saw Fika. The female monkey used to belong to one of his students back in '99, a young Canadian girl who had died in a tragic accident on the winding road down from the observatory. She'd hit a thick bank of fog and left the road. Almost a month went by before they found her body. The tragic part was that notes found beside her showed that she had managed to survive for eighteen days pinned beneath the wreckage of her TR-7 before dying of hunger and dehydration.

Astronomers no longer look through the eyepiece of a telescope. They rarely take photographs anymore. Nowadays they sit in heated control rooms gazing at computer monitors and TV screens. The stark volcanic summit of Mauna Kea volcano on the big island of Hawaii held eight observatories, Keck Two with its ten-meter mirror and array of latest scientific equipment being the acknowledged lord of the mountaintop. Its mate, Keck One, was just 285 feet away. Through the magic of interferometry, both telescopes together had a combined resolution seventeen times that of Mount Palomar's 200-inch reflector.

Twenty minutes later, the machinery that ran the 88 was all warmed up and the telescope responding well to commands. Copeland knew that Hamada often chose Mars or Antares for calibration purposes. Tonight, although it was just two hours from setting, Copeland decided to use Mars.

The astronomer glanced at his watch. He figured he had thirty minutes before the Japanese arrived. Calibration usually took about ten minutes. He instructed the control computer to locate Mars. Once it calculated the coordinates, the telescope drive motors whined into action and stars flew across the screen, drawn into dashes by the telescope's motion. Then, as the stars slowed, the red planet with its tormented surface drifted into the screen and stopped, shimmering slightly. Quite close was its largest satellite, Phobos.

Copeland knew right away something was wrong. The planet should be at the dead center of the screen.

It wasn't.

He sat back and folded his arms. The computer and telescope readouts were identical: right ascension of 16 hours, 02 minutes, 17.38 seconds, declination of -21 degrees, 47 minutes, 22.43 seconds. Yet the disc was clearly off-center.

The astronomer knew the 88 had just received its annual checkup, and it wasn't that unusual for little quirks to surface after the engineers had been digging around in the telescope's works. Out of idle curiosity he manually drove the telescope to center the image. Now the right ascension read 16 hours, 04 minutes, 20.21 seconds, with a declination of -21 degrees, 49 minutes, 18.12 seconds. A pointing error had definitely crept into the system. He compared the observatory's atomic clock with his Tag. They read the same.

Puzzled but unperturbed, Copeland realized that parallax and refraction played a greater role as the body approached the horizon, but those corrections had already been factored into the program.

For some reason Fika suddenly began to tear around her six-foot cage with all the speed she could muster in that short distance. Copeland gave the monkey a curious look as he considered that the instrument was nearly forty years old. Things occasionally broke down. The bright star Antares was close to Mars, so he commanded the computer to observe the star. The motors whined again, and two minutes later the bright red spark that was Antares settled into the exact center of the screen. Both its position and its coordinates were correct. There was no pointing error.

The frustrated astronomer tried two more stars at widely separated positions in the sky. He found no errors.

Although he had never heard of a similar occurrence, it almost seemed like some kind of localized observational inconsistency had crept into the process.

At that moment the control room door swung open and in marched the five Japanese astronomers huddled in fleece-lined parkas, even through the temperature was hovering around forty degrees. All wore happy smiles and were no doubt looking forward to the night's adventure. Japan had its own observatory on the mountain, but there was never enough observing time to go around. Copeland knew that the position of Mars was irrelevant for their observations, but at the same time he had a mystery on his hands. He was not prepared to hand over the instrument until he understood what was happening.

Five bows to the world-renowned Dr. Copeland took place, followed by several declarations of the most profuse gratitude that Dr. Copeland had himself come to operate the instrument for them.

Fika stopped her running around and let go a few high-pitched squeals, begging for attention. Copeland shook their hands and returned their cheesy smiles.

He knew the Japanese mindset inside out and backward. Those same five Cheshire grins would quickly turn into scowls of condemnation if something were to screw up their plans.

"Make yourselves at home; fridge is in the next room across the hall—lots of beer. Go easy though, at this altitude the effects of alcohol set in pretty darn fast. Still a few more minutes of fiddling to do. I'll give you a shout when everything is set to go."

No problem, no problem, they replied in sing-song harmony as they went after the beer. But the lone female in the group, a pretty little creature, walked over to Fika on her way out and put her face right up to the cage.

The young woman jerked her dainty nose back just in time to save it. She muttered something to the monkey in Japanese before leaving the room to join her companions.

Copeland stroked his raggedy beard as he considered his next course of action. He chided himself for taking this seriously. Known eccentricity aside, it was commonly accepted that Mars had not deviated from its orbit around the sun in millions, perhaps billions, of years. Nevertheless, something weird was going on.

Half an hour later the visitors began to grow restless. They had come to monitor a recent spectacular outburst of energy from a star in the constellation Pictor, not to drink beer. Since the control room door was wide open, they were able to watch Copeland tapping away on his keyboard. The five gradually made their way across the narrow hallway and one by one crept back inside the control room.

Copeland stood up abruptly, fixed them with a stern look, and took down the telephone receiver. He told the Japanese astronomers to be seated and punched four numbers on the observatory closed circuit.

"U.N. Observatory. Becker here."

"Dr. Copeland, Becker. Put Dr. Gallager on."

"Can't do that, sir. Dr. Gallager's up in the focus of the telescope."

"It wasn't a request, Becker. Go get him, now!"

Gallager, a born-again Texan who carried around a Bible in his briefcase, was over at the UN dome for the whole month of October, although Copeland had only a vague notion of what he was working on.

"Dan, that you? What the hell's this all about?"

Copeland could not blame the Texan for being upset. No one liked to be interrupted at the outset of a night's program.

"Sorry to disturb you, Rory. I just went through a routine setup and calibration on the 88, and the damn thing is acting real peculiar. I fed in the coordinates for Mars, and the disc came in two minutes off center."

Fika let out a piercing scream that made Copeland jump.

"What was that?"

"Our noisy monkey!" Copeland threw a marker pencil at the cage. "Stupid animal is all worked up about something."

Rory Gallager was a big, overweight man who did not look after himself. Copeland could hear him wheezing over the closed telephone line.

"I don't see there's much I can do if your machine is on the ropes. Two minutes of arc gives you what, three hundred thousand kilometers? Not too likely, is it? I suppose this close to setting, refraction could throw a screw into your readout."

"Nope, all factored in."

"Okay, so it's hardware or software. Maybe the CCD. How about your clock?"

"After Mars I tried Antares and two other stars. They came in perfect. That's the problem—far as I can tell, everything is working fine. And by the way, did you happen to notice all the meteor activity around Mars?"

"Matter of fact, I did. Seems to be a constant barrage, like there's a war going on up there."

"Exactly, which just happens to be in the same quadrant where those new comets showed up a few days ago."

"Hmm . . . interesting. I still say your problem's noise—thermal or readout probably. Either that, or some atmospheric glitch between you and Mars. Perhaps the meteors do come into play, though I can't see how. My best guess is your CCD is screwed up. Shut 'er down, come on over here if you want."

Copeland half-turned toward the five anxious faces. "Can't do that. Betsy is spoken for every night for the next three weeks. I have five astronomers from Tokyo University here right now—"

"Sorry, Danny boy. This sucker's tied up tighter than a fly's ass."

"I wouldn't think of asking you to do that. But I am asking for a favor, a big one."

"No harm asking, but the answer's probably no."

"I want you to run a check on Mars before it sets. That would tell me if it's my machine or something else."

Gallager chuckled away. "Something else—like the sucker's popped its orbit. Give me a break, Dan. Look, shut Betsy down and bring your little Oriental buddies on over here. They can watch some good infrared feedback from Orion."

"Ten minutes, Rory. That's all it will take. Then I'll know."

"You are definitely pushing the envelope, old buddy." Gallager took a few moments to think it over. "Well, you being the island's number one honcho, I suppose it's the neighborly thing to do. But you owe me."

Copeland breathed a sigh of relief. Of course the problem was technical, but he couldn't bring himself to turn over the 88 until he knew for certain.

"Thanks. I'll wait for your call."

The astronomer resumed his seat in front of the console and began to explain what was going on, but Fika interrupted him by rattling the hell out of her cage, screeching as she did so.

Copeland had never known the monkey to behave like this. He excused himself and went over to the cage. "What's got into you, Fika?"

The strangest look came over the tiny pinched face, almost as if the animal was trying to communicate. Her head was tilted to one side, dark eyes pleading with him. Probably just lonely, Copeland thought.

Then the sweet young face of Marie Quellet, the girl who had died so tragically, flashed across his mind. Her presence grew so powerful that Copeland could feel the hairs on the back of his neck bristle. He took a few deep breathes and then pulled the big black wrap over the cage. The little monkey soon halted her activity and settled in for the night.

The Japanese visitors had a rash of questions, but the bottom line was that an observational inconsistency had developed. They knew full well that data collected with faulty equipment amounted to a handful of rice. They put on long faces, folded their arms, and waited.

They didn't wait long. When the telephone buzzed, Gallager snapped, "Give me your current coordinates!"

Copeland had kept the telescope glued to Mars, in readiness for Gallager's verification. He began to read the screen when he noticed something that turned his blood cold. The last digit in both coordinates had changed; the RA now read .38, the declination .29. Each had advanced at several times the normal orbital speed. The startled astronomer read out the figures in a shaky voice.

After a moment's silence, Dr. Rory Gallager whispered, *"God help us all."*

TUESDAY

0915 HRS

✺

That morning brought some excitement to the dull but prestigious Southcott Golf and Country Club, located three miles east of Kennedy down near the ocean. One of the groundskeepers happened to be grabbing a coffee in the administration building overlooking the west parking area when he spotted a huge St. Bernard jump out of a big blue Chrysler. Astonished, he then watched Ms. Hennessey step out, a regular, followed by an old woman and a really big man.

Southcott being among the most exclusive clubs in the entire nation, guests were permitted only by prior consent and even then under strict rules. Jeb Soverign knew every regular member by sight and by name. He knew for a fact that the two people with Mrs. Hennessey were not members. But it wasn't the visitors that worried Jeb; it was the dog. Animals were not allowed on the grounds under any circumstances.

Rather than call security, Jeb, a sixty-eight-year-old fixture at Southcott, decided to head off the problem personally, before any of the senior members noticed the intrusion. Jeb liked young Mrs. Hennessey and knew she could be penalized for bringing a dog to the club.

He ran down the stairs, dashed out of the admin building, hopped across four tiers of bright fall flowers, and descended a short embankment to the parking lot. "Ms. Hennessey! Ms. Hennessey!"

Rachael turned around in surprise, saw who was calling her name, and began to walk back toward the groundskeeper.

Jeb doffed his aged 1955 Brooklyn Dodgers cap and pointed at Reggie. "Ma'am, I'd allow you'd better get that big ol' dog back in the car before someone spots him."

Rachael had so many other things on her mind that morning that she had not considered the potential danger in bringing Reggie along. The difficulty being, of course, that Mrs. Kelly—after urging Rachael to keep her nine-thirty tennis game and, further, that she and Brooks accompany her to Southcott—had insisted that the bloody dog come along. Rachael felt she was in no position to refuse an angel anything he, or she, or it, wanted.

"You see that little old gal? How about you go over and explain that to her. The dog is her idea."

"Sure, Ms. Hennessey, but it's, uh, just with you being the member and all, it's, uh, kind of your responsibility. Mr. B's just settin' up for his usual round of golf. He spots that dog . . . well, I sure don't want to see you get in no trouble."

Rachael cringed at the thought of being taken to task by the very person in the club she most detested. Baird had on a number of occasions made thinly-veiled attempts to seduce Rachael, and she knew he would not hesitate to use her infraction to tighten the screws a little more. She was aware of his reputation, of the ruthless intimidation tactics he had used to make his fortune in real estate. There were few kind words spoken about Charles Baird III, yet each year the old guard reelected him chairman of the ethics committee because he ran a tight ship.

Dressed smartly in a frilly white tennis skirt with a sporty mint-green top, she took Jeb Soverign by the arm and led him back to where the other three were waiting. "Allow me to introduce you to Mrs. Kathleen Kelly. Kindly explain to Mrs. Kelly, if you would, why this overstuffed creature," she cast a disdainful eye at Reggie, "is not allowed on the grounds."

Mrs. Kelly wore a set of pale pumpkin designer jeans with a rust blouse open at the neck. Jeb smiled down at the little old lady, thinking she might be Ms. Hennessey's grandmother, and told her the club rules about pets.

Reginald stood beside Mrs. Kelly, her right hand resting on his neck. He cocked his big head to one side and gazed up at the speaker as if he fully understood what was being said. Brooks didn't think Sarius was going to respond, but then a light came on in Mrs. Kelly's eyes and a grin spread across her shrunken features as the angel recalled Rachael's comments from the previous evening.

"Brooksie, I believe the time has come for us to meet this gentleman."

The old groundskeeper pushed his fuzzy eyebrows together but kept his advice to himself.

"Jeb, I'll tell you what—you go tell Mr. Baird that Kathleen Kelly wants a word. We'll meet him over at the pro shop. Go on now, catch him before he tees off."

Jeb was appalled at the request. "Jeez, lady, Mr. B'll blow a gasket if I haul him off the tee box. And you'd better not go bringin' your dog over. They'd call the cops, sure as heck."

"On your way, Jeb. Kindly announce our arrival."

His old brown face three shades darker than usual, the groundskeeper set off at a brisk pace. He knew all hell was about to break loose and now wished to God he had kept his nose out of matters that did not concern him. So much for trying to give people a hand, he thought.

Rachael threw her husband an exasperated look and said to Sarius, "Look, I would appreciate it if you stayed away from Mr. Baird. As it is, if he happens to spot this mutt, I'm toast. Did you plan this?"

Mrs. Kelly smiled knowingly as she took Brooks by the arm and set off in the direction of the pro shop. Over her shoulder she said, "Run along now, dear, or you are going be late. Your husband and I have work to do. And have a little faith, for heaven's sake."

Brooks half-turned and gave his wife a helpless shrug. He had no idea what they were doing here in the first place. Brooks had never once visited the grandiose development, never even been invited. It was a part of Rachael's life she kept to herself. But deep down he had always known his wife would be embarrassed to be seen among the cream of New York City's elite with her big blob of a husband in tow.

Rachael banged her tennis racket against her bare thigh, but managed to stifle the words that came to mind because she remembered Brooks's warning about watching her language. After a few deep breaths, she strode off in the direction of the courts more concerned than angry. She had an ominous feeling that she was about to play her last match at Southcott.

Since the building complex spanned five full acres of land, it usually took new members several attempts before they could confidently navigate their way through the maze of buildings and porticos and flower gardens that comprised the ninety-year-old country club. Sarius, naturally, did not have this problem, and headed straight for the pro shop with Brooks swiveling his head to take in the sights. Rachael's stories last evening had intrigued the angelic visitor, as did the game of golf itself, which seemed to a casual observer a foolish way to spend one's time.

Southcott's architecture was English Tudor in the grand tradition. The great house, which contained one of the finest dining rooms in the state, also offered two ballrooms and eleven large meeting rooms. Membership was limited to eighteen hundred American citizens at a modest cost of four hundred thousand annual, or one lump payment of four million for a lifetime membership, but was not available to Arabs, Jews, Orientals, Blacks, Puerto Ricans, Mexicans, or anyone whose ancestry could be traced to the Indian subcontinent. Southcott had one of the highest WASP ratings in America—and a waiting list seven pages long.

The man responsible for maintaining such high standards, Charles Baird III, was two days into his sixty-fifth year but could easily pass for ten years younger. Six feet tall, one hundred eighty-five pounds, a full head of sandy-brown hair with only a smattering of white above his ears, he could still lap his pool for two full hours without tiring. While waiting for Dermot Steel, the senior pro who had been his golfing partner for the past thirteen years, Baird noticed that the ninety-year oaks were beginning to yellow.

The season was coming to an end, but during the course of the year he had managed to shave off another two strokes. At the moment he was a four handicap, the best he had ever been during his thirty-four years of playing the game. He now held the lowest senior handicap in the club, which translated into the single most satisfying accomplishment of his entire life.

A cool breeze drifted in off the ocean a couple of miles or so to the south, but his light wool St. Andrews sweater provided just the right amount of warmth. He took a few practice swings with his new Callaway driver, feeling for the weight at the end of the tailored graphite shaft. It felt absolutely perfect, which caused Baird to smile. Another good round coming up.

When Jeb marched up to the number one tee box all out of breath, Baird wondered if the old groundskeeper had lost his mind. The tee box was inviolate. Once entered, it was sacred ground to all but one's partners. No one, under any circumstances, was allowed to breach this fundamental decree.

"What do *you* want?" Baird snarled.

Jeb held his cap tight to his belt with both hands and cast his eyes down at Baird's gleaming brown and white loafers. "Beg pardon, Mr. B, that new member, Ms. Hennessey, done brought in two guests, and a, uh . . . "

"Yes, man, spit it out!"

"A dog, that's what she brought. But—"

"What do you mean, *a dog?*"

Jeb's eyes rolled. He could feel the storm clouds gathering. "It's a big one Mr. B, and there's this old lady came with Ms. Hennessey said she wants a word with you." He reeled the words off fast as he could to make sure he didn't get interrupted again.

Baird caressed the head of his new driver as he glanced at his watch; two minutes to tee time, and his partner still had not shown. Overhead a big 777 out of Kennedy came close enough for him to read the warning sign beneath the left wing: NO SMOKING WHILE REFUELING THE AIRCRAFT. Baird was so accustomed to the murderous assaults on his eardrums that he rarely took notice.

He made a mental note of Dermot Steel's tardiness. There was no room at Southcott for tardiness on the part of any member of the staff. Just as there was no room for errors of judgment on the part of the members. Anyone but Rachael Hennessey, he would have exploded on the spot, but it was just possible that this unforgivable infraction could be the means of finally getting that cold-blooded minx to come around.

"Where is Mrs. Hennessey?"

"Uh, she was all dressed up for tennis, Mr. B. Over on the courts, I'd say."

"And this woman you referred to?"

"Said she's on her way." Jeb dared to raise his eyes, but only to turn around and search the grounds. Sure enough, the old gal and her friend were making their way to the pro shop. Much to his horror, so was the St. Bernard.

Baird almost dropped his Calloway in shock. In his thirty years as a member of Southcott, he had never heard of a dog entering the grounds.

It was simply too much. Even at fifty paces he could tell from her clothing that the woman was a commoner. And that big hulk at her side looked like a sumo wrestler.

"You there!" he said to the groundskeeper in a raspy voice. "Summon security, now! Have them remove these intruders at once, and I want you to personally escort that animal out of here. Get to it, man!"

"Yes sir, Mr. B. Uh, that little old gal just going in the shop, she's the one wants a word. She was mighty insistent."

But Baird had just about run out of patience. "Get out of my sight at once, you . . . you . . . you Negro! And tell Dermot Steel if he doesn't show up in one minute, his job is damned well on the line. If you dare interrupt me again, so is yours!"

❧

The two proper young men behind the counter in the pro shop could not believe their eyes. Looking for all the world like a pair of Mormon missionaries in golf clothes, they glanced at each other in amazement. Reggie liked the place at once and left his new mistress to have a sniff around.

After doing a quick scan herself, Mrs. Kelly strolled up to the counter and said in a sweet voice, "Morning, boys. I'll be wanting to get outfitted for a round of golf. Everything, from head to toe. Perhaps one of you nice youngsters can give me some assistance."

The kid looked up at Brooks. "Excuse me, sir. Is either of you a member of Southcott?"

Sarius pinched Brooks's arm and replied haughtily, "Not yet, young man, but if your facilities meet our standards, we just might consider joining."

The second kid's face darkened, and his voice took on a sharp edge. "That is quite out of the question. Nor can you purchase anything in this shop. Southcott is a private club. Didn't they tell you that at the gate?"

"Matter of fact, they didn't," said Brooks, getting into the spirit of things. He had no idea what the angel had in mind, but whatever it was, he knew he was going to enjoy it. "They welcomed us with open arms. Real friendly people you have down here."

The first attendant, his eyes nervously following Reggie's circuitous path in and out of the aisles of expensive clothing and equipment, said briskly, "I'm afraid a serious mistake has been made. I must ask you to leave the grounds at once, before I call security."

Sarius scanned the kid's mind, recovering his entire life experience in less than a second, then pressed Mrs. Kelly's wrinkled old face across the counter. "William Dunsmuir Smith. Yes, you seem like a nice young man, but in fact you are not. Far from it . . . "

✍

Since the senior pro was experiencing a severe bout of dysentery, all part of the angel's impulsive scheme, he was still nowhere to be seen; and by the time Baird tore through the doorway looking for him, Willie and his companion had both entered a kind of horrified hypnotic state.

Mrs. Kelly strolled up to the angry man and held out her hand. "As I live and breathe, if it isn't Charles Baird III. My late husband often spoke of you, but living away in Greece I never had the opportunity to meet many of Andy's old friends. I must say, you are even better looking in real life than on all those photos I have of Andy and you at college."

Although he did not want to, Baird took the brittle fingers into his hand. Andy . . . Andy . . . surely she was not speaking of Andy von Wilhem.

"Yes," Sarius went on in a grand voice, "my husband passed away in '84, as you know, and silly old me went ahead and married another over-the-hill billionaire. Blasted fool went off and got himself killed by a lightning bolt down in Botswana. Can you believe that? So here I am with two fortunes and nothing worthwhile to spend it on."

Baird caught the sardonic look on the big blob she had with her and stifled his suggestion that a decent wardrobe might be a good place to start. Looking down at the spidery crow's feet and protruding cheekbones, he wondered what Andy Von Wilhem had seen in this decrepit old granny. Thirty years ago she still would have been unsightly.

"A sad state of affairs, Mrs. . . . . ?"

"Kelly. But call me Kathleen. This is my dearest friend, Brooks Hennessey."

Baird stared at the big man in shock. "Rachael's husband?"

"The very same," said Brooks without holding out his hand. He'd never met Baird, but he'd heard enough stories.

Baird noticed the dog rummaging around out of the corner of his eye and had to fight hard to restrain himself. "I assume you're here to watch Mrs. Hennessey play tennis?"

"Not at all," Mrs. Kelly replied. "It's just that . . . well, the truth is that I left my equipment behind in Athens. Brooks doesn't play golf, but I do. Love the game. But I shall require a whole new wardrobe, plus a decent set of clubs. Then I thought, well . . . "

Her voice dropped so low that Baird had to lean close to hear the next words. The distinct odor of mothballs assaulted his nasal passages. "I was wondering if I might find me a real game—that is, a game with some hair on it."

"Hair?" Baird inquired, his ear almost touching the old woman's cracked lips.

"Bread, Charlie. Money. Cash dollars. I just *love* playing for money—a lot of money. Don't matter a damn if I lose it; just love the thrill. Gone and transferred a fair wad over to the Chase Manhattan down on Wall Street—and I intend to use it. What do you think—anyone around here be interested?"

Baird, a consummate opportunist, quickly set aside his anger over the dog and Dermot Steel's disappearing act. Although betting on the outcome of a game was strictly prohibited, occasional side bets between partners were not unknown. The bank she mentioned just happened to be where he conducted his own financial affairs, and Chase Manhattan's CEO was a personal friend. He tossed around the ramifications, did a quick overview of the entire scenario, then excused himself on the pretense that he was concerned about his missing partner, but assured Mrs. Kelly he would be right back.

He walked to the rear of the shop and exited through a door marked PRIVATE. One of the newer staff, the Marino woman, was working on some accounts. "Have you seen Dermot Steel?"

"Yes, sir. Mr. Steel came running through here fifteen minutes ago. He said something about the washroom."

The washroom! Steel was starting to behave like an adolescent. "I have to make an emergency call, Tracy. Please excuse me for a moment."

Although the accountant was fully cognizant of Baird's position in the club, she did not think it proper to leave personal records lying around. "I'll need a moment to—"

"Out, now! And shut the door behind you."

Her color rising, the young woman popped out of her chair and rushed from the room. Two minutes and twenty seconds later, Baird had Chase Manhattan's chief executive officer on the line. After the customary banalities, Baird told Roger Morris he needed a favor.

A small chuckle, then, "Cost you, Charles."

Baird explained about Mrs. Kelly and her mention of his bank. Morris hesitated. Revealing such information could get him into hot water.

"Sticky, Charles, very sticky. Might not be possible."

Baird was ready. "If this works out, I can promise your name will suddenly appear close to the top of the list."

"How close?"

"Top dozen for sure."

Morris was astonished. "You have that kind of pull?"

"I do."

"Why that means . . . next year!"

"Our average loss over the winter months is twenty members. You'll be in by April."

Class affiliations counted for a lot to snobbish New Yorkers, and belonging to the Southcott Golf and Country Club was considered pretty well the top of the heap. Morris told Charles Baird to stand by, put him on hold, then turned to his computer keyboard and typed in the code for the Wall Street branch. It took longer than expected to get Kathleen Kelly's account on the screen, and when her balance finally did come up, the CEO assumed there was a transmission error.

Aware of Baird's impatience, Morris telephoned the manager and asked several pointed questions. The answers confirmed the figure on his screen.

"*Charles!* This woman just transferred one point seven billion over from the Athens Commercial Bank."

Baird could feel the sweet glow in his belly. "U.S. currency?"

"U.S. currency. Came in yesterday morning. I must say, Charles, your friend appears to be filthy rich. You mind my asking—"

"No time now. I'll call you later this evening."

"Top dozen?"

"Roger, old buddy, consider it done."

Baird returned with a radiant smile on his face. He had forgotten all about Dermot Steel.

Placing one hand on Brooks's shoulder, Baird said, "William, this fine gentleman happens to be the husband of one of our esteemed members. His slightest wish is your command. Understand?"

Still shaken from the personal revelations the old woman had spouted, the young assistant pro bobbed his head rapidly.

Baird locked one arm into Mrs. Kelly's and led her toward the counter. "And this delightful lady, William, is my special guest. I want you to attend to her every desire. Mrs. Kelly shall require clothing, equipment, the works. Make certain she gets the best of everything, and put it on my account. Set up a tee time ASAP and call me in my office when she is ready."

Baird bent low to kiss Mrs. Kelly's scrawny knuckles. "My dear woman, I would be delighted if you would consider playing a round with me."

"Why, Charles, that would be just grand. Sure you don't mind?"

"Quite the contrary. I would deem it a great honor."

I'll bet, thought the angel as he twisted Mrs. Kelly's face into an acquiescent smile.

0430 HRS

❧

Copeland never truly believed that Mars had actually dropped out of orbit. This kind of irrational event was simply unacceptable to the scientific mind. Even if it were possible, evidence of the immense force required to shift a whole planet would be apparent. The big 88 could not detect such a force, nevertheless, over the next several intense hours during that terrible night at the top of Mauna Kea, the astronomer's initial skepticism slowly melted away in the face of unassailable reality.

Copeland and his five bewildered Japanese visitors discounted the computer baseline entirely and sat down with a book of tables and an old Hewlett Packard 200LX palm-top to manually compute the correct coordinates for Mars.

The red planet had long since set, but the original observations had all been recorded. They worked the figures every way possible, but the results never varied. For whatever reason, Mars appeared to be in the process of breaking free from its orbit around the sun. Dr. Gallager did not call again until four-fifty. His voice shook with excitement.

"After I got off the phone from talking to you, I got hold of Kevin Passmore at the radio observatory up at White Lake, British Columbia. They're the guys carrying out the galactic plane mapping project. Turns out three weeks ago they picked up a brand new source off in the direction of the heart of the galaxy. Very, very strong, Kevin says, a magnetic field that runs off the scale. They got in touch with Palomar right away, but they couldn't spot anything. Neither could the Hubble. Visually, this puppy's just not there."

67

Copeland knew where the Texan was heading—into another black hole.

"Yeah, I know what you're thinking. And at first that's what they figured, but they were wrong. Palomar arranged to have the newest XIT satellite take a look at it." The big x-ray imaging telescope had been launched in July. "They found the sucker—weak flashes every 56 seconds."

An extremely powerful magnetic field meant that the object was much denser than a normal star, and weak x-rays combined with slow rotation pretty well spelled it out. "A neutron star!"

"A neutron it is, and spinning so slow it's probably in its dying gasps."

When a star's normal-density core begins to implode, it releases vast amounts of energy into the star's outer layer. This in turn triggers a supernova explosion that drives the outer layers off into space. In this way the star's original million kilometer diameter can be reduced to as little as twenty kilometers over a relatively short period of time, but now contains a mass many times greater than the body it came from. Copeland knew that such a mass could reach densities in excess of one billion tons per cubic inch.

"Anyone figure out when the supernova took place?"

"I doubt they got that far along. There's always been so much energy in that sector of the galaxy that the radio boys were never able to separate this source from all the rest. Kevin is of the opinion that this sucker's got caught up in some kind of gravitational tango, presumably with another star, that ended up with the thing being catapulted straight at us."

Copeland's throat went dry. A star of enormous mass was headed this way. A mass so great that even at vast distances it managed to influence the gravity inside our solar system.

"Rory, is this for real?"

The Texan's wheezing voice softened almost to a whisper. "More real than you want it to be, old buddy because all you got so far is the good news."

Because they could hear only one side of the conversation, the Japanese were making wild guesses at what was taking place. All five faces were horror-stricken.

Copeland realized that the fetid body odor was his own. "What's the bad news?"

Gallager's voice became high-pitched again. "That itty-bitty star appears to be headed right down our alley. I mean *right* down our alley! Palomar's already named it—Omega. I've been on the blower to Bernstein for the last two hours. Turns out they already used all the info they could get their hands on to back-calculate the mass and come up with an educated guess at the temperature. But they couldn't tie down the speed and trajectory until I told them about Mars. They didn't know about Mars, so that's a big one for you, Danny boy. Now they got Omega racing through the cosmos at around 3,000 kilometers per second."

"God Almighty!"

The University of Hawaii's senior astronomer took a deep breath and shut his eyes before asking the next question. "Did anyone venture a guess on how far away they think Omega is?"

"Oh yeah, they told me. Did they ever! And it's not a guess, buddy boy. Three hundred ninety million kilometers, give or take a few million."

No wonder Mars was being pulled out of orbit. In astronomical terms three hundred and ninety million kilometers was just around the corner. Copeland's fingers scrambled to work out the numbers on his 200LX.

With his heart pounding out of control he yelled into the receiver, "Do you realize what you're saying? That's thirty-six hours from now!"

"Wednesday, six PM Eastern Daylight Time, to be precise. Just after lunch for us."

Copeland had to swallow a few times to activate his saliva glands. His thinking was getting muddled. "Are you telling me Bernstein honestly believes Omega is coming this way?"

"That, my friend, is precisely what I'm telling you. Know any good prayers, now is the time to start saying them."

Copeland was in a zombie-like state by the time he set down the telephone receiver. He continued to stare at the computer screen while his brain switched to automatic.

A body with, say, a mass twice that of the sun enters our solar system. It already had Mars, but the red planet would literally disintegrate well before it got close to impact. Whatever about Jupiter, the same could conceivably hold true for Venus and Mercury, even Earth, provided Lev Bernstein's calculations were correct.

Even a tiny tug from such an enormous gravity field would cause irrevocable damage. The entire atmosphere would be sucked into Omega's vast gravitational maw. Seven-tenths of the world's land mass would be covered by the oceans in their wild tidal surges, while thousands of violent earthquakes would effectively shatter the remaining segments into little bits. The eruption of every volcano in the world would block out the sun for months, perhaps years. A lesser, but still deadly side effect would see the release of millions of tons of poisonous gases from the earth's core into the darkened and stagnant atmosphere. Even if the earth did not spiral off into space, there was always the possibility that once knocked out of orbit the blue planet would fall toward the sun.

No matter how it happened, Copeland could not envision any survivors to such a catastrophe.

"Dr. Copeland! Dr. Copeland!"

The young Japanese woman was tapping his shoulder. Her doll-like face showed deep concern.

Copeland shook his head to clear away the terrible images. He stood up, took one last glance at the big 88 that he loved so dearly, gave his frightened colleagues a grim nod, then left the observatory forever.

1030 HRS

❧

S outhcott's senior golf pro was uncertain, even worried, about the prospect that lay before him. The woman seemed so old and frail he doubted she was capable of swinging a club without injuring herself. Dermot Steel was ex-Marine, slim and erect, with an old style crew-cut the same color as his name. A friendly, patient kind of person, highly regarded by the membership, he was astonished by Baird's proposal.

"Don't care for this, Charles. Don't care for it at all. The press gets wind of it, Southcott's reputation could get knocked. And that dog—what will the members think?"

Baird gave Steel an angry look but said nothing. His mind was surging ahead, wondering how high he could get her to go. The two men stood beside their cart, waiting for the fairway to clear. The old woman had declared herself a twenty-two handicap, which both men found hard to swallow. But her opponent was not about to protest—the lower her handicap, the better for him. With Baird's four handicap, this gave her a one stroke advantage on each of the eighteen holes. The game was match play, with the money riding on each hole. Except that Mrs. Kelly did not wish to name a figure until she teed off. This was unheard of, but Baird allowed it. If he was going to steal her money, he reasoned, she could do whatever she wanted.

Sarius had earlier scanned Dermot Steel's memory and extracted every technical term the man had ever used. The angel now had the same wealth of knowledge the golf pro had accumulated during his forty-two years of playing the game.

71

Brooks sat in his cart with the dog squeezed in beside him on the floor. Baird had almost croaked when Mrs. Kelly insisted Reggie come along. But Sarius would not relent. Either the dog came, or the game was off. Simple.

Greed won out.

The first hole was a par four, slightly downhill with a dogleg right. It was 180 yards from the men's tee box to get beyond the big oaks on the right and have a clear shot at the green. Baird went first. He didn't bother with the dogleg, but drove over the trees to land in the middle of the fairway 20 yards short of the green. His drive was 265 yards. He could not see his ball, but he knew exactly where it had come down. He stepped down and grinned at the pro, whose cart was stopped just behind Brooks's.

Mrs. Kelly stood beside Brooks with her right hand resting on his shoulder, which made the big Irishman feel more than a little uncomfortable.

She called out, "Good shot, Charlie!"

Brooks whispered, "You play this game before?"

"Contrary to a whole lot of wishful thinking, heaven is not inundated with golf courses. Wish me luck, Brooksie."

Brooks curled his fingers in the long hair on Reggie's neck as Mrs. Kelly strolled up to the woman's tee box. Blue and white Foot-Joy loafers, pale yellow slacks, a lovely blueberry Quantum cardigan, a wonderful full-brim Michelle McGann hat. Even her clubs, a set of Titleist woods with matching irons, looked professional. He couldn't help but wonder what the real Mrs. Kelly might have thought.

Reggie demonstrated his lack of interest in the game by settling in for a snooze. Brooks watched the dog get comfortable and scratched his ear fondly. He had no idea why Sarius wanted the dog along, but Brooks had to admit it was nice having the old mutt beside him.

He turned back just in time to see Mrs. Kelly strike the ball. It dribbled off the tee about twenty feet and stopped in the long grass well short of the fairway. Brooks groaned. Not at all what he had expected.

Baird groaned as well. He had a vision of large amounts of currency flying off into space. After that effort, he reasoned, she would not want to play for high stakes. Steel drove their cart closer to Mrs. Kelly, who continued to stare hard at the end of her driver as if it were the club's fault.

Typical amateur reaction, Baird thought. *Blame the club.*

"Bad start, dear."

The old woman, grim-faced, replied, "Too bloody right, it was. Well, let me tell you right now that I fully intend to improve, and right quick-like. So what's it to be, Charlie, hundred a hole?"

Baird's jaw dropped. "A hundred dollars?"

"You are a funny man, Charlie."

Baird gave a sigh of relief. "Hundred thousand, then. Well . . . I suppose if that is what you feel comfortable with."

Sarius leaned across Steel. He loved this part. "It's what *you* feel comfortable with, Charles. I don't have a limit."

Baird stared the eccentric old biddy in the eye as he searched for the right words. "The same applies to me, dear," he said lightly, but his tone clearly implied a challenge.

Mrs. Kelly withdrew and pursed her lips. "How do you know I didn't flub that ball on purpose?"

Baird almost choked trying not to laugh. Steel was not so lucky. He had just taken a swig of root beer and blasted it forth all over the front of the cart.

Baird felt like shooting him. "Allow me to apologize for my partner—"

Mrs. Kelly, her face still contemplative, cut him off. Coldly she said, "I can understand his reaction. After all, Mr. Steel just watched an eighty-two-year-old grandmother hit a golf ball twenty feet. Anyone would find it funny. How does a million suit you?"

The words were like an aphrodisiac to Baird. One million dollars a hole. He closed his eyes as if he were thinking it over. In fact he was saying to himself, with considerable fervor, *Thank you God, thank you God, thank you God . . .*

Looking up, he replied cautiously, "That is an awful lot of money."

"Yes," Mrs Kelly replied sweetly. "But you see, I don't intend to lose."

With this final statement, Baird felt exonerated. He gave Steel a quick glance, caught his bubble-eyed nod, and said, "Well then, dear, let's you and me play us some golf."

Sarius reached across Steel's chest. "Better shake on it, Charlie. Not that I don't trust you, but over the years I've noticed that the world is plugged with dishonest people."

Baird took her tiny, brittle hand in both of his. In a voice dripping with sincerity, he said, "You are so, so right, but you and I are not among them, are we?"

Sarius nodded. Greed was such a wonderful human attribute. "A perfectly accurate statement, I'm sure. Well, excuse me while I see if I can't recover from a bad start."

"Good luck, dear!"

"Thank you, Charles. You too."

As soon as she was out of earshot, Baird said, "Can you believe it? Eighteen million beautiful dollars! Oh God, I love this game."

"Problem is—she's nuttier than a fruitcake."

"Don't confuse eccentricity with mental disorder. Even if the old broad is a basket case, that stupid jerk, Hennessey, hasn't said a word. Any negative feedback, we can always point to his full complicity. And don't forget, the big turd is a newspaperman. Relax, Dermot old boy, we are in for the thrill of a lifetime."

"We?" Steel's mind was drifting off in a direction where it had never gone before.

Baird knew where he was coming from. He had been there himself enough times to recognize the symptoms. "Ten percent, Dermot. You get ten percent of the winnings. That's a promise. Thirteen years we've been playing together. You deserve something. One point eight million bucks. Think you can live with that?"

Steel's heart raced, and his mind raced. True, they were doing nothing wrong here. The whole thing had certainly been the old woman's idea, and she was accompanied by the husband of one of the members, who didn't seem to mind how she spent her money. The pro decided he could live with it.

"That's real nice of you, Charles. Real nice."

Mrs. Kelly used a five iron to get out of the rough. She chopped down, and up popped the ball in a fine arc all the way to the middle of the fairway just past the last oak, a good 130 yards. From there she would have a clear shot at the flag. Brooks smiled. Steel was impressed. So was Baird.

Although he sometimes followed the tournaments on TV, Brooks had never played the game. Ahead of him a smattering of tiny cloud shadows danced across the fairway. A light breeze ruffled a bed of wild roses behind the ladies' tee box, while a family of gray squirrels chattered noisily in the background. An osprey swooped low enough for Brooks to look it in the eye. The setting was pleasant and restful.

Only the fact that Mrs. Kelly was so tiny allowed her to squeeze in beside Brooks. Her new loafers rested on Reggie's back.

"How am I doing?"

"Good recovery. You, uh, happen to have eighteen million dollars lying around?"

"All under control, Brooksie. Trust me, and enjoy the game."

When Mrs. Kelly climbed back out beside her ball, she made a pretense of looking around for the yardage marker. But she already knew she was 157 yards from the flag. She also knew that Dermot Steel would expect someone of her age and size to choose a three wood. This she did, trying a few practice swings before taking up a position beside her ball. Her swing resulted in topping the ball, but she managed to get enough of it to run the ball to within forty yards of the green.

She climbed back in, and Brooks started up the cart. "He's two up on you already, and you're still away. You sure you know what you're doing?"

Sarius gave Mrs. Kelly's head a sad little shake. "Oh ye of little faith."

This time she took a wedge, gave the two men in the other cart a tiny shrug, then executed a fine shot that plopped the ball down four feet from the hole. "Well done, Mrs. Kelly," Steel called out.

"Four to get on," Baird commented in a low voice. "Best she can do is bogey."

"And a birdie gives you one million dollars."

The chairman of the ethics committee corrected his partner. "The *first* one million dollars."

"Right," Steel agreed with a grin. And one hundred thousand for him.

Baird took out his lob wedge, walked confidently over to his ball, took two quick practice swings, and plop—the ball landed softly on the green and rolled back to within three feet of the cup.

"Very nice, Charlie. Looks like you have me on this one."

Baird gave her a glittery smile. "Not over yet, dear."

Steel walked up and removed the flag. Brooks angled his cart for a better view.

Mrs. Kelly was first away. She studied the lie, figured there was a five-inch break, then squared herself to the line. Three small practice swings and a short tap sent the ball straight into the cup.

Steel removed it for her. "Nice putt."

Mrs. Kelly accepted the ball in silence and stepped back. Her opponent studied his three footer: downhill, with no break whatsoever, a straight-in shot. He stepped up and went through his putting routine.

A million dollar putt! thought Brooks. He was fully caught up in the excitement.

Steel was nervous, but he had watched his partner drain these short putts a thousand times. He had every confidence in Baird.

Baird tried to clear his mind of the obvious distraction. He aligned his putter and gently stroked the ball. The Nike Pro 2 cruised to within one inch of the cup, stopped, and hung there as if in complete defiance of gravity. The two men stared down in horror.

Mrs. Kelly glanced over at Brooks as if to say, *Told you so.*

Baird angrily tapped the ball in for par. But par merely tied him with the old woman. It was a carryover.

"Good par, Charlie," she said graciously.

But Charlie did not feel gracious. He stomped off the green, jammed his putter in the bag, and threw himself into the golf cart.

Brooks took Mrs. Kelly's putter. "Jeez, what a sore loser."

"You're right. Keep this up, he might blow a gasket before the day is out."

They set off around the green toward the number two tee box. Brooks said casually, "You don't talk much like an angel."

"How many angels you heard, Brooksie?"

"Not many, I suppose. None that I was sure of, anyway."

"So you don't know what angels talk like, do you?"

"Guess not. You a typical angel?"

Sarius smiled. "Typical? Probably not."

"Ummmm . . . and something makes me think you don't have permission to be doing this."

"Permission—pooh! You seem to be harboring the misconception that my activities are restricted in some way. Nothing could be further from the truth. I can, within certain limitations, do whatever I want. Same as you. Free will is free will, Brooksie."

The second hole was another par four, this time with a dogleg left, but with a pond on the right and a creek on the left. The fairway narrowed to less than 40 yards at 150 yards beyond the men's tee box, but it took a 200-yard drive to clear a thick grove of pines on the left and be able to go for the flag. The number two was considered the second toughest hole on the course.

Baird took the lead again, hitting his five wood 220 yards down the middle. It was superb execution.

Mrs. Kelly leaned close to her chauffeur and whispered, "Guess I'd better pull up my socks."

They drove ahead to the women's tee. Even though Brooks realized Sarius was just having fun with Baird, at the same time he found it just a touch scary that eighteen million bucks was up for grabs.

A pair of mountain bluebirds in early migration and well off course landed right in front of Mrs. Kelly as she was setting up for her drive. After studying them for a moment, Sarius held out his left hand. Both birds instantly fluttered up and landed on the gloved hand. Both were males, resplendent in pale turquoise with cobalt blue backs.

Turning to his astonished audience, the angel said, "Aren't they lovely?"

After the bluebirds flitted away into the sun, Mrs. Kelly went ahead and took her drive. It was weak, about 90 yards and well off to the right, but it deflected off the trunk of an elm tree down onto the paved cart path, where it took a big bounce to gain another 30 yards and land back on the fairway.

Her opponent muttered, "Luckier than a butcher's dog!"

Brooks chuckled away as he drove her to the ball.

Mrs. Kelly's second shot was longer and straighter, taking her just a few yards short of Baird. She had about 140 yards to the flag and this time, after some consideration, asked Brooks for her five wood.

Steel and Baird pulled in several yards behind them. "Old girl seems to know what she's about," ventured Steel, who hadn't spoken a word since Baird missed his three-footer.

Baird watched her third shot, which took her over the creek and onto the green but well beyond the pin. "Too much club," Baird said, but had to admit it was a damn nice shot for a pipsqueak granny.

His nine iron shot actually hit the flag pole and dropped two feet beyond the hole—a guaranteed birdie.

"Got her this time for sure," Steel said as they drove over the bridge. "Take a miracle to drop that forty-footer."

Brooks was thinking the same.

Sarius said, "I am learning something here today."

"Oh?" muttered Brooks, somehow sensing that his angelic passenger was not referring to golf.

"You know full well I can place that ball on the moon if I want, yet you still doubt my ability. Speaks volumes about human nature."

Brooks eyed the old woman who had died on the altar in the middle of Monday morning Mass. "Escorting a dead person around the most exclusive golf course in the state with eighteen million bucks on the line is not something I do on a regular basis. Takes a bit of adjustment. Perhaps I'll get the hang of it tomorrow, while you're in the process of selling Brooklyn Bridge to some rich Arab."

"The bridge, um? There's a thought." Sarius liked Brooks. He had not said so, but Brooks had a marvelous aura, and auras revealed a great deal about people.

Mrs. Kelly went off with her putter, her brows furrowed and her face determined. Baird marked his ball and backed away to allow Steel to hold the pin.

She studied the lie, saw that it was downhill over a hump with a good four-foot break from left to right. Problem was, once the ball got over the hump it would pick up speed and cruise well past the hole unless the alignment was perfect.

Mrs. Kelly set her feet, gripped her putter, bent over, eyed the flag, and gave the ball a good whack. Steel pulled the pin. The three men knew she had hit it too hard, but the speed of the ball did not allow it to meander much and it came drifting over the hump like a bat out of hell, hit the far rim of the cup, went two feet straight up in the air, and then back into the hole.

"Par," called a meek little voice from forty feet away.

Baird could hardly believe his eyes. It seemed like some kind of trick photography. He reset his own ball in a zombie-like state and tapped it in for birdie.

They were still tied, and the money would carry over once again.

0700 HRS

❧

"Yeah?"
The deep male voice threw Copeland off completely. "Who the hell are you?"

"Who the hell are *you?*"

"Jo-Ann's husband—that's who. Where is my wife?"

"Oh yeah, the starry-eyed professor. Sorry, Danny boy, she's gone to visit her parents."

"Damn! New York?"

"You got it."

"You the boyfriend?"

"Right again."

"When did she leave?"

"Sunday morning, took the kids with her. I've been appointed official house sitter. Anything I can do?"

"Not likely!"

Copeland slammed down the receiver. It took him a few minutes to recover from the knowledge that some jerk had moved in with his ex-wife. After nervously lighting a cigarette, he flipped through his address book, found the Hardings' number, and again tackled his telephone. It was just noon in New York.

❧

What prompted Jo-Ann Copeland to leave her husband in the first place had nothing to do with drinking, carousing, gambling, wife beating, or any of the usual lot. She left him because she was in real danger of

81

dying—from boredom. Last April, when she finally bit the bullet and broke the news that she was returning to San Diego, she also informed her husband that she was taking eight-year-old Dana and five-year-old Buddy with her.

Copeland, she found out shortly after they were married, turned out to be one of those one-dimensional academic creatures who was already married—to his work. Astronomy was his life. It occupied his every waking moment. His mind rarely came down to earth, but floated around in the heavens, sometimes for weeks on end. So after spending ten full years watching Professor Copeland drift from galaxy to galaxy while at the same time carefully observing the second, and this time successful, assault upon Hawaii by the Japanese, Jo-Ann decided she liked Mexicans better, and with just one week's notice, pulled the plug.

She had been back in San Diego for eight months, found a good job as a lab technician, got the kids settled into a school routine, and had become more or less reconciled to her new life. Best of all, she'd found a good man, one who smothered her with attention. Copeland had telephoned exactly four times, each time suggesting they might get back together, but putting no real effort into it. In her heart Jo-Ann had accepted the hard truth that he was better off without them. After all, she reasoned, there was no longer a need to divert his valuable time to mundane family matters.

So it was with a mild sense of apprehension that she took the receiver from her mother's hand that Tuesday as the clock struck twelve noon. Copeland's previous calls had always been around six in the evening, the last one less than one month ago.

"Danny, that you?"

"Hi, honey. I know this will sound crazy, but I want you and the children to fly back to San Diego right away. Forget packing. Go downstairs this minute and grab a taxicab. Will you do that for me?"

"Are you out of your mind? We just got in Sunday night. Besides, have you already forgotten what happened when I announced we were leaving? You spent about three minutes trying to talk me out of it, then said it was probably for the best. So why this sudden urge to see your family, Danny, tell me that!"

"Joey, listen to me. You know I have always loved the three of you, and I am the first to admit that I wasn't real attentive to your needs—"

"Attentive! *Attentive!* You miserable SOB! Whole frigging months went by when you didn't know we existed. Yeah, I'd say you weren't attentive." Jo-Ann ignored her mother's darkening features. Bad language upset her.

"All that is behind us now. The future is going to be different." He paused to get a grip on his emotions. "More different than you could ever imagine. You must come back, Joey, now, today. What I have to . . . tell you won't wait."

Jo-Ann was more than a little shaken. She had never heard her husband speak with such passion unless he happened to be describing the latest supernova.

"Are you okay?" she asked in a milder tone.

"I will be once you get here. Just grab anything that's available, and I'll meet you at the airport."

"Danny, Mom and Dad will be in Zurich for Thanksgiving. This is our family get-together. Even if I wanted to come, I couldn't."

"Have I ever lied to you?"

"You have a lot of faults, Dan Copeland, but lying is not one of them."

"Then believe me when I tell you it doesn't matter a fiddler's damn about Thanksgiving. It won't—look, just get there as quickly as you can. You have to be with me when . . . "

"When what?"

"I'll tell you that when I see you. And please, Joey, don't delay."

"Now you listen to me, Dan Copeland, there is not one chance in a million of me and the children—"

Copeland jammed his finger on the button. He couldn't bear to listen to her refusal. With his family beside him, he could accept the inevitable. Without them, it would be a first-class ticket to hell.

Jo-Ann's mother saw the tears and walked over to place an arm around her youngest daughter's shoulders. "You still love him, don't you?"

"Oh, Mother," Jo-Ann wailed, "of course I do. The nerve of the man! As if I'm going to flit across country just because he has some dark secret to share. What do I care about his secrets? The miserable rat—I hate him!"

"But dear, you just said you loved him."

"Don't try to confuse me. I have a life, I have a man who really cares for me. The last thing I need now is that jerk of an ex-husband on my case."

1510 HRS

ॐ

By mid-afternoon the two carts were making their way toward the final teeing ground. Baird turned toward his driver. "You ever know of a game being tied this long?"

Steel shook his head. "Tell the truth, I never thought it was possible."

Yet that is exactly what had taken place. They had played seventeen holes, and the two unlikely opponents were still tied neck and neck. Both men could barely withstand the pressure.

As Baird was preparing to enter the men's tee box for his final drive, two players who had just come off the eighth hole maneuvered their cart around a big pot bunker and motored up to Baird. He cringed when he realized who it was.

With that famous cheesy grin in place, David Stenberg nodded toward the strange entourage. "Charles, old boy, looks to me like you're heading up a circus act. Want me to slot you in for next week?"

Donald Olson leaned across Stenberg. "Dog got a handicap?"

Baird knew both men well, had played with them a number of times. He wasn't worried about Olson, but Stenberg's warped sense of humor could spell trouble. "Listen guys, how about cutting me a little slack on this? Come see me after and I'll explain everything."

Sarius, being the beneficiary of Kathleen Kelly's instinctive reaction to the famous pair, found out she did not care for either man. The old woman strolled up to Stenberg while Brooks slumped down in the cart as best he could.

"Hi fellows. How's tricks?"

Stenberg perused the old lady, taking in the sea of wrinkles, the bright colors and the big hat. "Who are you?"

"Nobody special. Who are you?"

Which was one question Stenberg never expected to hear. Olson chuckled and said, "Must be a Canadian."

Baird gritted his teeth. He had no choice but to make the introductions. "This is Mrs. Kathleen Kelly, the widow of an old school friend. Hails from Athens. Kathleen, allow me to introduce Mr. Stenberg and Mr. Olson."

"Charmed, I'm sure," the angel replied, but before he could say another word, Baird took the old woman by the arm and forcefully led her back to her cart. She turned around and gave the two men a big wave. "Nice meeting you."

"Sheesh—what an ugly old bat," Donald Olson commented as they drove away. Stenberg agreed. "She reminds me of one of those Egyptian mummies."

At that moment they were headed back around the pot bunker beside the eighth hole, but the cart took a sudden wild turn to the right. Before they knew what was happening, the two celebrities were lying on their backs with the golf cart sitting on top of them.

Ten minutes went by before the cart was righted and the victims on their way back to the clubhouse. When Brooks returned from helping out, Mrs. Kelly said, "I hope the dear boys weren't seriously hurt."

"Scratched and banged up pretty bad, but no bones broken. Funny thing though—Stenberg swears they were a good ten feet away from the lip of that bunker." Brooks climbed in behind the wheel and gave Mrs. Kelly a hard look. "Don't suppose you had anything to do with that?"

"Me?" declared the angel in wide-eyed innocence. "Perish the thought." Seeing that Baird was once again ready to tee off, she called out, "No matter who wins, Charlie, I want to tell you that this has been one heck of a game."

Baird listened to the scream of ambulance sirens in the distance. Couple of fat lawsuits on the way, no doubt about it. He cleared his head to get back down to business. He was about to complete one of the finest games of his life, but somehow, *somehow,* the old biddy always managed to keep up. Now the entire bundle was riding on the last hole. He had to reach deep for a smile.

"I couldn't agree more, dear."

Mrs. Kelly chuckled, her tea-stained dentures in full array. "I haven't had this much fun since Moses stymied the pharaoh."

Completely wacko, Steel acknowledged for the umpteenth time.

As they backed away to allow Baird to take his final drive, Brooks whispered, "Moses?"

"My previous visit," Sarius whispered back. "You know how the pharaoh died?"

Brooks glanced at the dead woman, but didn't respond.

"Choked on a fish bone. Not very romantic, is it?"

Baird leaned into his drive, seeking maximum yardage. This was always a gamble, but this time it worked for him. The hole was a par five, 463 yards, and his ball rolled up and stopped just short of the 150-yard tree.

Steel exclaimed, "Three hundred plus! Can't do much better than that."

Mrs. Kelly acknowledged this feat with a nod. "Onward, Brooksie. You feeling sorry for him yet?"

Brooks cracked a tiny grin. "Not a chance."

Mrs. Kelly's final drive was her best of the day, about 150 yards. Well to the right, but in play. Her next shot was even better, which placed her fifteen yards ahead of her opponent.

Just before Baird stepped out of his cart, Steel said passionately, "Do it, Charles. Do it!"

Baird loosened himself up, took out his eight iron, walked behind the ball, and carefully studied the line. He gripped his club, approached the ball, addressed it, then executed a perfect swing.

The ball exploded out of the turf, went high into the blue sky, and landed ten feet beyond the hole. But then the backspin caught and the ball rolled back to stop eighteen inches beyond the cup.

Tap it in, and he had an eagle!

Steel almost cried. He had to stop himself from running out and hugging Baird. In his mind he was already spending his one point eight big ones.

The old gal needed birdie to tie, eagle to win. Since she had yet to go one under for the day, her chances of achieving either were about the same as a snowball surviving hell. Steel sat back, tapped Baird on the knee when he got in, but kept silent.

He didn't have to say a word. They were home free.

Mrs. Kelly's ball was about 140 yards from the flag. She took a long time selecting a club, talking it over with Brooks, checking the wind. Finally plucking out her five wood, she approached the ball and took up her position.

Again she lingered, driving the two anxious men in the cart to distraction. Reggie poked his head up, appearing to take an interest in the proceedings. Mrs. Kelly wiggled the club in her hand, played with her grip, prepared to swing, then abruptly changed her mind.

She walked back to the cart, exchanged her five wood for a three iron, then took up her address position again.

Baird had to choke back his excitement. Long irons and women didn't mix worth a damn.

Like her opponent's shot, Mrs. Kelly's ball exploded in ragged clusters of grass and dirt. The ball vanished into the sun, but when Brooks caught sight of it again, he saw that it was headed straight for the flag.

Baird realized it was a good shot, but he was not upset. After all, it would have to come down close enough for her to drain it in one—extremely unlikely.

As luck would have it, Mrs. Kelly's ball came up well short of the green, but instead of the ball dribbling to a stop, it rolled forward.

And forward and forward, until it vanished from sight.

By now Steel was standing with one foot on the edge of his cart. His face paled when the ball disappeared.

"Not to worry" said the pro, although he was worried himself. "It falls off six feet in front of the pin. Her ball would have caught the slope and rolled to the back."

As both parties raced toward the green, Baird glared at his opponent with such hatred that Sarius could actually feel the force. As soon as the cart stopped, Reggie, sensing the excitement, jumped down and did a mad tear around the green. The second ball was nowhere in sight.

The four scrambled out and walked rapidly toward the cup. Looking down together, they spotted Mrs. Kelly's Titleist Pro V1, the very same ball she started out with. Brooks, somewhat in awe, realized that Sarius had just canceled out Baird's best effort of the day.

Mrs. Kelly stooped to extract her ball, stood up, and shook her head in disbelief. "Can you believe it? That is my very first eagle."

Brooks added, "Yeah, it's like a miracle."

Sarius gave Baird and Steel a few moments to get over their shock, then asked politely, "You going to putt out, Charlie?"

Charles Baird was forced to turn away to conceal the vicious rage that took hold of him. The big, drooling St. Bernard chose that moment to lift his leg and christen the front of their candy-apple red Toro golf cart, which, after all, did bear some resemblance to Rachael's Mercedes.

Baird threw his putter and missed Reggie, but hit the Plexiglas windscreen and shattered it.

Several members up on the main balcony were already in shock at the sight of a large dog running around the eighteenth green. They were rendered speechless when the chairman of the ethics committee put on his display of juvenile behavior.

After calling his dog over, Brooks placed one oversized arm around Mrs. Kelly's shoulders, just as he had done the previous morning before she died. "You did it! I still can't believe it, but you did it!"

Sarius seemed offended. "How could you have doubted me?"

The question was not intended to be frivolous, and Brooks knew it. "As you said, human nature. I guess it takes a whole lot to make us accept anything out of the ordinary."

"Brooksie, that just might be the understatement of a lifetime."

They arrived back at the pro shop well behind the losing team, whose cart had already been abandoned. "You really think Baird is going to hand over eighteen million bucks?"

"You're doing it again. Keep it up and I'll move out of your house."

Brooks was not dealing with one of his own species. This was a heavenly presence in his life, albeit a peculiar one. Since he was unable to discern an angel's thinking processes, he did not always know when Sarius was jerking him around. This made for more than a little discomfort.

Rachael stepped out of an archway leading to the main complex and walked toward them. She did a double take at Mrs. Kelly's outfit, then almost flipped when Reggie jumped out of the golf cart.

Mrs. Kelly whispered to Brooks, "Don't tell her about the bet. I want to do it."

Rachael marched up to the two. "I caught a glimpse of Charles Baird's face when he came in—like death warmed over. You didn't take that bloody dog out on the course?"

"Did so," said Mrs. Kelly.

"Dear God!" Rachael pictured herself being burned at the stake.

Brooks, excited, added, "Kathleen beat him. She eagled the eighteenth!"

Rachael was suspicious. She knew Baird was the club's top senior. "Did you really beat him?"

Mrs. Kelly took Rachael's arm and led her toward the pro shop. "Yes, dear, and I did it fair and square. Sort of. How did you make out with Jennifer?"

The younger woman stopped. Rachael did not let it show, but she was so elated that she could hardly contain herself. Jennifer Williamson was officially ranked Southcott's top player, and Rachael had trounced her in six straight sets.

"You know about that?"

"Good news travels fast. Backhand working much better today, was it?"

"Just a minute—did you have anything to do with my winning those games?"

Mrs. Kelly donned that same wonderful wide-eyed look of innocence. "Your husband hasn't left my side all day. True, Brooksie?"

Brooks grinned. "That's a fact."

As they went through the door, one of the junior pros came up to Mrs. Kelly flashing a smile. Ignoring the dog beside her, he grabbed the old woman's hand.

"Ma'am, I watched you come down the eighteenth. That last shot was . . . was unreal! Far as I know, that makes you the first woman in the history of this club to eagle the eighteenth. And congratulations on beating Mr. Baird. Not many people get to do that."

Mrs. Kelly shrugged. "Thank you, Gregory. Be a dear, would you? We're in a bit of a hurry and Charles has an envelope for me. Would you run up to his office and collect it?"

"It'd be my pleasure, ma'am. Be right back."

William, the young assistant pro who had originally ordered her off the grounds, also came over and congratulated Mrs. Kelly. It seemed that beating Charles Baird III was a sure road to popularity.

Rachael took in the triumphant blue eyes peeking out from under the grand sweep of Mrs. Kelly's Michelle McGann hat. "Did you buy those clothes?"

"Charlie purchased them for me. Isn't he a dear?"

"Charlie . . . Do you mean Charles Baird?"

"The very same, and here comes Gregory with my winnings."

Mrs. Kelly accepted the envelope with kind words, but did not open it. Soon as all three were back in the parking lot, she said, "Now we're going to have to hustle down to Wall Street before the bank closes."

Rachael watched Brooks place the expensive golf bag in the trunk. It was all done rather quickly, which made her suspicious. Once they were underway, she leaned over the front seat. "Let me get this straight. You actually bet on the game—with the chairman of the ethics committee?"

Mrs. Kelly nodded, and a foolish grin as wide as Reggie's butt spread across Brooks's face. Rachael knew something was up.

1615 HRS

～

Traffic in lower Manhattan was always in a snarl, more so since 9/11, so Brooks avoided the place like the plague. Although he made his living on Wall Street, specifically in the futures market, he rarely had reason to go there in person. Having just blasted through the Battery Tunnel underneath the East River, he began to navigate his way north along Trinity before darting across to Nassau along Liberty.

Brooks ignored the other drivers yelling at him. The bank would close in seventeen minutes, so he had pulled out all the stops to get over as fast as he could. Thousands of people who inhabited the financial district's jungle of skyscrapers were just now in the process of scattering in all directions like ants radiating out in search of food. The streets were clogged with humanity. Brooks paid them scant attention. After all, he reasoned, what could go wrong with an angel on board.

Rachael sat in the back by herself, silent, apprehensive. She was not at all certain about what was taking place. The St. Bernard had jumped into the front seat between the driver and Mrs. Kelly. It was Reggie's first visit to the big city, and he seemed just as interested as any first timer in the enormous buildings, all the more overpowering because the streets were so narrow.

Keeping up a head of steam through the maze of cars and bodies took some doing, but Brooks finally came to a screeching halt in front of the Chase Manhattan building and let off his three passengers. There was no question of finding a parking spot; he'd have to circle the block until they came out, which greatly annoyed him. Now that he had some idea of how Sarius worked, he didn't want to miss out on the action.

A pair of security guards hovering near the main entrance moved rapidly toward the two women. "Sorry, ladies, no pets. Out he goes."

The second guard went to reach for Reggie's collar, but jerked his hand back when the big dog bared his teeth. Mrs. Kelly patted Reggie's head. "You stay with these gentlemen and behave yourself."

To the guards—trim, athletic types in their late twenties—she said in a no-nonsense tone of voice, "You had better be nice to him."

She took Rachael by the arm and made her way across the massive foyer with its Italian marble floors and art deco walls toward an open teller. The middle-aged Hispanic woman smiled as she accepted the check from the old lady's hand.

Taking in her attire, the teller said, "Out for a round of golf, were you?"

Sarius returned her smile. "Indeed I was."

"Did you have a nice game?"

"Best game of my life."

"And the only one," Rachael muttered in Mrs. Kelly's ear.

"Good for you," said the teller. Then her jaw dropped.

The old lady stood on her tiptoes to lean over the counter. "Large bills will do nicely, my love."

The teller's face tightened. Instinct told her something underhanded was taking place. Rachael, who had not yet been appraised of the amount Charles Baird had bequeathed to her new tenant, said, "Could I see that, please."

The teller was only too happy to get rid of it. When Rachael saw the figure, she could hardly believe her eyes.

She managed to croak, "How on earth . . . ?"

"Million a hole. Charlie lost 'em all, poor dear."

Rachael studied the check with mixed emotions. Whatever else happened from here on in, her membership at Southcott was history.

Turning her back to the counter, she whispered, "Even if they cash it, which I doubt, you can't walk out of here with that kind of money. It would be insane."

Mrs. Kelly snatched the check from Rachael and gave it back to the teller. "Bank will be closing soon, dearie, so best you get started."

The teller, handling the check as if it were covered with warts, asked for identification, which Mrs. Kelly promptly presented to her, then marched over to the desk of a stony-faced matriarch. The older woman glanced at the check, glanced at the teller, glanced at Mrs. Kelly, pursed her lips, then declared, "Photocopy the check and her ID, and tell her to return tomorrow. This, I can assure you, is not Mr. Baird's doing."

Sarius, who had heard every word, noted that Mrs. Kelly's immediate reaction would have been, if she were still alive, to label the senior clerk an old battle-axe. The term was not familiar to the angel in that context.

When the check and ID were returned to her with instructions to come back tomorrow, Mrs. Kelly said firmly, "Out of the question, my love, since I shall be leaving town in the morning. Now kindly summon your manager so we can straighten out this matter without further delay."

When the matriarch saw that the customer was not about to depart without a fuss, she marched over to the counter and stared down at the offending party over the rims of her reading glasses.

"The bank is about to close, ladies. I must ask you to leave."

The angel zoomed through Harriet Marshall's memory banks, found her weakness, and said, "Now Harriet, is that any way to speak to Charlie's mother? If I thought for one moment that you were attempting to give me a hard time, I can assure you that my son would be on the telephone to his friend Roger Morris, who just happens to be your CEO, within minutes of our departing this building. Charles is a loving, obedient child and always does what his dear old mother tells him. Therefore—"

Rachael's sudden coughing fit threatened to get out of control, which prompted Mrs. Kelly to give her a stiff nudge before going on. "Therefore, you may be assured that the Baird account will depart the Chase Manhattan first thing in the morning, and Harriet Marshall will be out of a job before noon. Facts, my love. Now, go and have your chat with Mr. Seymour, but do move along. Time's awasting."

Harriet stiffened, but did not cave in. Thirty-three years in the banking business had exposed her to fraud in every conceivable form, even by little old ladies.

"I was not aware that Mr. Baird had a mother."

"You thought, perhaps, he arrived by stork?"

Harriet's color rose as the clerk and the other customer, an attractive woman in her mid-thirties, both burst into laughter. Flustered, she replied, "I meant—I thought his mother was dead."

"I am very much alive, as you can see." Mrs. Kelly glanced at the big Seiko wall clock: 4:28. Fifteen minutes after the bank shut its doors, the safe would close automatically. "Look, dear, I'll make it easy for you. Charles is at the Southcott Golf and Country Club." After reciting the number, she added, "Call him up and tell him his dear old mother is here to cash her check. Hurry now."

Harriet abruptly sensed that she was in real trouble. "At once, Mrs. Kelly. But your name, ah . . . "

"Charlie's daddy passed away in eighty-nine. Remarried, love. Happens all the time."

When Mrs. Marshall and the teller went off together, Rachael shook her head in disbelief. "I can't believe you are saying all those things. I never imagined an angel would behave like this."

Mrs. Kelly doffed her wide-brimmed hat and glanced over at Reggie, who had made himself comfortable at the feet of one of the guards. "The ends and the means, my dear. Simple logic, really. Besides, it's never wrong to play hell with the devil."

Harriet told the teller to go total up and stepped into the manager's office. She felt it was more proper for Mr. Seymour to contact an important customer like Charles Baird.

But the senior clerk was not prepared for the manager's reaction, who jumped out of his chair as if his pants were on fire. "Kathleen Kelly! You fool! You imbecile! Did you not think to check her account? Kathleen Kelly, you dumbass female, transferred one point seven billion to this branch just yesterday morning." A thin, nervous little man, Seymour jammed both hands to his cheeks. "My God, what have you *done?*"

Meekly, but with her heart pounding against her rib cage, Harriet Marshall replied, "But she never mentioned that she had—"

"Shut up and get out of my sight. Tell Betty to count out eighteen million, fast—she has exactly thirteen minutes! Make it hundreds and place the cash in two of our large bags."

Seymour tore through the door, spotted the old woman in the flashy golf getup, and hurried around the counter with his hand out. "My dear Mrs. Kelly, what an extraordinary pleasure. Gerald Seymour, the manager of this establishment. Please forgive my staff; they had no idea who you were. My secretary is counting out the money as we speak. Is there anything I can do while you're waiting?"

Mrs. Kelly half-turned to her completely puzzled companion and gave her an I-told-you-so nod. "Tell you the truth, Gerald, I was beginning to wonder if I was in the right bank. And yes, there is something—my poor Reggie. I did not appreciate your people treating him like an ordinary mongrel. His feelings are most certainly hurt."

The manager found nothing odd about this. Old folks, especially rich old folks, were entitled to their eccentricities. "Herman, bring Reggie over here at once!"

Herman glanced at his companion, who rolled his eyes in disbelief, then trotted the dog over to Mr. Seymour. Reggie affectionately nuzzled Mrs. Kelly's hand.

The manager ventured an opinion, "He seems okay, dear . . . ?"

Astonished as she was at the way events were unfolding, it suddenly occurred to Rachael that she might prevail upon her houseguest to make the stupid mutt stop sprinkling the front of her car.

But Sarius, who could move freely about the room in his true form, was at that moment inside the vault with Betty, watching her count the cash—eighteen hundred stacks of hundred dollar bills, hundred to a stack. Sweat was dripping from her nose as she began frantically tossing the stacks into two large gray canvas bags. By the time she exited the vault dragging the bags along the floor, the last customer had left, leaving the two women and Reggie alone with the entire bank staff. Eleven seconds later, three beeps of the alarm system signified that the vault was closed for the night.

The manager's secretary was panting hard when she arrived with the heavy bags. Seymour asked Mrs. Kelly if she wanted to count it.

"Of course not," she replied. "If I can't trust the bank, who can I trust?"

Seymour agreed wholeheartedly, then summoned the other security guard and instructed the two men to pick up the bags and follow Mrs. Kelly out.

Escorting them through the doorway, the manager said, "I do hope you will overlook Harriet's behavior. She really had no idea—"

Mrs. Kelly waved it off. "To forgive is divine, Gerald. Consider the matter closed. And thank you for being so considerate."

"My dear Mrs. Kelly, please remember that Chase Manhattan's facilities are at your complete disposal." He removed a card from his pocket. "If you should ever need anything . . ."

Mrs. Kelly took the card and gave the manager a lovely smile. "Of course, dear boy. I can just imagine how pleased Roger will be once he hears of your efficiency."

Brooks spotted his dog before he saw the girls and pulled over. An armed guard stepped off the sidewalk and walked around to the driver's side.

"You want them in the trunk?"

Only then did Brooks notice the two big canvas bags. *She pulled it off!* In shock, he mumbled, "Yeah, I guess."

Soon as the car's computer accepted Brooks's voice command to open the trunk, the two young men set about pushing Mrs. Kelly's new clubs back to make room for the sacks of money.

At that moment a big Wells Fargo armored truck came to a halt behind the two bank guards. A man jumped out with an Ingram submachine gun held in the ready position.

"Hey, Mr. Seymour, everything all right here?"

"Of course it is, Sammy." To Mrs. Kelly the manager said, "See, if you had come by tomorrow we'd not be able to cash your check. You're lucky we had this much on hand."

Mrs. Kelly fixed another grand smile. "Luck is my second name."

Brooks took all this in as he waited for the manager, a paper-thin man in his fifties, to open the front door for Mrs. Kelly, but Reggie jumped in first.

They were underway a few moments when Brooks caught a glimpse of his wife's face in the rearview mirror, primed as if she was ready to burst into tears. "Everything go okay?"

Sarius grabbed one of Reggie's floppy ears and gave it an affectionate rub. "Perfect, Brooksie, just perfect."

Rachael finally gave in, but instead of crying, began to shriek in laughter. "Dear God, Brooks, you should have been there. It was . . . it was—" and off she went again in gales of laughter.

Reggie gave a few excited woofs, Mrs. Kelly smiled contentedly, and Brooks was overcome with such a feeling of well-being that it was he who had to fight back tears.

1130 HRS

❧

Copeland played golf with General Martin, who commanded the Marine contingent over at Wheeler. So Copeland had no difficulty getting a helicopter to ferry him from the Mauna Kea base facility down to the airport at Hilo, where he managed to scramble aboard United's 9:15 just before the gates closed. Problems notwithstanding, he would arrive in Los Angeles around three local time, where he was on standby for a Delta 3:20 that would put him into La Guardia at 10:27 that night.

As usual, the flight was jammed with sunburned tourists draped in tacky clothes. Copeland was unfortunate enough to end up between two chatty, overweight gals from Kansas. He told them he'd be happy to trade seats, but one wanted the aisle and the other the window, and neither was prepared to move.

The women didn't say a whole lot until they found out they were both retired schoolteachers, then a full-blown barrage opened up across Copeland's bow. Twenty minutes of nonstop back and forth was all the astronomer could take.

"Look, ladies, I had a real bad night, and I need some peace and quiet, so either one of you trades places, *or you both shut up!*"

Sharp intakes of breath were followed by, "Well, I never . . . "

A few minutes of sign language resulted in the woman in the aisle seat trading places with the vulgar man with the beard. Copeland heaved a small sigh of relief and shut his eyes.

True, he was exhausted, but sleep was out of the question. Just as he'd pulled out of the observatory parking lot, he had watched the five Japanese astronomers flee the building as if the devil himself was after

101

them. No doubt the upper echelon had their own reasons for keeping the public in the dark, but he knew the media was bound to break the story before the day was out.

The end of the world was not something that could be kept under wraps. Too many people knew about Omega. Locally, if the Japanese didn't spill the beans, good old Bible-thumping Rory Gallager was bound to. Sounding the trumpet that would officially announce Armageddon seemed like a natural for Bible thumpers.

Copeland himself had not told a single soul about his final visit to the top of Mauna Kea. What was the point? Which might well explain Palomar's reluctance to break the news. *What the hell was the point?*

The physicist's old standby—cause and effect—continued to torment him. Gallager had referred to a gravitational tango: two or more powerful objects—they didn't have to be stars—entering into a dance of death, and one is hurled away with such speed that nothing short of a collision with another star could stop it. But Omega might travel a billion years on the same trajectory before encountering such an end because anything this small and this dense traveling at great speed was capable of passing through ordinary planets like a bullet through rain.

Which was one of the thorny little problems that did not sit well with Copeland's sense of logic. Although the universe was full of stars, their combined mass accounted for a minuscule percentage of the actual available space. The universe was in fact almost entirely space, and a given body, be it a spaceship or a castoff star, could theoretically travel forever without encountering another object. So what were the odds against Omega, which no doubt had started out many light years away, being shot directly at the earth?

This line of reasoning led, somewhat uncomfortably, to the possibility of the tiny star being knocked out of position by some influence that existed outside of space-time as we know them: some Force, or some Being, that lurked beyond the event horizon. A growing number of physicists tended to attribute unexplained cosmic phenomena to God, but Copeland was not one of them. Besides, he thought, what did it matter how Omega started out? It was coming right down the tube, and that was that.

"Drink, sir?"

Copeland opened his eyes and looked over the bottles on the cart. "Grand Marnier, double."

Both women ordered chardonnay. They were now about three hours out of Honolulu, and the school teacher in the adjoining seat, having worn down her companion, decided to give Copeland another chance.

Half-turning her stout frame toward him, she asked, "Have you heard the latest?"

"I suppose that depends on what you are referring to."

"Why, the end of the world, of course."

Of course. Any number of Internet sites continued to warn people that the final curtain was about to fall. Whole trainloads of books announcing their version of the end continued to sell beyond all expectations. Even though the original fear and paranoia sweeping the world had slowed to a trickle when the new millennium hype finally died away, the Mayan calendar scenario had brought the whole enchilada back onstage.

"Okay, so what is the latest?"

"Mars."

Copeland snapped his head around.

The teacher was pleased that she had his attention. "Our taxi driver told us on the way to the airport. He heard it from a party of Orientals he picked up at the Hilton."

Who likely heard it from another party of Orientals, the astronomer figured. Probably got a bit muddled in translation.

"What did he say?"

"Oh, terrible things. The Orientals were panic-stricken, he said. 'Panic-stricken,' his very words. The cabbie himself even seemed upset. Mars is on its way to earth, he told us, big crash coming soon, maybe even tomorrow. End of the world for sure, according to his passengers." She paused for a light chuckle. "Can you imagine? Mark my words, it will be on the front page of all those trashy papers before the week is out."

"I doubt it."

The nameless school teacher furled her eyebrows. "And why not?"

"You said tomorrow. After that there is nothing."

"I beg to differ. If you knew anything at all about the solar system, you would know that all the planets were set in place by Almighty

God. Only He has the power to move them. Can you give me one good reason why He would choose to do so?"

Religious fervor was not new to him, yet Copeland now found himself wondering whether, if he too believed in a Higher Authority, that might not lessen his inner sense of despair.

"You seem so very sure of yourself."

The undertone of hopelessness made the school teacher turn to study him. "Aren't you a Christian?"

Copeland's religion had been the universe. Now he couldn't even believe in that. "No, ma'am, afraid I never made it that far. But . . . "

"Yes?" she asked, aware now that he was deeply troubled.

When Copeland turned to her, she noticed one lone tear wandering down his cheek. "What if it were true?"

"Oh dear, surely you don't believe all this nonsense about the end of the world?"

"Just answer me, please. What if Mars really is about to crash into Earth? What if the world is going to end tomorrow? What would it mean to you personally?"

"Why, that would be the most wonderful news imaginable. It would mean that I'm going home."

The words were spoken with such utter simplicity and complete confidence that Copeland, from the bottom of his heart, said, "How I wish I had your faith!"

It was the most desperate cry for help Martha Grimly had ever heard. She was quite flabbergasted, but not for one moment did she consider shirking her duty.

"Oh dear," she said, wondering where to begin.

1715 HRS

❧

They drove home via the Brooklyn Bridge, only because Brooks loved the old girl. John Roebling's wonderful creation was part of his earliest memories. When it opened in 1883, a stunning symphony of wire and steel, not everyone believed she'd make it to the end of the second millennium. But here she was, fully operational well into the third millennium, an age many predicted would never arrive in the first place.

Not for the first time it crossed Brooks's mind that the sudden and dramatic appearance of a real live angel might well be tied to the new millennium.

He glanced across Reggie's chest to see that Sarius was taking in the sights. "Things look different through human eyes?"

"Indeed they do," the angel replied as he watched two small tugs pull a huge barge up the East River.

"What do you intend to do with all the money? I didn't think angels had any use for that stuff."

Sarius turned toward Brooks but couldn't see him with Mrs. Kelly's eyes because she was too short and Reggie was in the way. "What would you do with it?"

"Me? I'd put it back in the bank, where it's safe. Then I'd look around for a good place to invest it."

"Like the parable of the talents."

"Something like that."

It suddenly occurred to Brooks that Atlantic City was only a two-hour drive. He had a wonderful vision of Mrs. Kelly rolling the dice. They'd need a truck to haul away the loot.

The old woman shook her head. "Shame on you, Brooksie."

They came off the bridge onto Adams, took Fulton over to Flatbush, then headed southeast around the bronze war memorial at Grand Army Plaza and through Prospect Park, where the warmth of Indian summer had drawn the locals in droves. Brooks was on his way over to his office on Clarkson Avenue, where he had a few urgent matters to attend to.

He was fortunate enough to find a parking spot right in front of the single-story clapboard building that housed the *Village Review.* With no time to stop for lunch today, the instant he opened the car door he picked up the delicious aromas coming from the VIP restaurant, two doors away.

"Listen," he said to Rachael with his big brown eyes in full pleading mode, "why don't you go pick up some fries, maybe a pizza."

"Forget it, Brooks. We'll have supper soon enough. Missing one meal won't kill you."

"I'm not sure about that," Brooks moaned.

"Besides, we can't leave the car."

"I suppose you're right," he said as he lumbered off.

It was just five-thirty, with rush hour traffic in full swing. Mrs. Kelly had her head turned slightly left, as if she were watching the cars zoom by, but when she leaned forward with her chin tilted up, Rachael realized that the angel was staring at the massive complex across the road.

"It's a big hospital," Sarius declared.

"Third largest in the nation, they tell me."

"Perhaps we should stop in for a moment."

"At the hospital?"

"Yes, dear. There is a lost soul inside."

"No doubt," Rachael replied, but immediately regretted her unkind remark.

Kings County Hospital was the very heart of Brooklyn, in an area where she never felt safe. Why Brooks insisted on having his stupid little weekly published over here was something she had never understood. They were walking by now, tough-looking black youths in clumps of four or five, slowing down as they caught sight of the sleek Chrysler LHS.

Mrs. Kelly opened the door and stepped out onto the sidewalk.

"Wait a minute," Rachael called out. "What about the . . . you know?"

The old lady turned around. "Don't worry. Reggie is here."

When she began walking off at a brisk pace, Rachael jumped out too, ordered the dog to stay put, then poked her head into the *Review.* "Tell Brooks we're going over to the hospital."

Without waiting for an acknowledgment, she slammed the office door and set off down the sidewalk. She caught up with the angel at the pedestrian crossing just across from the hospital's emergency entrance.

"This place can get pretty hairy at times," she warned.

A sharp easterly wind made Rachael wish she had changed out of her tennis getup. Mrs. Kelly held tight to her wide-brimmed hat as she made her way along the circular entry and through the automatic glass doors. It was obvious that she knew where she was going, and Rachael followed her left across the crowded foyer to the main corridor, where two Puerto Rican cops, a fat older one and a skinny young one, were leaning against a scarred wooden stand in the aisle. Both men took more than a passing interest in Rachael's shapely bare legs.

When Mrs. Kelly tried to walk past them, the older cop put out his arm and stopped her. "Who you want to see, sweetheart?"

"It's my poor old sister. We just got the word. Veronica is dying."

Here we go again, thought Rachael.

The young cop looked slightly puzzled. "Veronica who?"

"Washington, of course. Sixth floor."

The old cop stood there impassively, blocking the way, while his partner dutifully flipped through several pages on a clipboard. A minute or so went by before the younger cop found what he was looking for.

"Yeah, Veronica Washington. Terminal ward, sixth floor."

"Can we go up now?" Mrs. Kelly asked politely.

The cop knew why his younger partner looked puzzled. White patients at Kings County were as rare as bikinis in winter. "Sure, honeybunch. You go on up and see your sister. This lovely senorita is your daughter?"

"Granddaughter, actually."

"Okay, off you go."

Already Rachael didn't like it. "Veronica Washington?"

Mrs. Kelly smiled, but made no attempt to explain.

They turned down the first hallway on the right and saw a cluster of twenty or more people, all dark-skinned, huddled around the elevators. The men and older boys began to mutter among themselves.

Rachael was nervous about sharing the elevator with them. "This might not be a good idea," she whispered.

When the doors opened, she managed to scramble into a corner where she was afforded some protection by Mrs. Kelly. Nevertheless, every single male stared at her with undisguised lust in his eyes.

"Hey, Granny, let me see 'dat thing."

One of the youths made a grab for the big hat Mrs. Kelly was wearing. He grabbed air. Puzzled, the kid tried again. Same result. The crowd began to snicker, their attention drawn away from Rachael. The next time the big kid—sixteen, eighteen years old, face pitted like a minefield—fixed one hand firmly on the old woman's shoulder.

"You quit 'dat bullshit, you hear? Now gimme 'dat hat!"

Sarius saw the huge hand before anyone else. It came out of nowhere and landed with such force across the back of the kid's head that he almost dropped to his knees.

The vast woman who had delivered the blow barked at her son, "How many times I tell you to respect your elders? You get home, Bartholomew, I learn you some manners."

They loved it. One guy called out, "Yo, *Bar-thol-om-ew,* your momma gonna learn you some manners."

On the sixth floor the doors opened onto a scene of pure bedlam. A pair of burly male nurses having it out with two paramedics had attracted a fairly large crowd of people who were evidently relishing the confrontation. The cause of the argument was a stretcher upon which apparently lay a child's body. The body was covered by a white sheet.

One of the nurses shoved the stretcher toward the two medics. "I'm telling you for the last time—get this stiff out of the hallway now!"

"And I'm telling you we don't take orders from no pansy-assed nurses."

"You dumb turd, this is not the effing morgue. She's dead! What the hell you bring her up here for anyway?"

"Who you callin' names? The kid wasn't dead when we got on the elevator. How were we supposed to know she's goin' kick off on the way up?"

The second medic leaned across the stretcher. "You go get a doctor, Charlie Brown. Have him tell us she's like, passed on. We ain't movin' till then!"

The same nurse rolled his eyes and looked around at the crowd. "You believe this crap? Dumbass medics don't know when they got a stiff on their hands. Look, numb-nuts, I'm saying she's dead. So move this stretcher out of the way—now!"

The grieving mother, who just moments before had watched a car driven by a drunk driver jump the curb and smash into her daughter, finally broke under the strain and leaped at the mouthy nurse with both arms flailing away. Before anyone could grab hold of her, a clenched fist struck the man smack on the bridge of his nose. Bright red blood squirted all over the white sheet.

Rachael shook her head in disgust. "Come on, let's get out of here."

Mrs. Kelly eased around the melee while glancing down at the stretcher. The youthful form was clearly outlined beneath the bloodied sheet.

The sudden charge of emotion put Sarius on full alert. He expected it, was ready for it, but the powerful tug on Kathleen Kelly's heartstrings forced him to stop. He placed one hand on the stretcher and glanced up at Rachael with a look of torment on his old woman's face.

Rachael was concerned that a full-scale brawl was about to erupt, and they were in the middle of it. "Better keep moving."

Then the impossible happened: Everyone in the hallway froze—except for Rachael Hennessey. Sarius began his inspection of the child's molecular structure, found the misplaced atoms without difficulty, then set about arranging them in their proper order. He did it with considerable reluctance, but he did it nevertheless.

As near as Rachael could tell, Sarius too was frozen in time. She placed a hand on Mrs. Kelly's arm but got no response. She shook the arm.

Nothing!

"Oh God!" Looking around, she saw mouths arrested in speech, grins anchored in place, eyes closed or partly open, arms poised in midair. And the second hand on the big wall clock behind the nursing station was motionless.

Rachael instinctively knew what had happened, and she was petrified. But just as she was about to panic, everyone began moving again, including Sarius.

The shouting grew louder as the enraged mother struggled to get free with the crowd egging her on. A piercing shriek brought the whole ensemble to a grinding halt.

Rachael's heart leaped into her throat when she noticed the white sheet moving. One woman fainted away into the arms of her husband. Everyone but Mrs. Kelly backed off from the stretcher.

Gradually, the body assumed a sitting position. When Mrs. Kelly removed the sheet, the smiling face of a pretty black girl turned to her at once.

"Did you see them?" she asked the elderly lady.

"Indeed I did, sweetie. Beautiful, weren't they?"

"Oh, yes! And they touched me! It was the nicest thing that ever happened."

The mother, an older version of her daughter, but now distraught to the point of insanity, came forward as if in a trance. When the child reached out for her, she jumped back.

Sarius took in the astonished faces and said to the mouthy nurse, "Just goes to show you, Charlie Brown, you can never be real sure who's dead and who's alive. Next time I suggest you check with the doctor."

Making light of it did nothing to offset the impact of Emma Lincoln's resurrection. Her mother finally found her voice and asked, "What was it that touched you, Emma love?"

"Butterflies, hundreds and hundreds, in every color of the rainbow; they played with me and even talked to me. Mommy, they *love* me. They all said they did, and I believe them."

Turning back to the old lady, Emma asked, "Will I see them again?"

Sarius leaned forward to whisper something in the child's ear while her mother's tear-stained face registered shock, disbelief, and wonder all at the same time.

The mother looked across the gurney at the old woman. "Who are you?" she asked in a low, husky voice.

Mrs. Kelly smiled at her, then grabbed Rachael by the arm and began to push her way through the crowd.

"You don't understand," the mother's broken voice called after her, "Emma's never spoke a word in her life. She's been deaf and dumb since birth!"

Sarius glanced up at Rachael and gave a quick little shrug. "You could hardly expect me to fix up some and leave the others."

A turn in the hallway left Emma and her mother behind. Desperately wanting answers, Rachael placed her hand on Mrs. Kelly's arm, bringing her to a stop.

"What is it, dear?" asked the little old lady.

"An explanation."

"Emma is alive. Why not just accept it?"

"I want to know how you did that."

"Did what?"

"You stopped the clock—everyone was frozen in time. How can you stop time?"

"Just moved outside of it. And took you with me. Not a big deal."

Rachael thought, *Sure, not a big deal.* "You brought her back to life, didn't you? But how?"

Sarius could not help admiring her genuine curiosity. "People still assume that at some moment in development God waves his magic wand and life is formed. Not at all. There is a specific order—a genetic code if you prefer—to all living things, and in that the human body is no different from other life forms. It is how the atomic structure is arranged that provides the spark of life. And when the natural order breaks down, for any reason, pain, sickness or death can be the result. So I went ahead and set Emma's molecules back in place. All of them. Wasn't my idea, I can tell you. My host, well, she kind of coerced me into it."

Seeing Rachael's mind frantically twirling about, the angel added, "You see, dear, atoms of iron or phosphorous or calcium inside the body are no different from those outside the body. It is only their arrangement that has meaning."

"But . . . doesn't God . . . ?"

"My dear girl, who do you think fashioned such marvelous designs in the first place?"

"Oh," Rachael replied meekly. Having just witnessed two miracles left her feeling rather unsteady.

But Sarius had said all he was going to say on the subject and moved briskly down the hallway. He stopped near the end at a door marked PRIVATE, twisted the knob, and walked in.

Rachael hesitated for only a moment or two, then followed the angel inside. It was a small room, and upon the narrow bed lay a thin, frail-looking man connected to an array of machines. He appeared to be unconscious.

"I thought we were looking for Veronica Washington."

"You might have noticed that the door was marked private. If I had used his name they would never have allowed us in."

"Who is he?"

"This gentleman happens to be one of the finest physicists the twentieth century produced. Except he doesn't know it. He considers himself a failure."

As she drew closer to the bed, it seemed to Rachael that he had been around for ages. "How old is he?"

"Ninety-seven, dear. And he has only a little time left. His name is Werner Reinhardt, born on the outskirts of a tiny village in eastern Austria. A terribly disenchanted person who spent his entire life, not to mention the family fortune, seeking the answer to the most fundamental question in all of physics."

"Which is?"

"Have a seat. Perhaps you might find out."

A large white marker board on the wall beside the bed was covered with random formulae that far exceeded Rachael's university math. She did recognize certain advanced symbols, but little else.

When Mrs. Kelly began to wipe the board clean, it seemed nothing short of sacrilege.

Rachael sat down on a cold metal chair and tucked her hands between her knees. *What now,* she wondered.

"Get away from there!"

The voice was weak, but it still held authority.

Turning around, Sarius marched over to the bed and fixed the old man's glasses on his nose. Rachael saw that his face was contorted in anger.

"Evening, Werner. How are you feeling tonight?"

"How dare you! Get out of my room—get out!" The professor tried to rise, couldn't, then reached under his pillow for the call button.

By then Sarius had placed two complete lines of equations on the six-foot-wide board. Stepping aside, he said with a broad smile, "Bet you don't remember this."

Professor Reinhardt stared hard and then gasped, "Why, that is my . . . my . . . "

"Precisely!" Sarius declared. "March 19, 1963—the nearest you ever came to combining general relativity and quantum mechanics."

For the first time the old man realized there was another person in the room, but he quickly swung his head back to the board. "This was never published. How . . . ?"

"Doesn't matter. Now, we'll have to start out by demonstrating the conditions under which space-time can be controlled. It sounds formidable, but a solid understanding of your four-dimensional world is essential before you can hope to grasp even the most elementary notion of the next dimension, because only there does general relativity encompass the quantum. Time in itself is a true continuum, and, despite the fervent beliefs held by so many of your colleagues, can never unhappen. On its own, that is. However, once in concert with space it can be expanded, deflated, stretched, shrunk, warped, curved, even spiraled, and ultimately the ends of time can touch each other and form a whole new dimension. You already know this, of course, but I will show you how it occurs."

Rachael noticed that the angel's manner of speech had completely shed Mrs. Kelly's Irish intonations. This was a teacher's voice.

"Early on in life you came to believe that each galaxy has its own configuration of time. While this is not entirely incorrect, whether or not it does has no bearing on the problem at hand. You should have looked deeper."

Sarius scribbled a few more equations, and then turned back to the dying physicist. "You see? By failing to allow for the variations in time in every solar system in a given galaxy, you were unable to factor in those massive disruptions to the overall universal fabric. Little wonder your calculations kept breaking down. Which brings us to the arrows of time. We can discard the psychological and cosmological arrows altogether. Those are red herrings. Only the thermodynamic arrow has meaning, although I will demonstrate that entropy does not necessarily increase with time, as stated in the second law of thermodynamics, only because the universe is not a simple closed order.

"I will prove to you that time can ultimately be understood, first by defining its four radii, then by computing the true radial centers. This is a difficult, but inherently logical process, one that is crucial to understanding unification. Why? For the simple reason that quantum gravitational effects interact more and more with classical relativity as the curvature of space-time increases.

"So here—" more clumps of figures appeared on the board, "—are the major steps we shall be taking: first, to search for all four centers—let's classify them as local, galactic, sidereal, and universal. It's okay to utilize the general concept of supergravity as you understand it, but the spin particle definition needs a much narrower interpretation. For the purposes of this discussion, strings can be disregarded in their entirety. As for the uncertainty principle itself, there are a few fundamental flaws that must first be addressed . . . "

Sarius lost Rachael at that point, and from there on she could only register the words. But those same words to Professor Reinhardt were like drinking from the fountain of youth. The terrible anger he had demonstrated upon awakening had turned into a child's wide-eyed glee. Every minute or so he would interrupt with one or more often-excitable questions, which the angel patiently and thoroughly answered.

Forty-five minutes had gone by when Brooks opened the door and let out a loud sigh of relief. Rachael placed a finger to her lips and motioned him to come in and shut the door. Professor Reinhardt hardly noticed him.

By now Sarius had wiped the board clean twenty-eight times. Rachael had counted them.

Sarius made no attempt whatsoever to acknowledge Rachael or her husband. As for Brooks, his primary concern was for Reggie, out guarding the cash. Desperate people lived in this neighborhood, and a whole lot of them owned guns.

Fifteen minutes later, Professor Reinhardt emitted a sudden loud gasp. After taking a sip of water from Rachael, he croaked, "If what you are showing me is true—"

"It is."

"Why, that has to mean . . . it means we are all . . . it means that even death . . . "

Sarius smiled. He had gotten through. Mastering the theory of unification would be a large step in human development. It was the first major hurdle on the long and difficult journey toward harnessing the ultimate energy of the universe: gravity. But the angel knew how far they had yet to go, and his intuition warned him once again that danger was close at hand for this unique species.

Big tears were now curling down Werner Reinhardt's parchment-like cheeks. "I don't know who you are or where you came from, and I dare not ask. But I want to express my deepest gratitude for making this the greatest day of my entire life. To think that I have survived long enough to have the glory of the universe explained to me, and explained so beautifully."

Misted over, his eyes could no longer make out the final, triumphant set of equations that bound together once and for all Einstein's eloquent postulation on relativity and Heisenberg's famous principle of uncertainty. Not only that, but proof positive had been rendered that the same benevolent hand that had formed the universe was still at work. A wondrous sense of peace settled in and took hold of the old physicist.

After a moment's silence, he whispered, "Yes, only an infinite intelligence could have conceived of such magnificent grandeur. I never believed in God, but your amazing work has brought Him to life. Now He is as real to me as Creation itself." Sunken eyes stared up at the diminutive woman standing beside him, and with great effort the dying man reached out and said plaintively, "Thank you for this. Perhaps . . . do I have to wait any longer?"

Sarius took hold of both hands. "Are you ready to go on?"

"Oh yes, I can hardly wait . . . now that I know the truth . . . "

With that final declaration, the professor's eyes closed, and a few minutes later his breathing slowly came to an end. A buzzer on one of the machines attached to the dead man went off, but when Sarius glanced at it, the noise stopped.

Rachael had been standing close to the bed, the glass of water still in her hand. She threw Sarius an anxious look. "Is he . . . ?"

Reverting again to Mrs. Kelly's voice, the angel smiled and replied, "Yes, I suppose he is, but only to this world. The reality, my child, is more profound than you can ever imagine."

Brooks stored this remark away for later as he drew close to the bed and gazed down upon the old man's tranquil expression. As happy a death as one is ever likely to have.

Little wonder, he thought, since the old physicist's most fervent wish had been granted. And he had literally died in the arms of an angel.

1830 HRS

❧

Baird was drunk as a skunk. A loud knock on his door brought him out of his stupor. "Bugger off, whoever you are!"

"Charles, it's me. Open the door."

Baird muttered, "I don't want to see any mes. I don't even want to see me."

This conjured up a slovenly grin, but it quickly died away when that horrible eighteen-million dollar shot reappeared. Baird could not shake it, and all evening long, like an alcoholic with the DTs, that wretched Titleist Pro V1 kept rolling and rolling and rolling until it finally vanished from sight, taking three quarters of his liquid reserves with it.

Steel pounded on the door again. "Charles, listen to me. Beth Marsden took a video of us this afternoon when we were on the eleventh hole. I want you to take a look at it."

Baird shook his head. Video—who cares? "Get lost, Steel, you pathetic twit!"

"We think there's some hanky-panky going on!"

This remark prompted Baird to get up off the floor, where he had been sitting with his back to the sofa and one bare foot up on a coffee table. He struggled to his knees, then to his feet, and navigated his way to the door with difficulty, in part because the room lay in darkness.

"Good Lord, Charles, you're a mess!" the golf pro commented when the door slid open. Baird's usually handsome face was twisted and flushed, the piercing blue eyes narrow and bleary, the carefully combed hair limp and straggly.

Steel stepped into the room and flicked on the lights. "The chairman of the ethics committee can't be seen by the members looking like this." He placed an arm around Baird's shoulders, spinning him about. "It's into the shower for you, my lad, and I'll put the coffee on."

Thirty minutes later, the two men exited the elevator on the main floor and headed for the Norfolk Room. But there was no sign of Beth Marsden. Steel was about to go searching for her when he saw a note stuck to the video recorder: *Sorry, couldn't wait, Barney had to leave. I saved it under Baird with today's date. I know Charles will enjoy it! Beth.*

Baird crept over to a sofa chair and carefully let himself down. He had a headache that would drop a mule.

Steel found the remote and took a seat close to the sixty-inch screen. The big Toshiba was one of three units used by Southcott's professionals to monitor progress by their students. It contained every known feature in the industry.

"Beth used her phone cam to shoot the final drives into the eleventh, which seem okay to me, but it's the putting that caught her attention while she and Barney were viewing it. I'll run through at normal speed first."

The Toshiba's reproduction quality was so true to life that when the old hag suddenly appeared, it took all the control Baird could muster not to run forward and try to throttle her.

"The eleven is a par four, you're on in two, granny is on in three. Okay, here's your putt, a twelve-footer . . . " The sound of the putter striking the ball came in loud and clear. "Pop, in it goes, which gives you the bird. Now, here she is, lining up . . . got a twenty-five-footer, uphill, with a big left to right break . . . takes a few swipes with her putter, looking very professional, I must say . . . positions herself, sets her alignment, looking good . . . then plop: up it goes, way too fast, but look at it curling now, wow, that's amazing . . . thing suddenly homes in like a cruise missile, then drops into the cup like a rock. She gets her par, the tie remains unbroken."

Baird was massaging his temples. "Sounds familiar. So the old broad's good with a putter. She has to be, because every damned hole she managed to dig herself out of trouble."

Reverse took a few seconds. Steel held down the forward button until he found the spot where Mrs. Kelly was just about to make her putt. "Watch again, and listen."

The putt was executed—a good stroke, and the results proved it to be the correct blend of weight and alignment. Baird could see nothing wrong. His face told Steel he had not yet made the connection.

"You hit the ball, you hear the plop. She hits the ball, silence. There is no sound when her putter makes contact with the ball. Beth was sharp enough to pick it up."

Baird straightened his posture. Beth Marsden was the only daughter of Henry Champion Marsden, Chancellor of Columbia University back in the fifties, who had gone on to make his fortune in South American copper. Beth inherited his entire estate. She was not only rich but held a Ph.D. in mathematics from Cornell; plus, she was a six handicap. Her advice and opinions were treated with a great deal of respect.

His brows furrowed in thought, Baird still could not envision what was wrong. Lack of a single plop hardly constituted a mystery. The ball was struck, it went in the cup. If it wasn't struck, it wouldn't have moved.

"This is crap, Steel. The broad hit the damn ball. It went in the hole. End of story."

"Ah," said Steel, grinning. "But did she hit it? That's the question."

Before Baird could reiterate his earlier comments, Steel touched the reverse button again. "I'm going to slow it down and blow it up by twenty. Keep your eyes glued to that putter."

This time the screen held only a gargantuan pair of Foot-Joy loafers, a giant Titleist Pro V1 golf ball, and a massive Ping putter. The putter went back in slow motion, came forward in a tantalizing arc, then . . .

Baird jumped to his feet. "Run it again!"

Steel was happy to comply. Baird moved close to the screen. The putter came in slow, almost to the face of the ball—when the ball took off of its own accord and went off-screen.

"Again!" Baird demanded. His headache forgotten, he stared intently at the moment of contact. There was no doubt. The putter never touched the ball.

He watched it in silence three more times, then went back to the sofa and sat down. "Beth make any comments?"

"She was reasonably confident that the ball was controlled by some kind of remote electronic device. If so, this Hennessey guy was obviously the operator, and the dog was their cover. No wonder she insisted on taking it along. You look at their cart, all you see is that big stupid mutt. And if you think back, Hennessey never once left the cart while she was putting. Neither did the dog. It was a setup, Charles. You've been had!"

Baird sucked in a deep breath and let it out slowly. "Amazing, isn't it? Now we've got professional con artists on the golf course—the last refuge of civilization. This world is going to hell in a handbasket."

"Beth wasn't all that surprised. The technology has been available since the turn of the century. She figured it was a just a matter of time."

"Yeah, and that one point seven billion supposedly transferred over from Greece was just more BS, just like her being married to one of my old college buddies—all part of their elaborate scam."

Baird could not quite figure where Rachael Hennessey came into play, if she did. He pulled the telephone into his lap. He had to scramble hard to remember Roger Morris's private number, but his mushy brain finally coughed it up. He would put a stop payment on the check. The offenders had left the grounds too late to catch the bank today, and tomorrow, when she tried to cash it, the cops would nab her.

Perfect! Baird was thinking of some way to reward Marsden when he caught up with Chase Manhattan's CEO.

He gave Morris a swift blow by blow, underscored the stop payment, then asked the big question: "We figured out how she ripped me off, but how the hell was she able to screw around with the bank's records?"

Morris did not see how that would have been possible and said so. "The funds might still have been deposited in our bank. Wealth, after all, is no guarantee of honesty."

"Roger, you're not listening. This is an effing scam, a real doozer. If I were you, I'd check into it right away. Tonight, if possible."

Though reluctant to do so, Morris acknowledged that he might have a problem on his hands. "Okay, I'll get onto it. In fact, Charles, give me your number and I'll get back to you ASAP."

After Baird put down the receiver, he smiled for the first time since the game. He'd get his money back, and life would return to normal. Plus, a valuable lesson had been learned.

"Both of us will need to testify," he said to Steel.

"A pleasure, I can assure you."

"I know most of the local judges. Those two will be put away for a long time, which should wrap it up for the old biddy, but Hennessey is still a young man. Twenty years should teach him some respect. His wife, though . . . that's another matter. You figure she's involved?"

Steel was fully aware of Baird's attraction to Rachael Hennessey. "On the surface, I'd say no. Then again, how could the other two have rigged all this without her at least knowing about it? And she brought them onto the grounds."

"She did, didn't she?" Baird mused. Then he grinned at the senior pro. "Play my cards right, this whole shemozzle might just put the lady's fate in my hands. Which means—"

He caught the phone on the first ring. "Baird here."

"You sitting down?"

The grin died instantly. "Go ahead."

"There is absolutely no record of a Kathleen Kelly making a deposit in any branch of the Chase Manhattan."

"But . . . but . . . what happened?"

"This is extremely serious, Charles. There is little doubt that someone has breached security, temporarily altered the records, then later fixed them up again. I just ordered a full-out investigation, but one thing is certain: We are up against a brilliant mind. The computer manipulation was carried out so professionally that it scares the hell out of me. If we have some twisted genius out there who has the capability to alter the bank's records with impunity, I can assure you that the entire nation is at risk."

It was becoming clearer to Baird now: The old hag was part of a larger conspiracy, probably Al-Qaeda or some other gang of extremists, out to break the banks; or perhaps, as Morris suspected, even to destabilize the country. "Then it's a good thing we picked up on this when we did. Now the cops can grab her when she tries to cash the check. You can—"

"Charles!"

"What?"

"She already cashed it."

The blood drained from Baird's face so fast that Steel rushed to his side. He thought the man was about to keel over.

Several seconds went by before Baird found his voice. The on-again, off-again likelihood of regaining his lost capital was taking its toll. "It was well after three when they left the club. How could—"

"They squeaked in just before closing."

"But *cash?* Do banks keep that kind of cash on hand?"

"Not usually, but from time to time unique circumstances do arise. Wells Fargo was pulling in just as she left. If they had arrived ten minutes earlier, she would have been given one or two million and told to come back for the rest. Bad luck, Charles. The timing went against you."

"Against me? The hell you say! I called you up for the specific purpose of checking her out. You went through the routine, told me she just transferred a ton of money over from Greece. I made a business decision based on information provided to me by the bank's senior officer, which turns out to be bullshit. Don't forget the confidence level, Morris. What do you think Joe Public is going to do when he reads tomorrow's *Times?* By week's end, Chase Manhattan won't even be listed on the damned exchange!"

"Charles, don't do anything rash. Be assured that the bank has your best interests at heart—"

"Cut the crap, Morris. You screwed up. I want that eighteen million back, and I don't care how you do it. You got one day to fix up my account. Thursday morning, I make the call."

"You are being entirely unreasonable. All I can do is report the matter, but I hardly think those felons will be waiting around for the police to come calling."

"One day, Morris!"

Baird slammed down the receiver. He had derived a certain amount of perverse satisfaction from putting the screws to Roger Morris. And the idiot deserved it. But deep down, other, darker thoughts were intruding. That prune-faced old bat had made him the laughingstock of the entire membership.

That made it personal.

1845 HRS

❧

In the early evening of the day following the grand event, after a particularly fruitful afternoon at the Harvest Rest Home over on 37th Street, it occurred to Mildred Manuel that Father Harry might be interested in knowing that Brooks Hennessey had an angel staying with him. All things considered, she had taken the death of her beloved friend rather well, perhaps because, in essence, Kathleen Kelly was still among the living, so to speak. All very confusing, thought Millie half an hour later, as she scurried along the cracked stone walkway leading to the rear of the rectory.

"You're looking fit as a fiddle this evening," said Father Harry, arrested in the act of spraying his late-blooming roses. "New man in your life?"

"New woman," Millie replied as she sat down on the concrete bench nearest the priest.

Her feet hurt, so she removed her shoes and placed the sole of her left foot on top of a huge steel bolt holding the bench secure. Like everything else in this neighborhood, it was tie it down or lose it.

Father Harry gave her a squinted appraisal. "Sister Mary's got a big pot of Irish stew on. Good stuff. Join the gang for dinner?"

St. Andrew's was a large parish, with ten priests in residence at the moment. Seeing Millie's frown, the priest quickly added, "Father Pumpfrey's gone to Jersey to visit his sister."

Few parishioners cared much for the former pastor, who had been demoted for a number of reasons, not the least of which was the permanent look of doom the man carried about him. All very well in Lent, but a terrible downer the rest of the year.

"Nice of you to ask, but I'm not all that hungry at the moment." She hesitated, wondering where to begin, then blurted out, "Tell me the truth, Father. You ever see an angel? I mean a real angel from right out of heaven?"

Harry Flynn turned off the tap. The dozen or so purple finches that had been enjoying the spray objected noisily. Each one had been born in this very garden, in the same nest up in the branches of the stately old elm that gave the south side of the rectory its summer shade.

Still dressed in his long black cassock from the five PM Mass, the priest plunked his rotund behind down beside his obviously troubled parishioner and removed his glasses. "You okay, my love?"

"Well as can be expected. Considering."

"Ah, so it's to be a mystery, is it? Well now, you have my undivided attention. Not a soul around to bother us. Go head, fire away."

Millie chewed on her lower lip for a moment, hoping she was not breaking a confidence or anything like that. "You know about Kathy?"

"Yes, yes. Terrible thing." Father Harry glanced at the finger where Mrs. Kelly had bitten him. "Happened right in the middle of Monday morning Mass. Frightened the devil out of all of us. How is the poor dear making out?"

"That's the problem, Father. She's not. According to her, uh, him—well, whoever, Kathy passed away Monday morning."

The pastor's eyes narrowed. "For the love of Pete, you know that's sheer nonsense. Sure I'd be the first to know."

Millie let out a big sigh. She knew it was going to be difficult. "I doubt it, because she's still alive. Sort of."

The pastor finished wiping his glasses on the hem of his cassock. Senility was something he encountered almost daily, but it saddened him to learn that this wonderful woman was fading away at such an early age. He took her right hand in both of his.

"Well now, me old darlin', tell you what—how about if the both of us go see if we can track Kathleen down, have a word with her? She's at home, I take it?"

"Un-uh. Moved in with Brooks Hennessey."

"Lord Almighty, if that isn't a fine example of Christian charity. Good for Brooks. Well then, after dinner we'll pop 'round, see how she's getting along."

"Won't find her there."

"But you just said—"

"You never answered my question, about angels. You ever see a real live one?"

Father Harry gave it some thought. A sudden flurry of Canada warblers on their way south dropped in from the sky and vanished inside a clump of pink floribunda still shimmering in the sun's dying light. The single male Baltimore oriole that had been perched on the edge of the picnic table stripping away the outer shell of a chestnut jumped up with a start.

"Who knows what form angels come in. Sure, there's been times in my life when I was left wondering. But no, I can't swear to you I ever saw the real thing. Why the sudden interest in angels?"

"Because Kathy's turned into one."

The priest tightened his grip. "Of course she has, the dear girl. That's hardly surprising, is it? And to tell the truth, I've always thought of you as an angel, an angel of mercy, doing all the fine things you do in this community."

"Says his name is Sarius."

"Who?"

"The angel."

"I see," the priest replied. It was worse than he thought. "Where is the angel now?"

"Already told you, over at Hennessey's."

"A real live angel. My goodness. What does this . . . "

"Sarius."

"Yes, Sarius. What does Sarius look like?"

Millie was beginning to grow impatient. "Already told you that too."

"Sarius resembles, ah, Kathleen. This what you're telling me?"

A cloud of confusion entered Millie's soft brown eyes. "Well, Father, the answer to that is yes and no. You see, Sarius and Kathy are really the same person—well, not *person* exactly, but you know what I mean."

Father Harry didn't have a clue what she meant. "How do you know all this, Mildred?"

She brightened up then, smiling a grand smile. "Sure we had a lovely dinner over at Brooks's place last night. She—he, came right out and told us."

"That he—she is an angel."

"You got it."

"Ah." How simple it was, now that he got it.

Millie lowered her voice. "Maybe I shouldn't be telling you this, but he didn't say not to."

"I'm sure it's okay—oh dear!"

At that moment, rounding the bend at the side of the rectory was none other than Bishop Alphonsus O'Rourke himself. He was in a dark mood, Harry Flynn noticed right away.

The priest rose to his feet, donning his best welcoming smile. He knew why the bishop had come. It concerned money. One way or another, it always did.

"Fine weather we're having, Your Excellency."

"If you say so, Father. Am I interrupting something?"

Millie stared up at the bishop, all decked out in his formal black attire. He always made her nervous.

"Mildred Manuel, Your Excellency, just dropped by for a visit."

"Then might I suggest that the visit is over. You and I have business to discuss."

Millie reddened, and the old priest shut his eyes. Rough night ahead, sure as the cross of St. Peter. St. Andrew's was run by the Redemptorist Fathers, of which Harry Flynn was the senior member.

"Father Tony's been working on the figures. I believe—"

"I am not in the slightest interested in Father Tony's figures. You happen to be the pastor of this parish. It is you and you alone who has the responsibility . . ."

Then a ray of light shot across Father Harry's brain. It was a sweet, clear thing, pointing the way. "Before you go any further, Excellency, I should tell you that Mildred's just seen an angel. Telling me all about it, she was."

The bishop was tall but well padded, giving the appearance of one who doesn't rush away from the dinner table. Beneath his smattering of gray-brown hair was a long, angular face, rimless glasses over cold blue eyes that rarely smiled, and a thin rubbery mouth that never sat still. Even in silence his mouth moved around, not unlike an old ewe chewing on its cud.

"Angels," said the bishop, chewing away impatiently. "Sounds like foolishness to me." He walked over to Millie, glared down at her bare feet, and asked, "Have you been drinking?"

"I have not!" Millie would have liked to tell O'Rourke to go get stuffed, but in truth she was afraid of the man. Kathy wasn't afraid of him, that's for sure.

"Well then, what's all this about angels?"

"It happens to be true."

Two crows, locals, swooped in to land on the lowest branch of the elm. They leaned forward and stared at the bishop, who in some ways resembled them, then exploded in a chorus of raucous cawing.

"Disgusting creatures! Yes, woman, go on. And kindly address me properly while you're at it."

Telling her parish priest was one thing. Telling the Grand Inquisitor was quite another. Millie clamped her mouth shut and fixed her eyes on the life-sized white marble figure of the Blessed Virgin off to her left.

"It's a touch complicated, Your Excellency," the priest ventured, after seeing that Millie had gone silent. "You see, it concerns a close friend of hers, Kathleen Kelly. You remember the dear lady, I'm sure."

"I believe so," muttered Bishop O'Rourke as he took in the rows of carefully manicured rose beds: thirty-two varieties he had been told on a number of occasions, many bright and cheerful even this late in the season. If only the old fool would put this much effort into running the parish. St. Andrew's was the largest of thirteen parishes in the lower section of the Brooklyn-Queens Diocese, and due in part to the low social order of the majority of its parishioners, was also the poorest of the lot.

But a big factor was Father Harry himself, who would happily run the New York marathon before standing up before his flock to solicit their hard-earned cash. Because of this reluctance, St. Andrew's had for the last several years lived off the charity of its sister parishes—a state of affairs, the bishop had emphatically declared only last month, that was no longer acceptable.

Orders had been issued. Orders had been disobeyed. And Harry Flynn was in big trouble.

"It's like this, Your Excellency . . . "

By the time the priest finished his tale, which he had embellished just a tad, O'Rourke was developing ideas of his own. He knew Brooks Hennessey to be among the wealthiest men in the parish, and he didn't stint when it came to the collection plate. But there was no doubt in the bishop's mind that Brooks could do far better, provided he had some incentive to do so. It seemed to O'Rourke that the Holy Spirit was sending him a message.

The crows had not let up in the slightest. O'Rourke picked up a pebble and threw it. The two black aviators immediately took wing, but in gaining altitude one of them left behind a parting gift. The dark gray splat landed right at the bishop's feet.

"There! You can't tell me that wasn't a deliberate act."

Father Harry struggled to keep a straight face. "Just Mother Nature at work, Excellency."

"Devil's own, they are. Tell me, Mildred, do you think your friend would mind if I dropped around for a chat?"

Millie pursed her lips. The whole thing had gotten completely out of hand, and she was sorry she had ever come by.

"Well, no matter. If there's an angel in Brooklyn, it is certainly my responsibility to go welcome him. Come along, Father. You too, my dear. You can make the introductions."

The priest's face fell. "Now surely, Your Excellency, you won't be wanting the likes of me along."

"It was not a request, Father," replied the steel-edged voice.

The delightful aroma of Sister Mary's wonderful concoction had already embedded itself in Harry Flynn's olfactory gland. He could almost taste it. Walking away from a good plate of Irish stew was akin to desertion. Not to mention madness.

"Can't it wait till after supper?"

But the prelate had already turned on his heel and was heading back out to the parking lot in long purposeful strides. The priest heaved an exasperated sigh as he took Millie by the arm and muttered his apologies. A few minutes later, the three were seated in O'Rourke's big black Buick, tearing off down Fifth Avenue.

The bishop was such a terrible driver that it was not uncommon for pedestrians to flee to safety at the sight of the Buick. Since the windows were heavily tinted, Father Harry knew most people assumed the car belonged to a drug dealer, a popular line of business in this part of the city.

The Hennessey residence was located just off Bay Ridge Parkway down near Shore Road, taking up more than an acre of land in a section of the community otherwise inundated with puny-sized lots. It was dusk now, and lights from the vast Verrazano-Narrows Bridge over to Staten Island could be seen three miles to the south. Back in the days when Rachael used to cook, Father Harry had enjoyed many a good meal here, not to mention partaking of Brooks's fine selection of imported wines. O'Rourke had not been around in those days. He had been parachuted in from some minor diocese in New Hampshire four years ago for the specific purpose of bringing south Brooklyn into line.

Rachael had taken it upon herself to whip up some Italian spaghetti. It was her mother's recipe, but until now she had used it for a minimum of six persons. In measuring out the noodles she had gotten mixed up and now realized there was barely enough for the three of them.

Sarius sat on one of the barstools, tiny feet several inches off the floor, finding it rather pleasant being part of a human family. The angel was recapping the day's highlights in Kathleen Kelly's wonderfully sardonic voice, and whenever Charles Baird's name came up, Rachael and Brooks would laugh until tears rolled down their cheeks.

Mrs. Kelly abruptly changed the subject. "How do you get along with Bishop O'Rourke?"

Brooks set down his glass of French brandy. "Well enough, far as I know."

"That's good because he just pulled up in front of your gate."

Rachael stopped stirring the spaghetti. "I wonder why?"

"No doubt dear old Mildred had a hard time keeping the news to herself. Gone and blabbered to Father Harry, who leaked it to the bishop. Now Holy Mother Church wants to know what's going on."

"Will there be any difficulties?"

Sarius was amused by her concern. "Like maybe my Green Card is not in order."

Rachael had seen the new bishop only from a distance, but even at a distance he didn't look friendly. She gave a start when the gate buzzer went off, but the face on the monitor was Father Harry's.

"Evening, Father," Brooks said. "Hear you brought the boss along."

"You must have a crystal ball. Mildred's come as well. You gonna let us in?"

"Sure. Drive right up to the front door. And don't worry about the dog if he shows up. Won't bite."

Brooks went out to greet the visitors. Reggie had been on one of his rare outside sojourns and arrived just in time to form part of the welcoming committee. Brooks was always pleased to see Father Harry. When the big Buick with its darkened windows came to a halt, he pulled open the rear door. But it was Millie who stepped out.

"Evening, Mildred. Nice to see you again."

Millie's face was a black cloud, and the sharp jerk of her head toward the driver's seat told Brooks she wasn't a happy camper. Father Harry rolled out behind her, still dressed in his black cassock. He gave Brooks a conspiratorial grin, but before Brooks could say a word the driver's door opened to admit the imposing figure of Bishop Alphonsus O'Rourke.

"Your Excellency, this is a wonderful surprise. To what do we owe the pleasure?"

O'Rourke was all smiles. "I heard a story. Wild one, I must admit. But Father Flynn here seems to believe there is some merit to it. Beautiful home you have, I must say. Fine dog too."

Brooks observed the shrewd blue eyes clicking off dollar signs. Thirty years ago he would have been expected to drop to one knee and kiss the holy ring, a big ruby, but these days it was sufficient just to shake the bishop's hand.

Rachael handed over command of the spaghetti pot to Mrs. Kelly. At least the house was tidy—a tribute to her Finnish obsession with cleanliness. Quickly doffing her apron, she gave herself a cursory once-over in the hall mirror. She wore a pair of Donna Karan blueberry jeans that hugged her slim hips and long legs, and a loose-fitting V-neck ivory cashmere sweater—hardly proper attire to receive church royalty. Then again, she thought, she already had the real thing in her kitchen.

When the prince of the Holy Roman Church crossed her doorstep, Rachael stepped forward and curtsied. This was the way high-ranking visitors were greeted in her native Finland. O'Rourke, who had purged all thoughts of sex from his mind upon entering the seminary forty years before, was surprised at his biological reaction to this blond beauty. There was a smoldering, yet virginal, aura about her, a yearning of some sort in those disturbing green eyes.

The bishop was a precise and measured man, an accountant by trade. As he quickly inventoried the splendid appointments surrounding him, especially the great rose-colored fireplace, it dawned on him that the five-armed bronze dancers at the entrance to the vast foyer bore more than a passing resemblance to the goddess Kali. While the garish impressionist canvases left him cold, a strange Egyptian-like figure propped in one corner intrigued him. He had to resist the urge to walk over and study it.

When everyone was inside, O'Rourke stood beside the fireplace and gave his formal blessing to the house and all who lived therein. Thereafter, at Rachael's invitation, he made his way into the living room, where he was at once taken by the extraordinary balance of color and fine furniture. It occurred to him that what was on display here was not so much wealth as good taste.

Father Harry turned right, into the kitchen, pulled along by the heavenly aroma emanating therefrom. The big St. Bernard trotted along behind the priest. He saw that Mrs. Kelly was in fine shape, all dressed up in a flared, gray-blue Spanish-style dress that looked pretty on her.

"Well now, me old love, you've come a long way since I last laid eyes on you. Just what is that delightful smell?"

"Rachael's specialty: Italian spaghetti direct from Finland."

"Ah, surely I'd forgotten about that." He crossed the large earth-tone kitchen and lowered his nose. "Fit for an angel. Don't suppose there'd be enough left over to feed a poor starving priest?"

Sarius smiled. A loaves and fishes scenario came to mind, but that would be plagiarism. "I expect if you spoke nicely to the lady of the house . . ."

"Ah, indeed I will. And I must say, you seem to have survived your thrashing quite nicely. Using contacts now?"

"Nah," Mrs. Kelly replied, lapsing into the vernacular. "Something knocked about inside me old 'ead, changed a few things around, I expect."

"Hopefully for the better," muttered the priest, recalling the terrible words used in church.

When Millie showed up beside Father Harry, he placed a hand on her shoulder and said, "Far as I can tell, except for the missing glasses and being all dolled up, I'd say we're looking at none other than the real Kathleen Kelly."

Millie was truly ashamed of bringing the church authorities into play. She gave Mrs. Kelly a hangdog look.

Sarius laid down the stir spoon and gave Millie a hug. He knew she needed it.

Brooks came into the kitchen and called out, "Kathleen, His Excellency would like to meet you."

"Already met me," Sarius replied, having summoned from Kathleen Kelly's memory banks the time and circumstances of their last meeting.

Brooks didn't push. He wondered how much the angel was prepared to reveal, if anything.

Father Harry was carefully watching the two of them. Finally he said, "I'm sure Mildred wouldn't mind stirring the pot for a few minutes. Come along, my love, you might as well get it over with."

On the way to the living room, he said in a low voice, "Mildred popped 'round this evening, kind of mixed up in her head, I believe she was. She claimed you were . . . well, an angel. A real one, right out of heaven."

"Silly girl," Sarius replied. "Get's a bit addled at times."

"That's what I thought. Well, no harm done. We'll just tell the bishop the truth, and that'll be the end of it."

O'Rourke was at that moment intently studying a vibrant El Greco. He had placed one hand on the loveseat beneath it and leaned forward until his nose was almost touching the surface. Unlike many El Grecos, the signature on this one was clear and legible: *Domenikos Theotokopoulos Epoiei*.

"My dear lady, surely this is not an original?"

"It had better be," Rachael commented dryly.

The large canvas depicted five golden angels in the foreground, apparently discussing the fate of a shining white city in the distance behind them. The amount of detail was astonishing. O'Rourke sighed, knowing only too well that the price of this single painting would carry St. Andrew's for three, perhaps even four years. Brooks Hennessey had money, no doubt about it.

"Here she is, Your Excellency. Mrs. Kathleen Kelly."

O'Rourke turned around, saw a very small and very ordinary old woman. She looked like one of the many he encountered every day, some of whom drove him batty. "Yes, indeed. We've met before, I believe."

"Bake sale, up at the parish hall. Two Thursdays ago. You dropped in for five whole minutes."

"Of course. You served me a cup of tea. Now, my dear, I want you to explain to me what Mrs. Manuel is going on about, angels and all such stuff. Wherever did she get such notions?"

Brooks rolled his eyes as he directed his wife toward the sofa. He leaned down and whispered, "This could get interesting."

1945 HRS

❧

Mrs. Kelly went over to the big leather recliner, but instead of sitting in it, she motioned to Father Harry, who promptly took his cue. O'Rourke declined Brooks's offer of a drink and sat down on the loveseat, crossed his legs, and spread his arms across the back like Christ on the cross. The five golden angels were poised above his head. Reggie wandered in from the kitchen and plopped himself down at Mrs. Kelly's feet.

Then, lo and behold, the frantic rush of rarely used wings grabbed everyone's attention. Arcturus hovered awkwardly in the doorway for a few seconds before deciding to set down on the divan beside the bishop. A sprinkling of small gray feathers fluttered in his wake.

"*Hyvä taivis!*" Rachael whispered in her native tongue, her mind racing ahead. "Brooks, get him out of here, now!"

Too late! The bishop had already extended his hand in greeting.

The parrot instantly seized the index finger and jerked back its head. A good chunk of flesh came loose from the bishop's hand and dangled from the corner of the parrot's beak.

Brooks grabbed the bird in both hands while the bishop's scream of agony could be heard down the block. Harry Flynn almost bit his tongue in two trying to maintain a straight face.

Rachael bent over O'Rourke and took hold of his bleeding hand. A few drops of blood fell to the carpet. "Your Excellency, I can't tell you how sorry I am. That's the second time today this monster has gotten loose. I can promise you he won't get loose tomorrow, *because he won't be here tomorrow!*"

When O'Rourke opened his eyes to check out his torn appendage, he found he was looking straight into Rachael's cleavage. She had leaned forward in such a way that her well-shaped bosom was completely exposed to his view.

"Big knockers to starboard!" yelled the parrot, as if he knew what the bishop was thinking. Brooks went to clamp a hand over his beak, but thought better of it.

"For God's sake, Brooks, get rid of that foul creature. Bring me a towel and some bandages and the first aid ointment. Hurry!"

But Sarius was reluctant to part with such fine entertainment. Mrs. Kelly held out her hand.

"Not a good idea," cautioned Brooks. The bird's entire repertoire consisted of bawdy language.

"Relax, Brooksie," said the angel as the big African Gray crash-landed on Mrs. Kelly's shoulder.

After Brooks left the room, Arcturus leaned forward as if to study how Rachael was tending to the bishop. In a slow, seductive tone, he said, "Nice pussycat, nice pussycat."

O'Rourke, keeping his eyes averted as best he could, was beginning to think the place was more like a circus—an overgrown dog, a foul-mouthed parrot, and now a cat. He especially did not like cats.

"Where is it?" he demanded to know.

Rachael had no idea what he was talking about.

Father Harry, praying that the good Lord would keep him from exploding, said in a deadly serious tone of voice, "I don't believe he is referring to a cat, Excellency."

The bishop was appalled. He could not help wondering now if he had entered a den of iniquity. Certainly the exposed breasts dangling in front of him were as sinful as anything he'd seen in years.

"Pissimoff!" screamed the parrot.

Rachael jumped up in shock. The damn bird was about to recite his list of Russian hockey players. There were five in all, each one more vulgar than the last.

She pointed her finger at Mrs. Kelly. "Don't you dare let him say another word!"

Sarius was enjoying himself to no end, as was Arcturus. It had been months since the parrot had this large an audience. "Jerkim—" was all he got out this time before the old woman's fingers pinched his beak shut.

Ten minutes went by before things returned to normal—the damaged finger treated and taped up, the vexatious bird silenced. Rachael and Brooks were again seated side by side, but feeling quite apprehensive. Arcturus had regurgitated just a small sampling of his seaman's lexicon. He was capable of far worse.

Standing to the left of Father Flynn with one hand on the back of the recliner and Arcturus comfortably perched on her right shoulder, the little old lady said to the bishop, "I understand St. Andrew's is short of funds."

O'Rourke was still recovering from having his finger ripped open. That, and struggling to expunge the two naked breasts from his mind. Although he didn't care for the tone used by Mrs. Kelly, he realized that it behooved him to see where this was leading.

Cautiously, he replied, "My dear woman, these days everyone is short of funds."

"So you're telling us this parish is no different from the others?"

The bishop sat up straight. Not only was this ancient person refusing to respect his office by addressing him properly, but he had the distinct feeling that she was talking down to him. Nevertheless, his four years in Brooklyn had taught him that parish politics played a big role in funding. Even though there was something going on here that he could not fathom, he was not foolish enough to pass up the opportunity to capitalize on his impromptu visit.

With the most sincere smile he could muster under the circumstances, the bishop replied, "I would not deny that St. Andrew's is in trouble." He glanced at the cherub-faced priest. "A great deal of trouble, in fact. There is even a possibility that if adequate funding is not soon forthcoming, we may have to close it down, or at least severely curtail operations."

Father Harry smiled back. Mrs. Kelly did not. "Define adequate."

The bishop's hackles went up. No one spoke to him this way. He tried to remain calm.

"The annual operating budget is just over eight hundred thousand, which is the amount that should be held in reserve, or at least be guaranteed so that the capital can be borrowed against the church's future income as the year progresses."

Brooks realized then where the eighteen big ones in the trunk of his car were headed, and with this knowledge came a tinge of regret. He wouldn't have minded if some of it had stayed with him.

The look that Mrs. Kelly shot him left no doubt in Brooks's mind that his avaricious notions had been monitored. It was a real bummer, having someone around who could read minds.

There was silence in the room then, as if the gauntlet had been thrown down. O'Rourke had a veneer of arrogance that rarely endeared him to others, but Brooks didn't yet know if angels felt the same kind of like or dislike for people that was implicit in human nature. Logic told him that angels, being godlike, were beyond human emotions, although Brooks knew of three dead Puerto Ricans who might not agree.

The bishop, on the other hand, wondered why this obnoxious creature was allowed to dominate the discussion. He wondered if she could be Hennessey's grandmother.

In a light, almost frivolous voice, Mrs. Kelly said, "As you can see, Your Excellency, Brooks and Rachael have done quite well for themselves."

"Indeed," replied the bishop, acknowledging the use of his title with a nod.

"And St. Andrew's has done quite well by them," added Father Harry.

Brooks didn't say a word. His name was being bandied about, but this wasn't his show.

Mrs. Kelly tucked her cheeks into a mischievous grin. "So now tell us the truth, Alphonsus, is it angels you're interested in, or money?"

O'Rourke's face lost color. This kind of familiarity was denied even to his own sister. "Madam, you are being grossly disrespectful. Father Flynn would do well to instruct you in the precepts of Holy Mother Church."

The grin vanished. "No doubt, with blind obedience to the hierarchy being uppermost on the list. Control the masses at all costs. Bend them to your will. Break them if necessary. To hell with Christian charity. Like the vast majority of such doctrines, your precepts have little enough to do with the teachings of Jesus Christ, I can promise you that. Ah, Alphonsus, you would do well yourself to research the history of how and why these so-called commandments of the church were originally contrived. It might make a better man out of you.

Perhaps a smidgen of humility might wind its way into that thick skull of yours, who knows?"

The bishop was incensed. Only by the grace of God did he manage to keep his cool. In a low, emotional voice he said, "May the good Lord forgive you for using such words."

"And may the good Lord forgive you and your ilk for believing that such nonsense originated with Him."

O'Rourke shot up like a bullet. His face became contorted, and for a second or two it looked like he was going to take a run at Mrs. Kelly.

He would not have gotten far in any case, because Reggie too had jumped to his feet, his upper lip curled back to reveal powerful canines.

"Squall coming in!" shrieked the parrot, hopping up and down on one leg. Sarius stroked the bird's throat to calm him down.

It took a few seconds for the outraged prince of the Holy Roman Church to find his voice. "How dare you, you . . . you . . . ungrateful person! I am the leader of this flock. I have your spiritual welfare at heart. And you speak to me like this. *How dare you?"*

Brooks kept a worried eye on Reggie. He had visions of more saintly blood being spilled over Rachael's royal blue carpet. Rachael herself stared down at the floor in embarrassment. As for Father Harry, although his face registered deep concern, he was having a ball. If Mrs. Kelly was getting all fired up for another show, at least this time it would not be at his expense.

"Dirty Mother!" screamed the parrot, who had obviously taken a dislike to the bishop.

Rachael covered her face with both hands.

"Don't be saucy now," said Mrs. Kelly pleasantly. As much as he would have liked to get into a detailed discussion about the church's spotted history, the angel figured he'd better move on before the guy busted a gut.

Smile back in place as if the previous discussion had never taken place, she continued, "The good news, Al, is that Brooks and Rachael, being the fine, upstanding citizens that they are, have decided to make you a generous offer. Interested?"

The bishop focused on the skinny neck, picturing his hands closing around it. It took every ounce of resolve to bring himself back down.

Sarius noted that this was the second person today who wanted to strangle Mrs. Kelly. After a full minute of standing there shaking, the bishop took a deep breath and resumed his seat.

"Good." Mrs. Kelly's hand slipped down the recliner onto Harry Flynn's shoulder. Arcturus muttered, "Steady as she goes," then settled down.

"You see, Al, old boy, we're talking a lot of cash here. Eighteen million to be precise, with one million for each of the other twelve parishes in south Brooklyn, one for the upkeep of your holy office, and five to St. Andrew's. That have a nice ring to it?"

Not for one moment did Alphonsus O'Rourke believe such prattle, but riled up as he was, he could not for the life of him figure out what was going on. Nor did Hennessey and his wife appear disturbed by this gratuitous pronouncement. Indeed, it was as if they had fully expected her to come out with such an idiotic proposal. The bishop did not believe in miracles, and yet . . .

He turned to the master of the house. "Brooks, what is all this about?"

"Just like the lady said, Your Excellency. Eighteen million, cash, all wrapped up and ready to go. Mrs. Kelly explained the terms. Accept them, the money's yours."

In desperation the bishop looked to Father Flynn for support, to see if he wasn't having a lapse of reality, but the old priest was rubbing his hands and quietly chuckling away to himself.

He believed it!

At that moment, Millie appeared in the hallway and Rachael beckoned her in. "I gather you were left stirring the spaghetti. All done?"

"I took the pot off the burner, but didn't mix in the herbs. You'd better do that."

Father Harry popped up from his chair. "Rachael, my love, I was sitting here remembering the old days, when you used to cook up your mother's recipe and I would clean out the pot. You don't suppose . . . ?"

Rachael felt a sudden pang of guilt. At that moment she realized that a big chunk of her life had disappeared without her even knowing it. Those were good times, the best of times. Before she knew it, she had crossed the room and thrown her arms around the chubby little priest.

"I *have* missed you, Father Harry. Promise you won't stay away from us ever again."

"Yes, my dear, but the same applies to you."

She nodded. The angel's arrival had changed things around, she knew that. Perhaps it was time she stood back and took a long look at where she was going.

The bishop was done reviewing his priorities. For sure, he had found no angel, just a snarky old woman with a big mouth; but if what she had told him was true, he was fully prepared to consider the sudden appearance of eighteen million dollars a first-class miracle.

"You must understand," he said to Brooks, "that your offer sounds much too good to be true. Are you telling me you actually have that money right here, in this house?"

"It's the truth."

"I see. But why in the world would you want to give it all to the diocese?"

"Gosh, Your Excellency, can you think of something better to do with it?"

"No, no," O'Rourke replied quickly. An unpleasant thought came to him. "It's not drug money, is it?"

Rachael took offense at that. "That is a disgusting thing to say."

"My dear lady, please forgive me. It's just that I find all this very confusing. You see, I didn't even know I was coming here tonight, not until Father Harry told me about Mildred's seeing angels. The coincidence somehow seems . . . so improbable."

Brooks glanced over at Mrs. Kelly, saw the twinkle in her eye, and knew she was prepared to let him finish it off. "It does, I admit. But I'm sure you would be the first to agree that God works in mysterious ways. And I must point out that you haven't yet agreed to Kathleen's terms."

The bishop slowly got to his feet, praying that he wasn't being caught up in some kind of devious undertaking. "Naturally, I agree. I might be an arrogant old fool, but I'm not crazy. The terms are perfectly acceptable, and I pledge to honor them to the letter."

Brooks stood as well, his six-six mass dwarfing O'Rourke's six-one, gave Mrs. Kelly a wink and said, "Follow me, Your Excellency."

Ten minutes later a stunned Alphonsus O'Rourke gracefully declined Rachael's invitation to stay for supper. He'd had quite enough for one night. Both heavy Chase Manhattan bags were tucked away in the Buick's trunk. Miracle or not, the bishop had only one thought in mind—to get away from this place while he still had his sanity.

WEDNESDAY

0115 HRS

⇛

Copeland arrived on the Harding's doorstep later than expected. He'd managed to catch his standby flight out of L.A., but the flight had been delayed for over an hour. There was absolutely no way he could have gotten to New York any sooner. Inside the L.A. terminal he had listened carefully, and indeed the subject of Mars breaking free from its orbit was floating around the building, but nothing about the killer star Omega. As far as the masses were concerned, Mars was just more end-of-the-world hype. No one took it seriously.

Jo-Ann's father claimed to be an international financier, but Copeland suspected this to be a convenient cover for something a bit darker than brokering money. Galen Harding spent half of each year in Europe, mostly in Switzerland. He was a cold individual, English by birth, who did not suffer fools gladly. The few times Copeland had met the man, he was always left with the impression that Harding considered his daughter to have married well beneath her station. A school teacher was a school teacher, no matter what his area of expertise. The mother, Lucia, was just the opposite: warm, gentle, nurturing, always a smile. More proof that opposites attract.

The Hardings lived in a small luxury condo on the upper West Side, just across the street from Central Park. They owned the entire penthouse floor. When Copeland motioned that he would like to get in, a uniformed man seated behind a semi-circular counter stood up, switched on the outside lights, then sauntered over to push a speaker button beside the thick glass doors.

"Sir?"

"My wife is visiting her parents, the Hardings, top floor. I'm here to join her."

The muscle-bound security guard eyed the late-night visitor suspiciously. He saw a bearded, graying man, sloppily dressed, with dark rings under his eyes. With no luggage. The guard had been trained to be on the lookout for trouble, and this looked like trouble to him.

"Folks usually say when they expect late-night visitors. Mr. Harding said nothing to me."

"It's a surprise," Copeland answered patiently.

I bet, thought the security guard. "It wouldn't be a smart thing to go waking up Mr. Harding this time of night. You'd better come back in the morning, buddy."

"It's Dr. Copeland to you, chum. And I just traveled halfway across the world to see my wife. Now, open this door before I kick it in!"

Copeland saw that he had the guy's attention. The guard, suddenly aware that he was on shaky ground, said quickly, "Okay, okay, I'll go check with the Hardings. Just hang on."

Jo-Ann's room was nearest the foyer, where the intercom was located. She hurried down the hallway to answer the buzz. "Yes?"

"Randy, down at the front door. Real sorry to disturb you, Mrs. Harding, but I got a man outside insists on seeing your daughter."

Dear God! She knew immediately who it was. "You are speaking to the daughter. Describe him."

Randy did, adding the name the guy gave him. Jo-Ann rubbed her eyes before saying, "Dr. Copeland happens to be my ex-husband. Let him in, but he is not to come up here. I will be right down."

When Jo-Ann stepped off the elevator ten minutes later, Copeland's heart leaped at the sight of her. He ran over and crushed the pretty redhead in his arms.

"I was beginning to think I would never see you again."

Shaken and confused, with Randy looking on with a sardonic grin, Jo-Ann pulled away. "You've been drinking!"

"You got that right." Copeland had availed himself of most everything he could get his hands on. At the moment he was still torn between spending his last day on earth in a state of drunken stupor or in a state of prayer with his family. "And that's not all. Yesterday I found Jesus."

"That's just ducky," Jo-Ann muttered. She glanced at the security guard, suddenly ashamed of having her private life bandied about in front of this big lug. "Danny, why don't you come back in the morning?"

Copeland shook his head emphatically. By morning the whole world would know. His own family should hear the news from him first. "It can't wait. Let's go upstairs. You have to wake up the kids, your parents too."

Jo-Ann Copeland had never known her husband to behave like this. "Look, I know whatever you have to say must be serious. But I can't go waking up everyone in the middle of the night."

A second elevator door opened, and Galen Harding stepped out. Dressed in an impeccably tailored dark blue dressing gown, he took in the scruffy former son-in-law, the distraught look on his daughter's face.

Moving closer to Copeland, who reeked of alcohol, he said, "You had better have a damned good excuse for disturbing my family at this hour."

Randy moved back to the desk, unlocked a drawer and removed his .357 magnum, just in case.

Copeland shook his head a few times, trying to clear away the fuzziness. He didn't feel anger, just frustration. "Nice to see you, too, Galen. Yeah, this one rates right up there. But I'd prefer not to go blabbering it around in a public hallway!"

Harding had heard enough. Turning to the security guard, he barked, "I will be speaking to your superiors in the morning about your allowing drunks onto the premises. Get him out of here this instant!"

Randy didn't have to be told twice. He tucked the .357 inside his belt and had a hammerlock fixed on Copeland before the echo of Harding's command had died away.

Jo-Ann turned to her father. "Can't we can put him up just for one night . . . "

Harding was adamant. "There will be no drunks under my roof."

Copeland struggled, but in vain. Randy was twenty years younger and outweighed him by eighty pounds. Harding held the door while Copeland was shoved out onto the landing. He managed to catch himself on the railing at the edge of the stone steps. Turning, he watched Harding forcefully turn his daughter about and walk her toward the elevator.

Copeland pushed his face up against the glass doors. "I came here to warn you," he shouted. "There's a neutron star headed this way! We have to trust in Jesus now—He's all we have left!"

Jo-Ann pulled away from her father and ran back to the glass doors. Copeland could read the pity in her eyes. "Oh Danny, what's happened to you?"

"You have to believe me! Even if it doesn't strike us, the close proximity of such an enormous gravity field will completely destroy this planet. Don't you understand? This is the end of time. *We are all going to die!*"

Even Harding felt a twinge of pity. Perhaps, he acknowledged, twenty years of staring into space could generate this kind of paranoia. Or maybe it was the booze, which had destroyed many a good man.

Randy walked up to the door and brandished the .357, make sure the drunk saw it. "Just another screwball, Mr. Harding. No shortage around here."

"Danny, call me in the morning, when you're sober. Okay?"

And she was gone. A minute later the outside lights were turned off and Copeland was left alone in the darkness.

0130 HRS

❦

That night, well after their visitors had left and the women gone off to bed, Brooks and Reggie were flopped down beside the pool enjoying the last of the mild October evenings. The Hennesseys' back garden was still crammed with flowers: petunias, marigolds, begonias, zinnias, dahlias. Scattered beds of delicate-colored roses, especially the large Arrillaga, gave off exquisite fragrances, as if there was something in the night air that compelled them to expunge their sweetness.

The floodlights were switched off, but this didn't hamper a visiting family of little brown bats from swooping in to snap up leftover summer moths. Crickets over at the fish pond sang joyfully, as if they thought spring was starting up again.

His head nestled securely on Reggie's warm belly, Brooks felt more content than he had for a long, long time. Sipping his Courvoisier, he recalled the astonishing events that had taken place during the last two days, the most memorable days of his entire life. Many thoughts wandered across his mind, but they wandered pleasantly, as if it didn't really matter where they ended up.

Even losing out on the eighteen million hadn't ruffled a single feather. A special kind of peace had taken hold of him, which he knew full well was due to their heavenly visitor. *If I could only get Rachael to come around*, Brooks thought wistfully, *everything would be perfect.*

She came from out of the darkness, silently, on tiny feet, and paused behind the big man long enough to catch his thoughts. Before taking on human form, Sarius had not felt much of anything for humans. They lacked the finer qualities he admired in other species, and while he found their more barbaric customs repugnant, now that he was, more or less, one of them, these notions were undergoing a significant change. Observing from within tended to alter his perspective more than he would have thought possible, and once again the angel realized he had to be wary of Mrs. Kelly's influence.

Reggie spotted her first, but Mrs. Kelly placed a finger to her lips and the dog remained still. They were such a perfectly matched couple, the big Irish-American and his big woolly dog, that the angel found the sight of the two of them cuddled up together rather pleasing.

She lowered herself to the concrete and leaned back against the St. Bernard. Brooks opened his eyes with a start when he realized they had company.

"Thought you'd turned in for the night."

"I suppose dear old Kathleen needs the sleep, but I don't. Fun day, wasn't it?"

"Sure was," Brooks agreed. "The look on the bishop's face when you told him off was worth the eighteen million. Miracle he didn't explode."

"O'Rourke's a good man, but he had a few attitudinal problems. Much of it is a carryover from the brainwashing he received about being a prince of the church, all that foolishness. Most men let it run off their backs, while others, like O'Rourke, drink up every drop. He honestly believes himself to be some kind of royalty."

Brooks chuckled. "I'd say you cleared that up for him."

"For the moment. And what about Rachael? Lightened up considerably, I'd say."

Brooks sighed. "Night and day difference since you arrived. It's like you brought her back to me. I mean, she's not really back, but . . . I couldn't believe it when she went over and gave Father Harry a hug. Yes, a bit of the old magic is there—I can feel it."

Sarius smiled. "Probably more than you think."

Brooks was enjoying a good Cuban cigar, a Saint Luis Rey, which he plopped back in his mouth for a few seconds, letting the rich aromatic smoke curl around his head. He turned to his visitor and said, "I've been meaning to ask you—where are your wings?"

"Birds have wings."

"Okay, no wings. What does my, uh, guardian angel think of your visit? Can you communicate with him?"

"Could if you had one."

"I don't?"

"Kids do, the little ones. Some adults do, but not many."

"Why?"

"You got six billion bodies crammed onto this planet, that's why. Not enough angels to go around. You see, it's only the three upper orders who are allowed to look after you guys. Us lower types have been classified as unsuitable."

Brooks completely missed the inflection of sarcasm, because finding out he didn't have a guardian angel came as a big shock. Like most Catholics, he'd always assumed that every human being in the world had a guardian angel.

"Something that's always bothered me—back in the old days, in the time of Christ and before, there seemed to be a whole lot of people caught up with evil spirits, which doesn't appear to be the case today. Am I imagining this, or . . . "

"You should have taken up theology, Brooksie, because you are absolutely correct. Guardians were one of the many special blessings that came with Pentecost. Before that, everyone was on their own, which made it easy for old Lucifer to do his thing."

After taking a few minutes to digest this rather sad revelation, Brooks asked, "What about these awesome powers you have: stopping time, bringing people back to life, not to mention cheating at golf. Is it the same for all angels?"

"More or less, even the fallen ones. You remember being inside the atom, when we came to the part where there was nothing but darkness?"

"Timeless space, you called it. Pure energy and intelligence."

Sarius considered explaining the difference between spiritual energy and physical energy, but knew it would be a waste of time. "That is essentially what I am."

"But you told us that is where God lives."

"God doesn't live. He is. I told you this is *one* of the places where God resides."

Brooks mulled over the startling and profound implications of God and His angels occupying the very same space, which just happened to be inside your average human-type atom. He soon decided it was too heavy for him to pursue and set off on a different course.

"So tell me about heaven."

"Heaven exists in another dimension. Even Professor Reinhardt would not have understood."

"Go ahead, take a stab at it."

Sarius reached back and plucked a tiny moth from Reggie's thick fur. He held it up to catch the light from the house. "Think you could explain the general theory of relativity to this little fellow?"

"Uh-uh."

"How about some basic math—two plus two?"

"Can't do it."

"Then why ask me about heaven? You can't even get a grip on four dimensions. How do you expect to understand twelve?"

Brooks was disappointed. After last night's journey inside the atom and today's lesson on unification, he'd figured a few descriptive passages wouldn't be a lot to ask.

"Okay, think of some wonderful experience from your childhood years—never mind, I'll do it for you."

A few seconds later, the angel smiled. "Nine years old, flat out in the long grass down by the ocean staring up at the clouds and pretending they were angels. Nice."

Brooks remembered. It was something he did to escape the turmoil that came from his father's constant drinking.

"Now take that experience and, say, multiply it by a factor of ten."

"Wow—that'd be something. Those were probably the most peaceful moments in my life."

"Say it was one hundred times more intense and wonderful than what you experienced—you with me?"

"I understand, sure, but I can't possibly imagine what that might feel like."

"One thousand times as intense—any ideas there?"

"Not a clue."

"A million times?"

"Lost me completely."

"Good. You getting the message?"

"It's beyond my comprehension to grasp."

"Congratulations—we just came full circle." Sarius tapped his arm. "Not to worry, you'll find out for yourself before long."

Brooks turned his mournful face toward the angel. Lowering his voice, he said, "But what about all the . . . "

"Screwing around?"

"Yeah."

Without looking at him Sarius asked, "When is the last time you slipped a bum a twenty?"

"Probably last week."

"That's right. Friday morning you gave away seventy bucks all told. Day before it was fifty. Hardly a day goes by when you don't help someone out."

The sudden switch made Brooks feel uncomfortable. Sure, he gave away a few bucks—because he could well afford to. Everything he'd touched in the last twenty years had coughed up wads of cash.

"One evening two weeks back you came across a young druggie, girl hadn't even reached her teens. Remember what you said after she propositioned you?"

"Something about church."

"Stop being modest. You told her if she spent an hour inside St. Joseph's, you'd give her two hundred bucks. She didn't buy it till you gave her the first hundred. Then you waited outside for the hour, made sure she didn't cheat. She came out, and you gave her the extra hundred, right?"

Brooks nodded. He knew he was a soft touch. There just didn't seem to be much he could do about it. "How do you know all this?"

"If you know it, I know it. So what prompted you to come up with the church number?"

"Guess I kind of figured if no one else would help her, God would. So I sent her in to see Him."

"Maybe you said a little prayer while you were sitting in your car?"

"Maybe. I don't remember."

"Sure you don't. Want to know what she did with the money?"

"Gave it to her pimp?"

"Not this time. When that youngster left you, she strolled right down to the bus depot and bought a one-way ticket to Rapid City, South Dakota."

"Wait a minute! I didn't know that. How can you know it?"

"Just played the old time trick—went back and watched her. Yeah, her mom and dad were almost basket cases from worry, and when she came marching through the door they literally soared with the angels, they were so relieved."

Brooks felt even more uncomfortable, because no matter how much money he gave away, he knew it could not undo the more personal transgressions he had committed over the years.

Sarius realized he wasn't getting through. "You ever set out to deliberately hurt Rachael?"

"Of course not!"

"You love her."

Brooks noticed it was not a question. "Very much."

Sarius finally released the moth and watched it vanish into the night. "Well then, since your playing around days are over, I'll just tell you it can become real serious if people get hurt. But . . . let me put it another way: I was down in Baltimore this summer and watched an old man, a beggar really, wander into a snooty neighborhood. Temperature was 101 degrees. The old man collapsed on this guy's lawn. The owner spotted him and came running out of his big air-conditioned house. The beggar held up one wobbly hand and asked for a drink of water. The owner went back inside, got the water, came out, and poured it on his lawn. Then he told the old man to get off his property before he called the cops."

Brooks waited, but it seemed like Sarius was finished. "I miss something?"

"Two hours later, the old man died of heat exhaustion."

"What a terrible thing to happen. So I guess that guy's in trouble."

"Big time, Brooksie. Big time."

Brooks listened to the street sounds blending with Reggie's contented snores. Brooklyn, his birthplace and namesake, was not a quiet place. Even Bay Ridge, considered a cut or two above the rest of the city, could get noisy. Besides the continuous drone of traffic along the parkway, there were radios and CDs blasting away at all hours, even a few shots fired from time to time. But Brooks had lived here all his life.

He rarely noticed anymore. Taking a deep pull on his cigar, he considered the angel's story.

After a few minutes, he said softly, "I suppose it's how we relate to one another, help each other out. That what you're saying?"

"That is *exactly* what I am saying. And that is *exactly* how all people will be judged. So you see, you're not in bad shape at all."

There was more to it than that, of course, and the angel was tempted to try and expound a little on the Baltimore incident, but knew it would be tough going.

There were many things Sarius wanted to share with Brooks, but held back because it would only confuse him. Considering where they were located on the evolutionary scale, Homo sapiens lagged well behind similar species in other solar systems. True, they were of moderate intelligence, but the inability to reason was their downfall. Even elementary logic seemed to elude them.

Which was not entirely their fault, Sarius knew. It was primarily due to Lucifer and his minions having declared all-out war on the human race. This species alone, in the entire universe, was now the recipient of all their cunning efforts. Nor did the Dark Side ever relent for one single moment of time. War had been declared, revenge was still being extracted, final victory for Lucifer was imminent. And Sarius knew no victory was more relished in the depths of hell than convincing humanity that evil was merely a Draconian myth fostered by the churches to keep their flocks in line.

How very clever was the Prince of Darkness. How very successful he had been.

Sarius accepted this truth. It did not upset him because the outcome had been foretold from earliest times. Despite the great powers given them, humankind was weak, indecisive, lacking any real force of will. But deep down, no doubt because he and Kathleen Kelly were essentially one, there was a kind of sadness that the angel had not anticipated and did not fully understand.

"Last night you mentioned other creatures in the universe, different life forms that inhabit other solar systems. I take it you've been to some of these places?"

"True, but not all by any means because the number and variety are limitless."

Brooks would have liked for Sarius to describe a few of them, but the angel's refusal to even attempt to describe heaven had made him reluctant to ask the bigger questions.

Sarius was finding it quite enjoyable that Mrs. Kelly's head moved up and down with Reggie's slow breathing. "That's what most angels do, especially the lower types like me. We move around. One of my personal favorites is a tiny planet about the size of Mercury. Place is close to you in astronomical terms, about three hundred light years away, and its inhabitants are minute animal life forms who communicate by means of quite lovely harmonic sounds. We call it the singing planet. Their heavy atmosphere tends to contain and reflect the tiny melodic trills they make, which over time developed into a life-giving source for the planet's inhabitants—in much the same way air became a life-giving source for human existence."

Although unable to comprehend music replacing air, Brooks found the concept incredibly appealing. A few minutes later he asked, "People arrive in heaven, I suppose they also wander around, take in the sights?"

"Can if they want to."

For some reason this made Brooks recall one of the scenes from *Oh, God!* "You ever come across George Burns in your travels?"

"Indeed I have." Sarius allowed a big smile to play across Mrs. Kelly's face. "Movie was great, wasn't it? Big hit Upstairs. Last time I saw George he was white-water rafting with Jimmy Durante."

"After they had, like, passed on?"

"Cute phrase, *passed on*. I like it. Yes, those boys had surely passed on."

"Isn't that something? I always thought of heaven as mist and clouds, tons of people standing around all day long singing praises."

"That happens, but not often. Special occasions."

"Okay, if George was shooting the rapids, he probably wasn't doing it at age one hundred. What, ah . . . how . . . do they, or can they . . . ?"

"No limits. George was seventeen at the time. Jimmy was sixteen. They were having a ball."

Now Brooks was really confused. "It's really hard for me to get a handle on how that works. I mean, if heaven is for all eternity, and one day these guys decide to go white-water rafting, even if they tried out every activity in the book, the time it would take to do everything over and over a hundred times is still just a drop in the bucket. What are they going to do the rest of the time? You know what I mean?"

"Sure, Brooksie. I know what you mean. Problem is, your present existence is time-based, and it's darned near impossible for human thinking to get beyond that. So let me put it this way: Say you arrive in heaven. Day one, you touch base with all your old friends and family, and then naturally you want to have a look around. Off you go, explore the universe or whatever. When that's done you return. Say in earth time that might take a thousand years. What comes next? Most anything, like playing Pebble Beach a few hundred times."

"You mean like a, uh, mock-up of Pebble Beach?"

"Hello, mock-up! The real thing, Brooksie, the real thing. Just like it is today."

"But if I no longer belong to this world, how can I—"

"Let's keep it simple. Think dimensional and nondimensional. Things with physical properties and things without. Think mirror image. You know enough about atomic physics to realize that only about one ten-trillionth is mass. So what happens with all the space left over? Like I told you last night, it's not empty space at all. Lots of good things going on there. Including the same activity the present neutron or whatever happens to be engaged in at the moment, except in another dimension. Everyone who arrives in heaven is turned on by dimensional physics. It's a lot of fun."

"So the bottom line is, there's two Pebble Beaches?"

"Uh-uh. Millions, more like."

"Wow! That sounds really exciting. But even that doesn't explain the time versus activity scenario."

"As I said, you do the tour, you play a few games, sit and yack with everyone you've ever known or heard about, then you make choices."

"Choices?"

"There's no time here. One moment is the same as the next. You're always on day one. So, after doing everything you can think of, you decide what you want to retain."

"Retain?"

"Memories. You want to hold on to the problems you had ascending the north face of Everest, you do it. Maybe one or two other things. Then you dump the rest."

"Dump?"

"Is there an echo out here? Pay attention, Brooksie. Yes, dump, as in expunge, as in delete from the hard drive. If you choose to dump everything, as most everyone does, then there you are, day one in heaven. You just arrived. You start over."

"So you're saying everything is always fresh, always new?'

"Forever and ever, Brooksie. That's what heaven is all about."

Brooks tried to wrap his brain around this, couldn't, then moved on. He was fully aware of the golden opportunity that lay before him, of the angel's willingness to tell all, so to speak, but it didn't seem that important anymore, and he was content just to enjoy the company of his heavenly visitor. The silence went on for some time, as Sarius too was deep in thought.

Finally the angel said, "Rachael can't get to sleep. You should go in and talk to her."

This suggestion automatically conjured up resistance. Rachael had made it clear on a number of occasions that her room was off limits, and Brooks did not care to risk the fragile truce that had come about due to the angel's presence in their lives.

"Go on, the girl is waiting for you."

"Waiting?" Brooks found that hard to swallow.

Sarius wondered what it would take to get him mobile. "Get off your fat ass and go see your wife."

Brooks got to his feet. "Angels usually talk like that?"

"We already had this conversation, Brooksie. Get going."

Rachael's room was just across the hall from her husband's, but it might have been in Jersey for all the good it did. Brooks put his ear to the door, listened, heard nothing—no music, no TV. He didn't think it was such a good idea, but dared not turn away because he was acting under orders. His faint knock brought an instant response.

"Incredible!" His clothing told her he hadn't yet gone to bed. "I just called out to her in my mind, asking her to send you in. And here you are."

Brooks smiled his shy smile, the same one that had swept many a woman off her feet, except this time he really was feeling shy.

"So don't just stand there—come in!"

She was wearing a translucent silk top in pale indigo that barely reached to her thighs. It was very frilly and incredibly sexy. Brooks had not seen his wife dressed this way for a long time. The sight of her gorgeous figure took his breath away.

She reached out and took his hand, led him to the bed, and ordered him to sit. He did as instructed, still not having spoken a word. When she proceeded to undress him, his breath began to roll out in great clumps of air, as if he were hyperventilating.

"My God, Brooks, relax, will you? I won't bite." Rachael grinned, displaying a set of teeth that matched the rest of her. "Then again, I just might."

Unbelievable, Brooks thought, as she shoved him backward. He wondered if he wasn't witnessing another miracle. Rachael had never behaved this way. Even in the early days of their marriage she had always been passive. Now her cheeks were blazing, her lips open and moist, her green eyes smoldering.

"Scared?"

Brooks wasn't really scared, but he figured it was time to find out if he was dreaming. Over the next two hours the couple made love so many times Brooks lost count. Twice he begged for mercy: "Wait a minute, wait . . . " But Rachael would not wait. She had a whole lifetime to make up for.

0200 HRS

✑

Copeland sat on the steps for a while, puffing away on a cigarette and feeling sorry for himself. He had been trying to cut back, but comparatively speaking, lung cancer looked pretty good to him at the moment. Staring at the darkened tops of the great oaks across the street in Central Park only served to deepen his sense of despair.

Passersby, lovers, and crooks eyed the lone man suspiciously. There was a hotel just down the street, but Copeland felt a desperate need to seek out a familiar face. He knew a good number of people in the city, but none well. Then he recalled that Martin Alyward, an old Harvard buddy, lived somewhere over in south Brooklyn. Alyward, a confirmed bachelor and brilliant theorist, had visited Copeland in Hawaii several times over the years, and Copeland had stayed with him during the 1998 World Astronomical Conference sponsored by Columbia.

He stood up, still a bit unsteady, and made his way down the steps. He walked out to the curb where he was fortunate enough to wave down a cab after only a twenty-minute wait.

Half an hour later, the cab pulled up on the corner across the street from Owl's Head Park in southwest Brooklyn, where Shore Parkway swung back toward the ocean. The Jamaican driver had managed to get the address from control, and then located the street with little effort. His diligence earned him a hundred dollar tip, which truly surprised the driver as his passenger did not seem the sort to award lavish tips.

Greatly relieved to see the little white stucco house, Copeland leaned against the gate to collect his thoughts before going in. For the first time since arriving in New York he glanced up at the sky and saw with mixed emotions that some cloud cover was moving in. He did not dwell upon the horror of the errant star bursting through the cloud cover and almost instantaneously smashing the earth into smithereens. At 3,000 kilometers per second, by the time Omega's spectacular entry was visible with the naked eye, it would all be over.

The media would have the story by now, although he did not see them taking it seriously at first. The idea that a killer star might be headed this way was the stuff of tabloids; plus, human nature being what it is, most people needed to look death in the eye before they were prepared to acknowledge it.

A single ring of the doorbell caused the lights to go on. Seconds later the door opened. A young, dark-haired man holding a large revolver stared at Copeland in silence. The sight of a second handgun in less than an hour conjured up visions of the NRA going door to door passing out free samples.

"I'm looking for Dr. Alyward."

"Who is looking for Dr. Alyward?" Sharp, high-pitched voice, very much on edge.

"Dan Copeland, University of Hawaii, a friend. Is Martin at home?"

Then the young man did something completely unexpected: He burst into tears. The gun crashed to the floor and he all but collapsed into Copeland's arms.

Copeland was astonished. He half-dragged the sobbing man into the living room and set him down on a beige sofa. A big black cat Copeland remembered as Spook darted out from behind an armchair and vanished into the kitchen.

Leaving the emotionally distraught young man on the sofa, Copeland went into the main bedroom. He wondered now if Martin was sick or had an accident. After a quick inspection of both bedrooms, he realized that this stranger was the sole occupant. He wandered back to the living room, dropped heavily into an old basket chair, and waited.

A few moments later, a pair of dark eyes, almost coal black, fixed upon him. A lovely pair of eyes, Copeland could not help noticing even as certain unsettling thoughts began to take shape.

The smile came slowly, hesitantly. "I am Armand. You and Marty were good friends. He told me. He thought highly of you. Sorry about the theatrics. It's just that I . . . "

The voice died away when his lower lip began quivering. Copeland expected another rush of emotion, but Armand managed to pull himself out of it. "I was supposed to let you know. Marty asked me to, but I . . . I couldn't . . . I can't . . ."

"Armand, tell me what happened."

"Died. Last Tuesday. Stupid, *stupid* doctors! Promised Marty at least two months. Eight days was all he got. Hate doctors. Positively *hate* them. Doctors don't know *anything!*"

Copeland closed his eyes, thinking how unfair it was that he had been condemned to live out his last day on earth with this grief-stricken young man. "AIDS?"

"What do *you* think?"

"I see. You got it as well?"

"What a stupid question!"

"Sorry. How long did they give you?"

"Who cares? I'm a dead man."

Big deal, Copeland thought. He walked over to the television and switched it on, then fiddled with the remote until he got CNN.

"Hate television, positively *despise* it."

Wolf Blitzer came on, standing in front of the White House. He didn't look so good. "Listen up, Armand, something here might interest you."

"That's highly unlikely, don't you think?"

"Oh, I don't know. You decide."

"—no response from the president. As you can see, the lights are on, and I know he is just as shocked as the rest of us. The press conference called for four AM, which would be two hours after the devastating news was first released from Mount Palomar, has now been delayed again. It seems . . . "

Blitzer gulped a few times, and the hand with which he held the mike was trembling. Copeland grabbed the phone, dialed, and said to the speaker, "CNN, Galen, old boy. Turn it on. Now!"

He slammed down the receiver but immediately regretted his impulsiveness. He had just destroyed his family's last few moments of peace.

The veteran reporter raised the mike to his mouth with difficulty. "It seems, well, rather pointless I suppose, especially in light of the comments made earlier this morning by the chairman of the Joint Chiefs. General Delaney confirmed that even if the combined arsenal of the entire world's nuclear powers were to be applied in an effort to deflect the killer star from its deadly trajectory, it would be futile. If you tuned in earlier, you would have caught Dr. Savage's emotional countdown of events, leading up to the final moments, when at approximately six PM eastern daylight time this evening, a star named Omega will smash into the earth. The ensuing fireball will . . .

"Sorry, I'm a bit shaken. Ladies and gentlemen, this is not a hoax. This is not a nightmare you will wake up from. This is real. The rumors going around the last few days are true. Mars did break free from its orbit several days ago, but the cause has only now been accurately determined. For whatever reason, a small but immensely powerful neutron star is headed straight for us at a speed thousands of times faster than the fastest rifle bullet. Its trajectory will bring it so close to the earth's gravity field that a collision is inevitable."

He stared at the camera for several seconds before going on. "Ladies and gentlemen, it is my terrible, terrible duty to report to you that just a few hours from now, this planet and all its inhabitants will cease to exist. Yes, the doomsday prophets will finally have their day. Armageddon has arrived. I hope it makes them happy.

"As to the probable cause, the best scientific minds in the world can only speculate. According to Mount Palomar's Dr. Savage, a great many unexplained phenomena occur in space all the time, and this is just another example. Dr. Sanders of the University of Southern California believes that a plausible explanation of Omega's unlikely trajectory cannot be forthcoming and, in fact, may lie outside this dimension entirely, his primary argument being that the odds against striking our small planet from an outset point that must have been many light years away are several trillions to one. Others, such as Harvard's Dr. Exner, are just as adamant that the forthcoming catastrophe is well within the known laws of physics.

"Dr. Robillard of Washington State University has a somewhat different view. He believes that the seeds of our destruction were planted right from the beginning. This is all the time the human species has been allotted, period. The alarm clock was set at the very beginning of time, during the formation of this galaxy, and it is now ready to go off.

"Whatever the reason, the truth is that only a miracle can save us. To put it more succinctly, only the direct intervention of God Himself can save the human race from certain annihilation. Assuming He wants to, that is. Back to you, Bernard."

"Thank you, Wolf. It's unbelievable, folks. Utterly unbelievable. But, well, I have to tell you that everyone in the studio is still at work, and we intend to stay here as long as possible. Now, I understand that the one man who just might have some answers to this final human tragedy is ready to speak to the world. Peter, are you there?"

Copeland took small comfort from knowing it was his discovery that provided the vital missing link in the puzzle. Considering it now, he realized that both Venus and Mercury would be forced out of orbit, perhaps even themselves be drawn into the shattered remnants of the initial collision. And afterward, even with the killer star safely on its way out of the solar system, if and when the combined mass of the four planets fell into the sun—providing Omega did not destroy the sun as well—the entire solar system would be thrown out of alignment. Interstellar collisions took place all the time, yet . . . if this solar system collapsed, he reasoned, it was entirely possible that our wounded sun could be redirected into one of the sister systems in the galaxy.

What then? Would the damage be contained in this galaxy, or might it spread into adjoining galaxies?

Armand had dropped to his knees in front of the television. He turned and stared at Copeland with a quizzical cant to his petulant mouth. "They're lying, aren't they?"

Copeland went back to the chair. Spook took a sudden liking to the visitor and bounded onto his lap. The deeply troubled face of the Roman Catholic pontiff flashed across the screen.

Turning to Armand, Copeland said softly, "I guess we humans have always considered ourselves to be something special, something higher than the creature that crawled out of the slime and learned to stand upright and use its brain. Now we know the truth: that we live on an average planet in an average star system. And we are all about to die. There is nothing special about us after all."

Copeland looked back at the hunched figure on the television screen, listened to a few words, but knew there was no comfort to be found on this man's lips. "Ironic, isn't it, that just yesterday, for the first time in my life, I really began to believe in a universal being, a loving God who cares deeply for us. How could I have been so stupid? One thing's for sure, if there is a God, He doesn't give a damn what happens to the human race."

In a louder, somewhat hysterical voice, Armand said again, *"It's all lies!"*

"You saw Blitzer's face—the poor guy's crapping his pants. Nope, I'm afraid it's game over. Six point five billion people, not to mention several billion lesser type critters, are about to become the greatest barbecue of all time."

"I don't believe you!"

Armand abruptly popped up and raced back to the door. Snatching up the enormous .455 Webley, he shouted, "You were sent here to torment me, weren't you, to drive me over the edge? Do you take me for a fool? This video is some kind of trick. They can do *anything* with film these days. I hate you, Copeland, positively *hate* you! Out of my house this instant. Get out!"

Copeland had not expected this, and the notion of being thrown out twice in one night summoned up considerable resistance. He truly didn't think Armand had the guts to pull the trigger and remained seated with his fingers scratching the cat's neck.

"Settle down, son. I admit it's hard to swallow, but I've known about it since Monday. I—"

The shot sounded like a cannon inside the small quarters. It tore away a chunk of the chair beside Copeland's right shoulder. He jumped up in shock. So did Spook.

"You bloody idiot!"

"Out!" Armand screamed as loud as he could. *"Out! Out!"*

Copeland didn't say another word. Thirty seconds later he was back on the street, having a hard time believing that his friend of thirty years had actually taken in this paranoid little rat. Copeland hadn't even guessed that Martin was gay.

He assumed everyone in the vicinity would have heard the shot, though he doubted if anyone would report it. What was the point? He peered into the darkness of Owl's Head Park across the road, spotted a few figures in the shadows, and quickly concluded that it might not be all that safe to hang around.

Being tossed out of two places in one night was a real bummer. Welcome to New York, Dr. Copeland. Enjoy your stay. Sure.

He was cold sober now. He tried to recall where he was located in Brooklyn, but could not; he had never driven in the city. The lights on a huge bridge in the near distance told him nothing. Manhattan was surrounded by bridges.

He glanced at his watch: 2:40. Jo-Ann would be ready to listen to him now, probably sitting in front of the television shivering in fear— the very thing Copeland had wanted to avoid until he could be there with her. He set off down the street in a kind of mindless daze without even thinking about where he was going.

0330 HRS

❧

Earlier that evening, after reality had set in, Charles Baird III quickly set about reducing his options to two. Now that his man had assured him Mrs. Kelly was staying with the Hennesseys, it would take only one phone call to arrange the kind of raid he had in mind: to rescue the cash, to squash the old bat who had bamboozled him out of the eighteen million, to teach the Hennessey goon a good lesson, maybe break his legs.

But the kind of men who carried out such assignments did not work for nothing. The police, on the other hand, did.

Baird did not have many scruples. Murder? Well, he could easily rationalize putting down a slimy sewer rat. He relished the idea of putting her down. Like one of his Kentucky thoroughbreds that wasn't up to snuff. The appeal was so great that he was fully prepared to pay fifty grand for a clean job. But too many people would be able to tie him to the deed. No smoking gun, but it wouldn't take a genius to make the connection.

Enter Captain Tom Lyman, the man in charge of the 68th Precinct, activated by a call from his boss, Commissioner Harrison, one of Baird's poker buddies. Lyman lost no time putting his team together, taking personal control of the operation, and the four unmarked cars were on their way to Hennessey's place just after three-thirty in the morning. Baird rode with Lyman. He thought the bulletproof vest unnecessary, but what did he know about dangerous criminals?

They were about ten minutes away from Bay Ridge when a call came in from the dispatcher. It was a female voice. "You there, Captain?"

169

The cop in the front passenger seat handed the mike back to Lyman. "Yeah, what is it?"

"Want me to cancel your Rotary speech this evening?"

Lyman wondered what the hell now. Practical jokes were not unknown at the 68th. "Any particular reason?"

"Wolf Blitzer just announced that the world is going to end around six. Your talk is at eight."

Lyman was annoyed, plus a bit embarrassed. The turkey he had in the car with him was a personal friend of the commissioner, meaning that Harrison would know every little detail about what went down tonight.

"You listen to me, Lindsey, I hear any more of this nonsense, you're up on charge. And stay the hell off this frequency unless it's an emergency!" He glanced at his passenger. "I inherited a bunch of smart-asses. Think they're all stand-up comedians."

Baird shrugged. He'd heard stories himself, some star about to come crashing into earth. Probably more of that Mayan calendar crap.

It went without saying that anyone belonging to the Southcott Golf and Country Club had money, so Baird was not surprised to see as they drove by that Hennessey had perched himself on a fair chunk of real estate—and the rambling white stone house itself looked pretty impressive, what he could make out from the road.

Baird and the officer occupied the rear seat in the first of the unmarked cars. They both knew Brooks Hennessey ran the *Village Review,* but this kind of money had not come from publishing a local weekly paper.

"Guy's got a few bucks," Lyman commented.

No wonder, Baird thought, pulling off those kinds of capers. He leaned forward to scan the four-story residence, the eight-foot-high stone wall, security camera at the gate. "Yeah, but I have to ask myself who'd want to live in Brooklyn if he could afford to go someplace else. Maybe he inherited it."

"Not from his old man. Paddy Hennessey was a cop; guys knew him said he was a real lush, typical Irish booze artist. Old days, this precinct was full of 'em."

Baird grunted. "Gate looks like a solid sheet of steel. How do you intend to get in?"

Lyman didn't answer. There were three ways he could break through, but only one had been available on short notice. After they completed the reconnaissance drive-by he always insisted on before setting up a raid, two cops were dropped off at each end of the block. Soon as everyone was in place, Lyman would close off the street.

When Rachael heard the light knock on her door, the glowing clock face told her it was close to four. With her wrung-out husband snoring peacefully beside her, only one other person remained in the house.

She grabbed a bathrobe on the run, then pulled open the door. Sure enough, it was Mrs. Kelly, a grim look on her tiny face.

"Sorry dear, more visitors. Not nice ones this time. Better roust Brooksie. I'll turn the lights on, get ready to receive them."

"Who is it?"

"None other than the chairman of your ethics committee, plus a few friends."

"Damn! I don't suppose he wants his money back?"

"Wouldn't surprise me in the least. Charlie *was* a devil of a poor loser."

When Rachael went to call Brooks, Sarius reverted to his true form and popped out to scan the activity along the street. It didn't take him long to get the picture, including the fact that the police were armed to the teeth.

The angel knew full well that he was responsible for the raid. He also knew that this series of events could not have taken place without his initial involvement, so it stood to reason that he was free to deal with the repercussions any way he chose.

Lyman had just given the order to close off the street when the house lights went on. Creeping along the sidewalk about fifty feet from Hennessey's gate, he stopped dead in his tracks. "Figure they made us?"

Lieutenant Ben Driscoll was tight to his commander's butt. "We only cruised by once. Don't see how."

Lyman had been born and bred to make decisions. Senior officers did not stand around pondering their predicament. They took action. He spoke into the tiny mike on his left shoulder: "Mandoli, get your men to reef the gate, now!"

"On their way, boss."

A mobile jaws-of-life contraption, known as the Breaker, came from the opposite direction to where Lyman was standing. The two cops pulling it stuck the Breaker's nose into the narrow space between the gate and the stone pillar and began to rotate the flywheel by hand.

Brooks watched the kitchen monitor in astonishment. "I don't believe this is happening."

"Better give 'em a shout before they rip it apart."

"Hey, you stupid jerks, all you got to do is push the red button. Thing's lit up like a Christmas tree."

The cops jumped back when the speaker sounded off and the floodlights came on. They looked to Lyman for direction. The captain ran the last few yards. He did not like the way things were unfolding.

"Hit it!"

As the fifteen-foot-wide gate started to swing open in the direction of the house, the twelve cops who were huddled against the stone wall either side of the gate began to bunch up, waiting for word from their commanding officer.

Decked out in gold pajamas and black robe, Brooks worked the camera controls, counting at least a dozen cops. Baird was nowhere in sight. "Bulletproof vests, assault rifles—sheesh! Guys must figure they're closing in on Mafia headquarters."

Brooks saw that Rachael's face had grown distraught. Reggie went to the front door and barked to get out. He turned to Sarius. "Any suggestions?"

The old woman cracked a toothy grin. "Same one I gave you on the golf course."

Faith was a wonderful thing, and at that moment Brooks knew everything was going to be okay. He gave Rachael a little squeeze. "Just more entertainment, honey. Nothing to worry about."

"But what will the neighbors think?"

Mrs. Kelly had donned a lovely pale peach robe that flowed behind her as she walked. "Let's go meet the boys in blue."

Rachael had grabbed a heavy winter robe by mistake. Just as well, she thought, considering she had nothing on underneath it.

The minute the front door was pulled open, Reggie tore across the front lawn at full speed, making Brooks realize once again that the dog was able to relate what he saw on the kitchen monitor with what was taking place outside the gate. Smart dog, Brooks was thinking, when a burst of gunfire startled him.

He glanced at the angel. "Reggie!"

Mrs. Kelly's lips formed a solid line. She looked angry. She shot down the steps and strode purposefully across the lawn, Brooks and Rachael at her heels.

"YOU THERE! REMAIN WHERE YOU ARE! Empty your hands and hold them above your head. Do it now!"

The cops were fewer than twenty paces away, a tight little cluster of flak jackets and helmets with weapons cocked and ready to open fire again at the slightest provocation. The St. Bernard was down in the middle of the driveway, his blood already creating tiny rivulets in the concrete.

Rachael screamed the instant she saw the dog. Brooks was paralyzed. Sarius was busy fighting off Mrs. Kelly's dark urges.

The senior officer came forward slowly. He was the only one holding a handgun, which he kept pointed at Brooks's chest.

Lyman was a veteran, a man who had come face to face with too many bad surprises over the years not to be cautious even in the face of victory. "Check it out!" he roared at Driscoll. "The yard, all the rooms, garage, everything. Don't come back until it's clean. Keep an eye peeled for the cash and electronic gear."

At that moment a head peered around the stone pillar. Sight of the downed St. Bernard gave Baird a nice warm glow.

"These the ones?" Lyman asked when Baird came up beside him. The three suspects seemed frozen in place, hands in the air, eyes fixed on the still carcass.

Baird had expected to encounter some resistance. Except for the dog, there was nothing. He was disappointed, but at the same time pleased that Rachael had not been harmed; with her hair tousled and her Ms. Cool façade absent, she looked positively radiant.

"Yeah, it's them—in the running for rip-off artists of the year. Too bad it didn't work out. They tell you where the money is?"

"Not yet. But I imagine they will want to cooperate."

Brooks tore his eyes away from Reggie's still body and glared down at the cop, lowering his hands at the same time. The cop backed off.

"No matter what prompted this raid, I can personally guarantee that this will be the final act of your career," Brooks said. "Baird is not the only one with friends in high places."

Baird sneered. "Big words for a con man. Pay no attention, Captain, you did a first-class job. Just read them their rights and find my money."

"You're too late, Charles," said Rachael, her voice charged with intensity and her green eyes seething with hatred.

Baird smiled. "It's not nice to lie, Rachael. You see, I can smell money."

"That's your arse, Charlie, all that rich food." Of course this was Mrs. Kelly speaking, but Sarius found the powerful impulses difficult to resist. "It's all given over to charity, for the betterment of your fellow man."

"That's a pile of crap!"

Brooks shook his head. "All gone, Charlie, like you'd better be before Mrs. Kelly gets mad."

Baird stepped forward. "Careful!" Lyman warned.

But the big Irish blob didn't scare him. "So what's she going to do, throw a fit?"

Once again recalling the three Puerto Ricans and their tiny mounds of ash, Brooks said softly, "You had better hope she doesn't."

But in fact Sarius, being vigorously prodded by the person whose body he occupied, *was* ready to throw a fit. "Get up, Reggie, stop fooling around."

The dog leaped to his feet, then bounded the few steps to stand beside Mrs. Kelly. The four cops who'd stayed behind couldn't believe their eyes.

Sarius shook Mrs. Kelly's head in disgust. "You fellows are kinda mixed up, aren't you? This is not a nudist colony."

There was not a stitch of clothing left on the intruders: no glasses, helmets, no rings or watches, no fillings in their teeth. The transition was instantaneous. Each man, including Baird, was naked as the day he was born. Captain Lyman had even lost his hairpiece.

Brooks placed his arm around Rachael's shoulder. "Here we go." The guns, like the clothing, had vanished.

Rachael glanced down at Baird, who had lost his power of speech, grinned, and said to Brooks, "Not much to get excited about, is it?"

Brooks would have traded a year of his life for a camera. The eight men who had gone in to search the house came streaking across the lawn bare-ass naked. "*Captain! Captain! What the hell's going on?*"

"She's a frigging witch!" declared Baird, as he withdrew to the street in haste.

Tom Lyman didn't have to be a genius to realize he had lost control of the situation. "Everyone out of here—*move!*"

Reggie took off after the retreating cops, getting really close to sinking his teeth into Lyman's butt before Brooks whistled him back.

Rachael was laughing so hard she slumped down on the lawn. Brooks shook his head in amazement. "We're gonna have to find you a new tennis club for sure."

"Can you just imagine them arriving back at the station house?"

Brooks nodded. "Those guys will remember this one for a long time."

Rachael used her husband's arm to pull herself up. Mrs. Kelly stood in front of them, still facing the open gate. A handful of people had gathered there, looking in, no doubt under the impression there was a great party going on.

Rachael touched the old woman's arm. "Thank you for giving us Reggie back." She glanced up at Brooks, seeing the tender look on his face and feeling her own heart leap with joy. "And thanks for everything else you've done. Life has been so wonderful since you arrived. I just wish you could stay with us forever."

But the angel was silent. Still and silent. Brooks walked around to look the old woman in the face. He was shocked to see that her gaunt cheeks were damp.

"What . . . ?"

Rachael moved out in front, where the floodlights from the entry caught the sorrowful features. Tears were the last thing she expected to see. She threw Brooks an anxious glance and in quiet astonishment asked, "Why are you crying?"

"Angels don't cry," Sarius replied between sniffs.

"Those look like tears to me—oh, I see what you mean. Then why is Mrs. Kelly crying? Is it because you have to leave?"

"No dear, I don't have to go anywhere."

"Then what is it?"

"It seems that you must."

"But . . . I don't understand."

Sarius had been staring hard at a bearded man standing beside the open gate. The angel forcibly extracted himself from Mrs. Kelly's overpowering sense of grief and said, "You might as well come in, Dr. Copeland."

0415 HRS

❦

As he drew closer, the stranger's desperate, haunted features hinted at his being someone who had recently undergone a terrible ordeal.

"Who is he?" Rachael whispered into Mrs. Kelly's ear, setting aside for the moment the mysterious words used by the angel.

"As it turns out, Danny here is the bearer of bad tidings. Very bad tidings."

Copeland took a few hesitant steps forward. He hadn't the slightest idea what was going on, other than the fact that he was standing in the driveway of a large estate, large by Brooklyn standards, staring at three people in their pajamas. Having just watched two dozen naked men run down the street in panic, who appeared to have fled this very place, he wondered now what might have caused their mass exodus. These three seemed normal enough. They were like rungs on a ladder: the tiny grandmother who had called him by name; a tall, attractive woman, and one huge man.

Plus an overgrown St. Bernard, now vigorously sniffing his crotch.

"Cut it out, Reggie!" ordered the big man as he stepped forward with hand outstretched. "Brooks Hennessey. My wife, Rachael. I guess you already know Mrs. Kelly."

Copeland watched his hand vanish, hoping it would emerge intact. When it did, he moved closer to the old woman. "I don't believe I do. Are you an astronomer?"

"Not a professional like you. But I know a thing or two about the heavens."

Rachael would have laughed, except she knew something serious was going on. She was also becoming chilled. "Why don't we all go inside? I'll put the coffee on."

Mrs. Kelly linked her arm into Copeland's, directing him to follow Brooks and Rachael toward the house. She glanced up at the puzzled newcomer. "Third time lucky."

"Excuse me?"

"Being kicked out twice in one night doesn't do much for the old ego. But you're safe here."

"That's an odd word to use under the circumstances."

" 'Tis, I admit. Safe for the moment, anyway."

Having the brittle limb linked into his gave Copeland an odd sensation, like a mild electric current running along his arm. "How would you know what happened to me tonight?"

"You see, I'm a bit of a clairvoyant. Runs in the family."

The astronomer and the old lady ascended the steps together. "So you must be aware of . . . "

"Am now. I suppose congratulations are in order, since it was your finding out about Mars that allowed the big boys to get a handle on Omega."

Those words could only mean one thing: Someone had gone public. He figured Rory Gallager or the Japanese astronomers. Short-lived as it was, Dan Copeland's name would be inexorably linked to the final moments in time.

Sarius did not bother to correct the astronomer, though he did think it an interesting coincidence that one of the key players in the endgame scenario had landed in Brooks Hennessey's garden in the middle of the night.

The sound of a racing motor behind them caused the two to turn around in time to watch a taxicab disgorge none other than a stressed-out Mildred Manuel before tearing away in a squeal of burning rubber.

"His last fare," Millie said in relief. She looked in rough shape. "Little devil almost killed us both."

"For heaven's sake," said Mrs. Kelly as she walked back to meet Millie. "You know too!"

"It's everywhere. All the radio stations have gone crazy."

"What is?" asked Brooks from the top of the steps.

"The end of the world!" Millie replied in a slightly hysterical tone. "Didn't you . . . I mean, I thought everyone . . . "

Mrs. Kelly lowered her eyes. "We were having too much fun to notice."

Millie had been torn between walking over to church or coming down to see Mrs. Kelly, or at least her angel. She gave the bearded stranger a nervous nod, wondering if he might be another heavenly visitor.

Reggie too seemed upset, because he started to moan for no reason whatsoever.

Brooks reached for Rachael's hand. A very real layer of fear suddenly enveloped him. To the angel he pleaded, "Please tell us what is going on."

Sarius nodded toward Copeland. "This gentleman happens to be none other than the prognosticator of the Apocalypse, the portent of darkness for you and your kind."

"Meaning?"

"Meaning six o'clock this evening, Brooksie. That's all she wrote."

"Meaning?"

"You stuck on replay? The game's up. The party's over. Your insignificant little planet is about to be ripped apart!"

This was spoken with such vehemence that Rachael flinched. "That is utterly preposterous!"

Flopped down beside the refrigerator, Reggie's ears poked up when the two women raised their voices.

"I wish it were," said Copeland, puzzled by the old woman's use of the possessive pronoun. "But it happens to be true. I doubt if a single organism will survive the impact. From here on in, we're on borrowed time."

"Borrowed time," the angel repeated softly, having already applied the extent of Copeland's knowledge to what Millie had heard on the radio. Borrowed time indeed.

"What damned impact?" Brooks demanded to know. He had been on a flat-out roller coaster ride ever since Mrs. Kelly's death Monday morning, and things were tightening up inside him.

They were all in the kitchen now: two women, two men, one dog and an angel. Sarius deferred to Dr. Copeland. "You tell 'em, Dan."

Millie, trying to be helpful, said, "It's on TV—every channel."

"Forget the TV. You're about to get it from the horse's mouth."

Copeland reluctantly took one of the bar stools and leaned his left arm on the counter. He was thinking he should have grabbed the taxi that dropped off the other old woman.

Sarius said, "Take a look through the window behind you."

Copeland swiveled about, saw the same bridge he had noticed earlier in the distance. It was clogged with barely-moving traffic.

"Every bridge in the area is the same. Another twenty minutes or so, people will start abandoning their cars. You're not going anywhere, Danny boy, so you might as well relax."

Copeland sighed. He was tired, hungry and afraid to die; but for some reason he felt entirely at ease with these people. "Okay, it goes something like this: A long, long time ago, somewhere deep in the heart of a distant galaxy . . . "

When the telling was done, Brooks stared long and hard into the sad and beautiful eyes of the woman he loved so much. Now that they had found each other again, it was over.

Rachael knew what her husband was thinking, and it made her angry. "It's not fair!"

"Millions of people throughout the world are having that same thought," ventured the angel, although he did share her opinion. Lack of any reaction to his ridding the world of the three young hoodlums who had repeatedly attacked Mrs. Kelly was a strong hint that the end might not be far off, but he hadn't the slightest reason to suspect it was just a matter of days.

Rachael turned on the angel. "You knew all along, didn't you?" Her words were harsh, accusing.

Mrs. Kelly shook her head. "Did not."

"You expect us to believe that? You know everything! How could you not know about . . . about . . . "

Brooks walked over to his wife, who was standing with her back against the counter, and placed his arms around her. "Calm down, honey."

A tiny wooden bird emerged from a Dutch cuckoo clock over her head, tweeted five times, then retreated. Everyone in the room, including Sarius, automatically registered the time: just thirteen hours to go.

Copeland did not understand why Rachael was beating on the old lady. "Look, even if we'd known months ago, what difference would it make? The star can't be stopped. Knowing about it doesn't alter anything."

"That's not the point!" Rachael declared, her eyes moist and her temper rising. "He should have warned us."

"Who?"

"Sarius."

"Oops," said Millie.

"Who the hell is Sarius?" Copeland demanded.

Only downcast eyes answered his question, as if the whole gang were guilty of something. After a few moments of awkward silence, Mrs. Kelly took a deep breath. The angel did not see any point in keeping his identity a secret.

"She means me."

Copeland shrugged, thinking, *So what! The old girl could have a dozen names if she wanted.*

Sarius said, "So what! The old girl could have a dozen names if she wanted."

Copeland's heart took a few unscheduled leaps before settling down. He forced a smile. "Okay, you already told me you're clairvoyant, and you can obviously read minds. But I still don't see—"

"Oh for heaven's sake!" Rachael said. "Tell him."

Sarius bared Mrs. Kelly's yellow dentures. "I'm an angel."

"So's my mother," said Copeland, wondering how his initial assessment could have been so far off the mark. He would have sworn these were all regular-type people.

"Your mother deals cards at a blackjack table in Vegas. She's no angel."

Just for a moment Copeland felt a touch uneasy. Then he chided himself for actually wanting to believe that this old gal might be someone special. Even though he knew zip about what might actually constitute a divine presence, he could plainly see this shriveled old granny was not one. Then he noticed that the other old woman, the newcomer, was staring at him as if he were about to explode or something. Her worn clothing and bedraggled appearance prompted him to wonder if she was the cleaning lady.

When Rachael placed the coffee pot on the table, Copeland gave his head a good shake before asking, "You got anything stronger than this?"

Brooks was more than ready himself. He went off to the dining room, grabbed the three-tiered liquor cart and wheeled it back into the kitchen. "No beer, but most everything else you can name."

When Brooks began piling bottles on the kitchen counter, sight of the Grand Marnier reminded Copeland of his first and only lesson in Christianity.

The old woman looked up in surprise. "You got religion last night, on your way over from Hawaii? That's really something."

Copeland accepted a crystal brandy snifter from Rachael and pulled the bottle toward him. "I'm jumping on the bandwagon while there's still time. That what you think?"

Mrs. Kelly's eyes narrowed. "I can't help wondering why a learned man in your particular profession would not at least be curious about the truth."

"What particular truth do you have in mind?"

"In your case, Dr. Copeland, the greatest of all truths: how the universe was formed."

"If you're talking about God, where I come from God is the guy who gave Charlton Heston the Ten Commandments. At least He was up until yesterday, when a nice lady went out of her way to explain a few things. It's all a bit confusing for me at the moment. In any case, how can you be so sure God created the universe?"

"I watched Him do it."

Copeland sighed as he poured himself a large drink. This was definitely his night for wackos.

Brooks took a seat beside the astronomer. "You might as well face up to it. Mrs. Kelly really is an angel. She's proven it to us enough times."

Copeland gulped down three ounces straight. The orange fire in his throat felt absolutely marvelous. "I wander aimlessly down the street, go into someone's yard, and here's this angel. I suppose Elvis is around back."

Rachael paid little attention to the conversation. She was feeling guilty about her outburst. She wiped her eyes and gave Mrs. Kelly a sheepish look.

"I understand, dear. The news was enough to send anyone around the bend. It was a terrible shock to me too."

"What are you going to do?" Rachael asked.

Sarius stared back at the young woman, not at all liking her question. "I am sorry, my love, truly sorry. You see, short of God's own intervention, there are only two ways I know of to stop the neutron star from reaching earth. The first is to alter Omega's path, which can be done only by its being attracted to a body of similar mass, and none exists in this part of your galaxy. Or if the star were to suddenly implode and convert all its mass to energy. Which is entirely possible, by the way, because aging neutron stars are notoriously unstable. When their degenerating particles finally do achieve maximum density, gravity overwhelms pressure and implosion is instantaneous. Of course, if this were to happen, not only the earth, but your entire solar system would vanish inside the hole that it formed."

Copeland poured himself another shot of Grand Marnier and quickly gulped it down. This little old gal had stated, with all the confidence in the world, that an imploding neutron star would create a black hole. This was hardly news, but the notion that a degenerating stellar body fifteen miles in diameter possessed the ability to gobble up an entire solar system was definitely not an accepted postulation. If that were true, it could well explain certain abrupt changes in the cosmic fabric.

The astronomer found this premise highly exciting and took another drink. For the scientific community at large the jury was still out on the final fate of neutron stars, but Mrs. Kelly had made this profound statement as a matter of fact.

It was at least enough to convince Copeland that there was more at work here than met the eye.

By now Sarius had unscrewed the caps on several liquor bottles and sniffed the contents. He selected a bottle of O'Darby's Irish Mist—probably Mrs. Kelly's own preference coming into play—and poured himself and Millie each several ounces.

Rachael shot Brooks an anxious look, who cautioned, "You'd better go easy on that stuff. It's pretty strong."

"That's good, Brooksie, because it seems to me if there ever was a reason to get cocked to the gills, this is it." She raised her glass, gave an old Irish toast in Celtic, which no one understood, giggled, then downed half the contents of her glass.

"Wow!"

Millie was horrified. "This is not . . . it's not right. We are all going to die!"

"Right you are," agreed the angel, chuckling away. "Except for good old Kathleen, of course. She went and beat you to it."

"Well then, shouldn't we all be over at church praying?"

"Can if you want, my love, but I don't see why. You've made your statement in this life, and a fine one it is. Spending your last few hours inside a church is not going to earn you more Brownie points, believe me."

This was not Catholic dogma by any means, yet Brooks realized the angel was right. What was done was done. It was too late to get down on bended knee and beg forgiveness. He poured Rachael a shot of akvavit, a big one. For himself he selected the Courvoisier X.O., the same cognac he had been drinking earlier out by the pool, when everything seemed perfect with the world. Little had he known . . . .

Copeland had been intently studying the supposed angel. There was nothing at all to distinguish her from a thousand other old grannies, except for being a tiny runt of a thing.

"If you're an angel, how about showing us what you truly look like?"

"Wouldn't be very exciting. You see, my true form happens to be nondimensional. No mass at all, not even a little bit."

"Which, of course, is impossible."

Sarius found this amusing. "Congratulations, you just wiped out the entire angelic realm."

A glance at the master of the house told Copeland that the big man was buying all this at face value. The wall clock read five twenty. It would be dawn soon, dawn of the last day of human existence. Jo-Ann would be frantic by now. Yet he was in no rush to get away.

"Okay, say you have no mass. That means you must be entirely energy."

"Now you're getting warm."

"But . . . converting mass to energy can only be accomplished by—"

"Forget Einstein. Besides, who said anything about converting?"

Copeland's train of thought slammed into a brick wall. He protested. "Even the most elementary laws of physics—"

"As you understand them."

"Okay, as I understand them. But no living creature can start out as pure energy."

"In that, my lad, you are entirely correct."

No living creature. Copeland's pulse jumped again. This was getting spooky.

"How much do you know about Omega?"

"Only what you know and what Mildred has heard. However, from that I can deduce that the star is small, twenty to twenty-five kilometers in diameter. Considering its speed and trajectory and the degree of alteration in Mars orbit, it seems to be quite dense, perhaps around thirteen solar masses—"

"No way! Sixty years of research puts the most optimistic projection at three solar masses. One point four is normal. Thirteen is . . . beyond reason."

"Thirteen—pooh! Try forty."

This declaration took Copeland's breath away. He cursed the alcoholic fuzziness inside his skull as he desperately tried to work out the figures.

"But . . . but, that kind of density would exceed half a trillion tons to the cubic inch. How can such a body be stable?"

"Just told you, they aren't. At that density the slightest change in pressure can set the little devils off. Happens all the time."

"Do they implode?"

"Only the heavier ones. Obviously, in lesser masses gravity will lose out, and those will disperse in the usual manner. And well over one half die natural deaths, with gravity and pressure held in continuous equilibrium until their fires burn out."

"White dwarfs."

"What you call white dwarfs are not neutron stars, but ordinary stars that burn out over time. And they are reddish brown, not white."

Copeland tugged at his beard. Notwithstanding the fact that he had only a few hours left, his disastrous night had suddenly turned into one of the most thrilling moments of his entire life.

He decided to go right for the top. "I don't suppose you know anything about black holes?"

The slightly tipsy angel waved Kathleen Kelly's free hand back and forth. "White dwarfs, black holes—such foolish names. They happen to be perfectly normal gravity funnels."

Copeland set down his drink and leaned forward, his eyes dancing with excitement. "What happens when—"

But Rachael had no intention of wasting her final hours listening to a lecture on astronomy. "Excuse me. Mildred, you can have the bedroom at the end of the hallway on the second floor. Dr. Copeland, the room next to it is yours if you want it. Each has an ensuite bathroom."

Then she took her husband by the hand and declared, "Brooks and I are going back to bed."

1325 HRS

❦

The normal capacity of St. Andrew's was two thousand and seventy—seated. Another six hundred could be accommodated in the aisles, but they had to stand. This many again might be added by crowding around the three main altars or by filling up the foyer or by packing people around the great pipe organ in the overhead choir loft.

They had begun to arrive even before the first light of dawn, long before the doors were open, and by early afternoon on the day the earth was to be destroyed, the old church had somehow managed to squeeze in well over four thousand desperate souls. Another eight hundred or so had managed to grab a foothold somewhere on the three-tiered white granite staircase leading to the iron-studded twin doors at the main entrance, now held open by the pressing bodies. Two less imposing side entrances each held another three to four hundred.

Scattered around the front of the church, up and down the street in both directions, were several thousand more, not all Catholics by any means, or even Christians, but many who up to this moment in time had professed no faith at all. Faced with their own mortality, they had suddenly become believers, or at least half-believers, on the off chance that there might be a God after all, so they wanted to get in a prayer or two before it was too late.

The word was out now. Not everywhere in the world, but wherever the media could reach. Word that it was time to call it a day. Although chaos had replaced the general order in most places, there was no insurrection to speak of. The criminal element, too, had to make their peace before the coming of Armageddon.

Fifth Avenue, as far as the eye could see in either direction, was clogged with abandoned cars and buses. Yet this was the very heart of lower west side Brooklyn, a place rampant with activity day and night. Now, aside from the relatively small clump of humanity that had attached itself to St. Andrew's, only a handful of frightened people could be seen darting along the street.

Because the end was close at hand.

Several signs stating as much had appeared in the windows of abandoned shops like so much graffiti. Not all began with REPENT! *Rejoice, the Kingdom is at Hand,* and *Jesus, Savior of the World, has Come!* were common proclamations. A big sign carried on the shoulders of an old black man read simply: THE END IS HERE.

Brooks and his entourage, having sadly abandoned Reggie and their car several blocks away, intended to circumvent the frantic crowd by going along 59th Street to the rectory door at the side of the church. St. Andrew's was a Redemptorist parish, its large attached rectory providing accommodation for as many as two dozen priests. Having served as an altar boy for seven years, Brooks knew how to get to the sacristy from the rectory, provided he could get into the rectory.

Repeated presses on the doorbell brought no response. He jerked hard on the big brass latch. Locked! "I'm not surprised. We'll have to push our way through one of those side entrances."

Copeland glanced back down the street. "Not a chance."

"I just know we won't get in," declared Millie while wringing her hands. She was the one who had insisted they come.

"Mildred's right," Rachael agreed nervously. They had waited too long. "Maybe we should go back home."

"Try the door again," Mrs. Kelly suggested.

Brooks glanced down at the old woman beside him, catching the twinkle in her eye. He had merely to touch it and the door swung open on its own.

In they went, into the hushed interior of the rectory with its oak paneled walls and its fine old furniture. The blend of lemon oil mixed with cigar smoke was not unpleasant. They encountered no one on their journey, and a few minutes later arrived at a big arched door marked CHAPEL.

Inside were seven priests seated in a semicircle in front of a small alabaster statue of Christ the Redeemer. The priests were not praying— they were arguing. Their heads jerked around in surprise.

Brooks was embarrassed. "I'm really sorry for this. Just trying . . . you know . . . "

Father Pumpfrey threw a dark look their way, started to lecture Brooks on privacy, but Father Flynn cut him off. "Can't fault a man for using the old noggin. Nice to see you ladies. Too bad the timing's not better."

Young Father Ryan got to his feet. He had known Brooks in school. "The altar's just as packed as the nave. So is the choir loft. Be tough to find a spot anywhere."

"Go on," said Harry Flynn. "We're still working on our game plan. I'll be along in a few minutes."

Father Ryan's prediction was accurate enough, except Brooks had another trick up his sleeve, which took the five around the back of the great marble pillar right of the main altar to emerge into a tiny nook no one had yet claimed. Being head and shoulders over the mostly Hispanic parishioners crowded around the altar allowed him and Rachael and Copeland a clear view of the entire church, but Millie and Mrs. Kelly could not even see the altar. He returned to the chapel, excused himself again, grabbed two chairs and brought them back. Perching themselves upon the chairs, the two older women now had a perfect view of the terrified assembly.

Brooks could not spot any ushers. Near as he could see, there didn't seem to be any control at all, just noise and confusion. The century-old stone building echoed with wailing, whining, moaning: an entire symphony of human despair in full operatic voice. He did not envy the pastor the terrible chore ahead of him.

Oddly enough, even though Brooks dearly loved St. Andrew's, he now regretted giving in to Millie. He would have preferred to live out his last few hours at home.

Copeland was experiencing the worst hangover of his life. He had consumed a huge amount of alcohol since leaving Hawaii and was now paying the price. Still, it was his first time inside a Catholic church, so even the pain inside his head and the extreme anxiety he felt did not completely blot out his natural curiosity. The black crucified Christ on the left altar intrigued him. The dramatic sculpture was attached to a gold and silver cross with a crown of golden thorns surrounding the hanging head. Copeland found the visual impact quite overwhelming. He wondered at the Son of God being portrayed as black, but supposed there was no reason He should not be.

After a few minutes he shifted his gaze to the main altar itself, a twenty-foot-high alcove worked in whitish-amber marble. It, too, contained the crucified founder of Christianity, this time in rich buff marble, with the life-sized figures of a man and woman standing near the foot of a large wooden cross. High up behind the altar were five magnificent frescos which he took to be saints or early leaders of the church, and higher still, twenty-four life-size angels gazed placidly down upon the stricken congregation.

He was attempting to read the Latin texts beneath the frescos when Sarius leaned down and whispered in his ear, "Some of the big guys: Moses, David, Jesus, John the Baptist, and Paul."

When Harry Flynn finally put in an appearance ten minutes later, a great cry went up from the front of the church: "Confession, Father. We want to go to confession!"

In grim silence the old Irish priest made his way between his anxious parishioners, stepped up to the marble pulpit and switched on the microphone. He was not wearing Mass vestments, only his black cassock—appropriate dress for the occasion, as the entire European contingent and most of the Hispanics were dressed in black.

An overpowering sense of fear predominated the assembly, so real in form that it had created an odor all its own. Their faces alone— Hispanics, Italians, blacks, Irish, Asians—told him the whole gang was scared stiff, as sorry a sight as Harry Flynn had ever laid eyes on. Many were actually trembling in holy terror. And no wonder—a killer star, no less, was about to smash the earth into little bits.

"Okay, calm down, calm down. *Calm down!* That's better. Now you probably heard the Holy Father announce this morning on the news that he's given dispensation to all priests throughout the world to administer the Sacrament of Penance in general, which does away with the need for individual confessions. So let us begin this morning by saying the Confiteor: *I confess to Almighty God . . .* "

Harry Flynn was fully cognizant of the heavy burden that had been placed upon him and his brother priests, and if what the media were screaming over the airwaves was true, it was shaping up to be their final burden. He did not blame his parishioners for seeking refuge inside the house of God; it was, after all, a natural place for Catholics to come in their time of need. But what possible words could a simple old priest like him use to alleviate their fears?

After the last amen had died away, he held out both arms. "Are you truly sorry for all the sins of your past life?"

Everyone inside and outside the church within reach of his voice shouted, *"We are!"*

"Then let us all recite a sincere Act of Contrition: *O my God, I am heartily sorry for having offended Thee . . .* "

When the brief but intense prayer was over, the priest said, "By the power vested in me by Almighty God through Holy Mother Church, I hereby absolve you of all your sins in the name of the Father, and of the Son, and of the Holy Spirit. Amen."

A big sigh of relief went up from the crowd. Harry Flynn took a deep breath and smiled kindly at his flock. "Father Pumpfrey will have Mass and Holy Communion in a little while, which will be followed by Benediction of the Blessed Sacrament. Then we'll be saying the rosary until . . . as long as necessary.

"Well then, now that we have that behind us, I want to address this idea that some wayward star is about to come crashing into earth. And it's a terrible thing, to be sure. It reminds me of the time when the apostles were caught out in a big storm at sea while Jesus slept on in their boat. The poor buggers were scared out of their wits—every bit as scared as you are right this moment. For them it surely was the end of the world. The Bible tells us they woke the Master and begged Him to save them. Do you recall what Jesus said?"

The old priest rolled his eyes over the thousands of panic-stricken bodies crowded before him, waiting for the noise level to taper off before going on. "He didn't say, 'Don't worry, everything will be fine.' Not at all. He said, 'O ye of little faith!' The Bible doesn't say so, but I always suspected He was a bit teed off. After all, that very evening at Peter's house, those same fishermen had watched Him perform dozens of miracles. They knew Jesus Christ was the Son of God! They should have known He was capable of protecting them from harm. But you see, they didn't! *Because they did not believe!* They began to whine and snivel, just like you lot are doing right now. Jesus didn't make a big deal out of it. He just stretched out His hand and commanded the winds to stop. Then He went back to sleep."

Having spent a good part of the night in prayer and reflection, Father Harry's original prognosis had waned under the relentless onslaught of his colleagues. Up to this moment he was unclear as to the direction he would take. He realized now that his indecision had vanished.

Thank God!

Harry Flynn pounded his fist on the lectern and shouted in a loud voice, "I don't care who you are or what you do, if you don't BELIEVE in the power of Almighty God, then you deserve to have this neutron star come crashing down on your head! Now listen to me: The reason you are Catholics in the first place is because you believe! In case you didn't know, it's time someone told you that what separates you from the rest of the herd is your faith! A Catholic without faith is an empty shell—nothing! Less than nothing!"

The priest was yelling so loud Brooks's ears were ringing. Twenty-one years at St. Andrews, and no one had ever heard Father Flynn raise his voice, let alone yell at them.

"Didn't it ever occur to you for one minute that you are being tested? That your faith is being tested? That the faith of the entire Christian community is being tested? It was Jesus Himself who told us that faith can move mountains. You might argue, sure, an ordinary old mountain—but Father, this is a killer star! And I say, *how dare you limit the power of God?*

"Who do you think created the cosmos in the first place? You think it sprang from nowhere, just some random event? We are talking about the entire universe—billions upon billions of suns just like ours, trillions upon trillions of planets and moons and comets and asteroids and black holes and everything else that makes up the heavens—even killer stars."

There wasn't much racket now, just the occasional sniffle and a few bawling babies.

"The only question we need ask ourselves is whether this is the end God intended for us. If it is, then we should acknowledge it, confess our sins like we just did, and get ready to meet our Maker. And if I truly believed for one split second that the world is about to end, I wouldn't hesitate to say so. Sure I'd be administering the final sacrament right this minute and reaching out for that one-way ticket to paradise.

"You know, after hearing the news last night, I knelt down and asked Almighty God if Homo sapiens is about to become the dodo bird of the galaxy, the passenger pigeon of the universe. Isn't that what they are telling us, that we are about to become extinct? And yet . . . and yet, those same experts readily admit that just because we happen to be in the path of some derelict star as it speeds through the cosmos should not be regarded as anything out of the ordinary. Which makes perfect sense to me. After all, we know that a whole lot of strange and wonderful things happen up there in the heavens all the time, stuff we cannot begin to understand or even imagine.

"According to the news reports, most astronomers agree that this is merely the result of some dramatic but natural event that occurred many, many years ago in a far off section of the galaxy. It is not the hand of an angry God bearing down on us. Regardless of what my brother priests might tell you when they get up here, nothing I have seen or heard so far tells me that Almighty God has chosen this star as some neat way to get rid of the human race!

"This morning, with that very thought in mind, I managed to find a few minutes after the phone went dead to check out the dozens of scripture readings that describe the events associated with the last days. And you know what—only one of many signs and wonders described in the Bible has appeared on the horizon: the bit about stars falling from the heavens—loosely interpreted that is, because the little devil is not exactly falling.

"I'll tell you something else: The word of God is crystal clear on what constitutes the end of time, and the common ground between the Old and New Testaments is speed. 'For as the lightning cometh forth out of the east and shineth even unto the west, so shall be the coming of the Son of Man'. Speed! The end of the world will happen with the swiftness of a lightning bolt. In the twinkling of an eye. The Bible goes on to tell us that not even the angels know the hour when the Son of Man will appear in all His glory.

"So there you have it: This Omega star is old news now. The scientific community knew about it weeks ago. I mean, everyone knows about it!

"Listen to me now: I'm not knocking Islam, but you won't hear Harry Flynn go around yelling *Inshallah!* then bowing down in subjugation to accept my fate. Absolute submission to what we might interpret as the divine will is just dandy if you want to remove your brain first and lay it on the sidewalk. Because God gave us *brains* to think, and He gave us *guts* to act! And you know as well as I do in this day and age it takes guts *and* brains to be a true follower of Jesus Christ.

"So as true followers of Jesus Christ we have every right to demand that Almighty God get rid of this rogue star! And if this happens to be some queer trick He dreamed up to scare the pants off us, we're telling Him flat out we don't care for His tactics. So I'll give you fair warning: If there are those among you who honestly believe these are your last few hours on earth and want to spend them in quiet prayer and meditation, you've come to the wrong place. Harry Flynn's church is no place for quitters. Now kneel down, close your eyes, and I'll say a prayer on our behalf."

Many in the petrified congregation had found enough room within their paranoia to slip in a touch of wonder at the tone old Father Harry was using with his Creator. "If he keeps this up," Brooks said to Rachael, "the damn thing will be here within the hour."

Sarius was not so sure. Seizing God by the shoulders and giving Him a good shake was always a dangerous ploy, but when one looked Death directly in the face, there seemed little downside to laying it on the line.

Father Flynn took a deep breath, jammed his own eyes tight together, and when he spoke again his voice had lowered a couple of notches. "Lord, I'll be the first to admit we haven't done such a great job of putting the talents You gave us to good use. We make lots of mistakes. We stumble all over the place. We continue to screw up. Yes, and we haven't aspired to perfection like You wanted us to. But damn it all, we're *trying*! We're trying. And if we haven't given up, why should You?

"Truth is, it seems to me like Lucifer and his cohorts got too much control, and at times I even get the feeling there's not a whole lot of help coming down from Your side. So don't go giving up on us so easy. You agreed with Abraham to spare Sodom if he could find ten just men. Ten! This church alone, inside and out, has *ten thousand!* Do they count for nothing?"

"Poor Father Harry," Millie whispered to Mrs. Kelly.

"The guy's completely off his rocker!" Copeland declared, astonished at what he was hearing. The last thing he had expected to find inside a Catholic church was a raving lunatic priest.

A shocked Brooks Hennessey glanced down at the astronomer. "I believe you're right. Old Harry's lost it."

The hands on Rachael's watch read 2:18. Fewer than four hours to go until the end of time. Stricken as she was, her heart went out to Father Harry. She had not expected this wonderful old man to proclaim outright denial. The Omega star was on its way. It would strike the earth. Everyone would die. Copeland had said as much, and the angel standing beside her had confirmed it. There was nothing anyone could do, not even Sarius.

Nevertheless . . . the priest's words had planted a tiny seed of doubt. In the biblical sense his postulation was entirely correct. But Rachael could not help wondering if they might be witnessing the final, undeniable proof that the Bible was more fiction than truth, like most people assumed it was anyway.

Sarius was also troubled, but for different reasons. Rachael's meanderings had carried over into the angel's own subconscious mind even though he had not sought them. He found this odd. The angel moved through a doorway and stood in the streets of Jerusalem and there listened to the condemned Son of Man explain to His disciples that even He did not know the hour when the earth would be destroyed. The priest had wisely pointed out that now everyone knew.

Mrs. Kelly abruptly excused herself, stepped off her chair, and squeezed by Brooks to make her way over to the right-hand aisle. Her diminutive size allowed her to navigate the packed crowds and reach the side entrance, but it took considerable effort to thread her way through the hundreds of bodies crammed onto the church steps.

Across from the front of St. Andrew's, having paused beneath a small red awning that proclaimed the Los Pinas Grocery, Sarius turned to study the big stone edifice. He felt uneasy, even nervous. His superb intelligence pondered the cause of these unusual sensations, which he knew for once had nothing to do with Kathleen Kelly.

The gap between Omega's discovery and eventual arrival could only mean that the Last Judgment would not be appearing as foretold throughout the ages, like a thief in the night. The logical conclusion under the circumstances seemed to be that God had changed His mind and decided to allow humanity this little time to make their peace with Him.

Was that it? Was this the final show of mercy before the great God of Justice rose up in judgment?

The old priest, whom Sarius quite liked, had taken off like a house on fire. He claimed his people were being tested. Tested? The angel found this perplexing. He had only to cast his angelic vision into the western sky and see the truth for himself. The tiny star with its deadly mass almost fourteen times that of the sun was on its way. It would strike the earth with such speed that it would pass through in seconds; yet the planet's inhabitants would not die as they thought—by fire and water. They would suffocate.

Omega's enormous gravity field would strip away the earth's atmosphere while it was still seventeen million miles distant. The planet's puny gravity would be quickly negated, then reversed. Following the loss of air, the entire eastern seaboard would be ripped from its moorings and pulled toward the star in countless shattered fragments, manmade structures first, followed by lakes and oceans and great chunks of land mass. The remainder, after being turned into mush by the enormous shock wave, would be scattered throughout the solar system.

It seemed unfair to the angel, not only because the human experiment was about to be terminated, but because he had been allowed only a few moments of time to be among them. Observing in the flesh had created a kind of attachment that was outside the angel's normal range of sensation.

Angels do not love in the human sense. They do not form attachments. They are spirit beings of pure energy and intelligence, supposedly impervious to emotion in any form.

Yet here he was, a lowly, insignificant creature of the Realm, loving with as true a love as the most emotional mortal being, fearing with their deepest fears, and being swept along with as much passion as Father Harry at the notion that it was all about to end.

Since Mrs. Kelly was the lone person to occupy the west side of the street, several women in the crowd kept glancing her way with puzzled expressions. The tiny Irish woman had attended St. Andrew's since first moving down from Boston in 1947, so her face was a common sight to the regulars. It suddenly occurred to the angel that even in the depths of their own despair, these women were concerned about her welfare.

Standing there in his borrowed human body, listening to the air raid sirens wailing away in the distance, smelling the smoke from a nearby building fire, Sarius was overcome with a bitter sense of frustration. Preventing the holocaust was beyond the parameters of his capabilities, yet his mind whirled around and around at a speed that could not be measured. He continued, desperately now, to scan the history and dimensions of human existence, searching for clues. It was a futile task.

Even if by some stroke of genius he was able to find a way to divert the gravity star, he would most certainly not be permitted to do so. By now it was painfully obvious that the Creator had declared this experiment a failure.

In the midst of such deeply troubled thoughts, something remarkable happened.

The angel began to grow angry.

0000 HRS

❧

A direct audience with the Lord and Master of the Universe was so rare that Sarius could recall only three times since his own inception that such an event had transpired. Two of those had been to enter a plea on behalf of a dying world. The third was to seek permission to destroy a species that had become permanently mired in depravity.

All had been denied.

So it was with no real hope of success that the angel made his request to the great Metatron. He and Kathleen Kelly were no longer enjoined, but there was little doubt that her earlier influence was at least partly responsible for pressuring Sarius into sticking his neck out.

Even though Earth was but one of a great many developing worlds, the father of all angels was perfectly aware of the imminent destruction of the human species. But he above all others knew better than to question the Wisdom of the Ages.

"It is not proper for one belonging to the Ophanim to seek audience with the Master," was Metatron's response. "Besides, have you and I not witnessed the deaths of countless worlds? I realize this one is special, but we have known for some time that Earth's failure was in the winds. My advice is to put it from your mind and accept the consequences of human iniquity."

Angels do not communicate by sound, but by impulse. Therefore, Sarius had to quickly suppress his instinctive rebuttal before it turned into thought.

Humbly, as befitting a member of the lower orders, he said, "I have watched them closely for fifty years, great Metatron, and I would be the first to agree that this small planet is rampant with vile transgressions. If they were merely another race of transgressors, I would hardly seek to lengthen their existence. But lately I have noticed that their desire to unite with God on a higher level has taken on new urgency, which I suspect is related to entering the new millennium. Whatever the reason, it is clear to me that they are only now, finally, learning the right path. They must be allowed more time."

Since this was the same angel who only a short time earlier had terminated the lives of three young men, hopeless though they were, his passionate plea came as a surprise to Metatron. "You seem to think highly of them, though I cannot see why. They are hardly a noble species."

Nobility had a far different meaning here than it had on Earth. It was essentially a combination of purity of spirit and a loving, child-like obedience to God, a concept too simple to be grasped by most human adults.

"It is unfortunate that they have remained in their primitive state for so long, but everyone knows why."

Metatron began to grow impatient. He did not feel it proper for someone of his high office to enter into a philosophical discussion with a junior angel. An inflection of haughtiness crept into the big boss's thought impulses.

"They were given the means to resist and chose not to use it. Now it seems the Master has decided to end the experiment. Who can blame Him? So you are wasting your time, and mine. Go now. You are dismissed."

Since the dimension of time did not exist within the Kingdom, Metatron's comment was largely rhetorical in nature. And Sarius was not going anywhere.

"I refuse to be dismissed. What do you say to that?"

Metatron's aura, already the greatest in the angelic realm, flared to such an extent that his reaction was picked up in the farthest reaches of the Kingdom.

"How dare you show disrespect?"

"I came seeking an audience, and you scorn my efforts. If I belonged to the Seraphim or Cherubim, would you act this way? I think not. If you insist on denying me, I will go forward without your permission. I doubt if you can stop me."

Metatron's thoughts became so jumbled that he could not get a clear sentence together. He could only bluster. Sarius decided to wait no longer, and, not without considerable trepidation, projected his spirit energy into the void.

In order to appear before the Throne, it was necessary to draw free from all temporal barriers. There existed, within this nondimensional embodiment that formed the Eternal Light, the Absolute and Everlasting Power of the Omnipotent Presence: the Face of God, the Holy of Holies, a sight longed for throughout the ages.

Due to an embryonic and indissoluble spatial nonconformity with material structure and created mass, God could not be portrayed to those outside the Kingdom. Brooks had asked Sarius to describe his Master, but how does one describe an infinite being that holds the very bounds of Creation within His bosom?

Although they could not be seen with human eyes or grasped with human intelligence, there resided within the Presence not one, but Seven Golden Rings of Eternity. It was common knowledge to the inhabitants of the Kingdom that the First Ring held all of paradise, and the Second, the totality of all creations: past, present, and future. The Third Ring held secure those spirit energies that had been originally sent out from the Source—the souls of humankind. The Fourth Ring contained the Blessed One, He who had been chosen to renew God's covenant with humanity, while the Fifth Ring embodied the Great Spirit, the conveyor of all mercies and hope.

Inside the Sixth Ring were six dark crystals, each holding six primary reaches of the Underworld; so was the number of the Beast and of all evil spirits stamped upon Eternity: 666!

The Seventh and central ring remained a mystery. Not even Metatron understood its composition. Sarius had learned that it held more energy than all the outer rings combined, but beyond this inceptive knowledge he had no idea, although it had occurred to him more than once that this final ring might well be the actual Source, the Power that fueled All: *the very heart of God!*

Upon reaching the foot of the Throne, Sarius's own aura quickly vanished inside the great Light that was God.

"Why?" asked a deep voice from out of the light.

Sarius did not expect that his presence would be immediately acknowledged. And the last thing he expected to hear was the spoken word.

This single word rendered the angel speechless.

"Metatron is a wise and faithful servant, but he sometimes lacks perception. You may speak freely."

Sarius attempted to recover his dignity. He was unable to see God. No one, to the best of his knowledge, had even determined the actual form that gives birth to the Light. "The odor of death lies heavy upon the earth, Great Lord and Master. Why must it be so?"

"Tell me why it should not be so."

Sarius gathered all the intellectual resources at his command and began his postulation. He had earlier considered the tack he would take and now entered his plea without hesitation.

When he was finished, God said, "Your words are well chosen. And now you wish me to divert the star."

"Yes, Master, and quickly, before their own star system collapses."

"Too late for that."

"Too late! But—"

"Your actions are out of character for one belonging to the Ophanim. Have you come to love them so much?"

Sarius could not declare with certainty that what he felt for Brooks Hennessey and the others was love, but he was inclined to believe it was. "I admit they have become . . . special to me."

"And you believe that allowing them more time will make a difference?"

"I am sure it will."

"What if I said you were wrong?"

Sarius had no answer for that.

"Surely you saw that they lack nobility."

That word again. "Yes, Master. Metatron has already brought this to my attention. However, I must remind my Lord that it was Your own plan to share Your Spirit with them that prompted Lucifer's rage. Under his command the entire powers of hell have descended upon this poor planet. Is it any wonder they cannot aspire to nobility?"

These words teetered on the very bounds of disrespect, but Sarius realized by now that desperate measures were required.

God's reply was tinged with sadness. "This cannot be denied. Truly, they were destined for greatness; indeed, the highest honors in the heavens were reserved for them. But they have not achieved greatness. Iniquity has become the dominant force in their lives."

"Not for all, Master."

"Not for all. But the forces of evil have far too much control over the hearts and minds of this weak species. They have spurned my first commandment and everything it stands for. Now their true god is technology. I see no purpose in prolonging the inevitable."

"So Lucifer has won after all!"

This time there was no reply from the Throne, only a eerie, pulsating silence. A silence, Sarius knew, that was anything but what it seemed. The angel waited and waited, but no sound came forth. Finally he asked, "Master, is this truly the end for humanity?"

"What has been established as due process cannot be altered."

Sarius assumed God was referring to the killer star. The angel had just finished reviewing the circumstances that had given birth to Omega. It had achieved its present trajectory some eight million years earlier, and although any number of similar stars or gravity funnels along the way might have deflected the star, it had never deviated from its original course. This had only one meaning to the angel—that Earth's inhabitants had been granted a fixed period of time to acknowledge their Creator or, in heavenly terms, to achieve nobility.

After another long silence, the angel said, "So there is no hope."

"None."

At that moment, if he had a head he would have lowered it in sorrow. If he had eyes, he would weep. If he had knees he would fall upon them and beg for mercy. But Sarius had no knees to bend, and within this Sanctuary, no surface to touch even if he did.

For in God's final proclamation lay the futility of all creations past. This one would fare no different than all the others.

"Lucifer foretold this! He said—"

"I know what he said."

"But Master, You shared Your own Spirit with them. You sent the Holy One to rescue them. You gave them the Paraclete to keep them steadfast in faith."

"All for nothing."

"They need more time to open their minds to the truth. I know they will change. Even now, I can see the changes—"

"The answer is no!"

Sarius forced himself to take the human equivalent of three deep breathes. "You knew all along that they never had a chance. Tell me then, what was the point?"

"Sarius of the Ophanim, it is not for you to question the One who created you. This is not a foolish game you are playing. The taking of three lives was an unwarranted act and overlooked only because the end was close at hand. But be assured that your meddling in the larger picture will not be tolerated!"

With these final words a ferocious spiral of light from the Throne knocked the angel all the way down to his own level. Dazed and distraught, Sarius covered up his embarrassment as best he could while his fellow Ophanim fled in panic.

News traveled fast within the angelic realm, instantaneously, in fact, and his provocative actions had given rise to suspicions of rebellion— a word so feared among the heavenly host that not one of the 1.5 million Ophanim who happened to be around at the time came to his aid. They huddled far off in the distance, in sight, but barely.

In regaining control of his powers, Sarius realized that he and the earth now had something in common: Both were in real trouble.

1500 HRS

❧

Mrs. Kelly's sudden appearance beside Millie forced her to grab hold of Copeland's shoulder to keep from falling off the chair. Brooks turned around at Millie's muffled screech and heaved a deep sigh of relief at the sight of Mrs. Kelly. The thought of trying to get through this without her was almost more than he could bear. The angel had been gone for a full hour, and Brooks was beginning to think they would never see her again.

"Where did you get to?"

"Topside, Brooksie, for a little chat."

Rachael forced her way around her husband. She pointed her finger to the sky, and in a wide-eyed whisper asked, "You mean . . . up there?"

"Yes, child, up there."

Having spent the last eight hours listening to the old woman expound on everything in the universe, Copeland was now a believer. Angel or not, she was, without a doubt, the most gifted and intelligent person he had ever met. As a result, the astronomer had all but forgotten about his wife and children. Only a tiny pang of regret accompanied the knowledge that he would never see them again. He leaned forward around Millie's skirt to catch every word.

Brooks's sense of relief vanished when he caught the look of dejection on Mrs. Kelly's face. "I guess you didn't fare too well?"

"Big fat zero."

Copeland, his believer's eyes ablaze with excitement, asked, "Who did you see?"

"The only one who can stop the star—the big boss Himself." Sarius did not feel like playing around with the word *see*.

Mass was just getting underway again, with all ten priests in residence taking part. The crowd was growing restless.

Brooks asked, "Did He bother to explain why?"

"Not to the likes of me. That would be much like your president being asked to explain his foreign policy to a street bum. Ah well, doesn't matter a hoot now. Earth is going down the tube. It's all over for you guys." Once again caught up in Kathleen Kelly's emotions, the angel looked Brooks Hennessey in the eye and stated plaintively, "I want you to know that I tried my best."

With Mrs. Kelly standing on the chair, she and Brooks were almost nose to nose. Brooks felt an almost desperate urge to hug her, to console her, to express his gratitude for her efforts, but did not think it proper to embrace an angel. Softly, he said, "I know you did."

There was no organist, but Father Harry insisted that Mass begin in the usual way, with a hymn. Young Father Ryan started out in his fine Irish baritone.

Now fades all earthly splendor,
The shades of night descend;
The dying of the daylight
Foretells creation's end . . .

In light of the pastor's vigorous denial that the end really was nigh, Brooks thought the selection inappropriate. Unless, of course, the old priest was finally coming to grips with reality.

The hour hand on Brooks's watch was touching three. Three hours remaining. Father Harry's brief infusion of hope had already faded away. It had been a futile gesture, at best providing a few moments of distraction.

Sarius was still reeling from his brief appearance before the throne of God. Nothing in his experience had led him to believe that the Lord of Creation might behave in such a callous manner. Even Metatron's words had been unnecessarily harsh under the circumstances.

The angel quickly reviewed the many covenants between God and man. Sublime promises had been made, promises that would not now be kept. It seemed inconceivable that the Creator of the Universe would renege on His word. But there it was. He had even grown angry at Sarius's appeal for mercy. The Greatest of all Beings had considered the angel's behavior irrational. Yet to Sarius it was God's behavior that was capricious in the extreme.

Why?

The lowly Ophanim fell into a state of torment. The somber ceremony unfolding before him was not even taking place. He did not see it. He saw the Son of God, the Redeemer of humanity, dying on a tree. The pain of His passage had been so great that the entire angelic host had been forced to turn away. The great archangel Michael had been banished to the farthest reaches of the Kingdom because it was feared that he above all others would not stand idly by and allow his Master to suffer so.

This was the supreme act of love, the ultimate covenant between God and man. It was the heavenly life preserver thrown to a drowning species. Now it was being jerked away from them.

Why?

Sarius withdrew totally into himself. Someone looking at Kathleen Kelly would think she had fallen asleep standing up. There was not a single movement in her frail body.

The angel opened his mind to every conceivable possibility that might allow him some small insight into God's decision to abandon the human race. What terrible offense had they committed to incur the Master's wrath?

Sarius had been around people for fewer than fifty years, but during that time he had absorbed the contents of a number of major libraries in several countries. This knowledge provided him with a good perspective into human development. He also knew that the God of human history, at least in the latter days, had always behaved like a gentle, loving father, slow to anger and quick to forgive.

The angel was reasonably certain they were the only species within this present universe that had been granted the promise of eternal life. Other species had evolved to far greater levels of intelligence, but even those superior beings had been offered no future beyond the grave. Only humanity held the promise of eternal life. Only humanity had been awarded the spark of godliness. So why abandon them now, when their journey was just beginning?

Sarius saw no logic in destroying something so precious and unique. He did not see their reluctance to acknowledge God as Lord and Master as their fault. Under the circumstances they could hardly be expected to behave differently. Plus, it greatly disturbed Sarius that God seemed so willing to accept defeat, and thereby award total victory to the Powers of Darkness. He could easily imagine the rejoicing that was even now taking place within the great vaulted halls of the Underworld.

Brooks had been watching the angel closely. When he saw the tiny head abruptly drop to her chest, he reached over to steady her. Mrs. Kelly's eyes opened with a start.

"You okay?"

"Course I am."

"Looked like you were about to fall over."

"Don't worry about me, Brooksie."

A phrase used the previous evening came back to Sarius: *We're on borrowed time.*

All angels possess the ability to arrest time, a necessary device often used by Guardians in the performance of their duties. If he wished, Sarius could delay the inevitable by wrapping a time band around the earth. This would effectively bring to a halt all activities within the earth's solar system, though it would not stop the Omega star. It would, however, slow down the star, since its speed could not exceed that of being able to reach earth before it was due to arrive in the first place.

But freezing time was strictly a temporary measure, the parameters of which were governed by a stringent set of physical laws. He would not be able to hold the band in place for long.

The temperature inside St. Andrews had risen dramatically, and so had a few tempers. This made Father Harry feel sad. Even with death breathing down their necks, aggression still raised its ugly head.

Since this Mass was not part of the normal church calendar, he had to personally select the three Bible readings. The first usually came from the Old Testament, so he had chosen a passage from Isaiah. It was old Father Brennan who made his way to the pulpit with difficulty and, in his gravelly ninety-two-year-old voice, began to read.

For a small moment have I forsaken thee,
But with great mercies will I gather thee.
In a moment of indignation have I hid my face from thee,
But with everlasting kindness have I had mercy on thee,
said the Lord thy Redeemer.
This thing is to me as in the days of Noe, to whom I swore,
That I would no more bring in the waters of Noe upon the earth:
So have I sworn not to be angry with thee,
And not to rebuke thee.
For the mountains shall be moved, and the hills shall tremble;
But my mercy shall not depart from thee,
And the covenant of my peace shall not be moved . . .

Dark thoughts began to seep into the angel's consciousness. Sending a deadly neutron star straight at the earth hardly constituted a covenant of peace.

From where he stood on the chair, the tilted head of the crucified Christ stared down at the angel.

Sarius stared back.

Ten minutes later he moved out of the church, slowly at first, rising above the dissipating clouds, and then far above the earth. With one final, lingering look back at the blue planet, he projected into the cosmos.

Millie's scream caused everyone at the front of the church to look in her direction. The pastor of St. Andrew's had just sat down after the gospel reading. Father Divine, an Australian and one of the finest orators in the business, was getting started, but stopped dead at the scream.

When Father Harry realized it was Mrs. Kelly who had fallen off her chair, he muttered under his breath, "Not again!"

Brooks knew right away that the angel no longer had possession of her body. She had fallen forward partly across Copeland's shoulder, and Brooks used his bulk to clear a spot on the floor to lay her out. A ring of concerned faces stared down at the poor dear.

Brooks touched Mrs. Kelly's forehead, recoiled at the deathly cold flesh, as if she had been dead for hours. He did not have to feel for a heartbeat, but did so anyway.

This time she truly was gone. Brooks glanced up at Rachael, his eyes misty. It was like losing two friends at once.

The old pastor managed to squeeze through. "Oh dear," he said upon seeing the color of her face. So much for Millie's belief that Mrs. Kelly was an angel.

"Gone for sure this time, is she?"

Brooks nodded. He could hardly believe it. Her last words had been: *"Don't worry about me, Brooksie."*

Copeland was astonished at the deep sense of loss that came over him. He had known the woman for only a few hours, but it was as if he had known her for years. His overpowering desire to remain by her side had caused him to turn his back on his family. Now that she was gone, he felt truly lost.

The priest gave Mrs. Kelly his final blessing and stood up. He placed a hand on Rachael's shoulder. "That's twice this week Kathleen Kelly's died on my altar, but I'm afraid this time the poor darling won't be coming back. Ah well, if these doomsayers get their wish, we'll be catching up to her before long."

Father Divine was still at the pulpit, waiting for permission to continue. Father Harry asked Brooks to cover up the victim, then nodded toward the pulpit.

The Australian was five minutes into his sermon, not even warmed up yet, when a peculiar thing happened. A lady's bandanna began to float upward.

It had come from the middle of church, and those at the rear watched in mild curiosity. It seemed peculiar, as they had all seen balloons float into the sky, but never a bandanna. That one was thirty feet into the air, heading not straight up, but angling toward the altar, when another joined it.

From there on matters deteriorated rapidly. A number of piercing screams came from outside the church, rendering a stunned silence among the parishioners inside.

Copeland knew what was talking place. The back of the church behind the altar was facing southeast, the same direction where he had seen all the comet activity, where Mars used to be. He also realized that Earth had broken free from its orbit.

He reacted to this knowledge by freezing up.

Brooks saw the terrified look on the astronomer's face. "What is it?"

Copeland could not even find his voice. Brooks had to shake him to get an answer.

"We're losing gravity! Omega has started to suck up our atmosphere!"

Brooks looked out over the congregation and saw that the light had taken on a brownish tinge: dust! It was rising all around them. He pulled Rachael close and in quiet desperation asked Copeland, "This mean we're all going to suffocate?"

"Yes—maybe, I don't know! The entire surface will come loose next. Everything, and I mean *everything*, will start heading toward Omega! No wonder Mars popped its orbit. The mass of this thing is off the scale."

From the rear of the church a third kerchief began rising. Women with long hair felt it lift from their shoulders. The little tots began to feel the shift in gravity. Down the street a gun went off, the first of many.

Father Flynn had heard the stranger's terrified outburst. He knew now that all claims of imminent danger were true. He quickly unlocked the golden tabernacle, removed the Monstrance and set a Sacred Host inside it. Then he pushed Father Divine out of the way and placed the Blessed Sacrament on the podium.

After appealing for calm, he said, "Kneel down now, and we'll pray the rosary."

The eight-hundred-year-old prayer was, after all, a proven fortress of strength in times of great danger. The pastor assumed that his Protestant colleagues, who had long ago spurned all devotion to the Blessed Virgin, were at this moment reciting the Twenty-third Psalm. And rightly so since the entire planet had just entered the valley of the shadow of death.

The crowd was close to all-out panic now, as more and more untended items continued to drift upward. Small children, who did not realize they were about to die, began casting pages of the church bulletin into the rapidly-thinning air.

Father Harry refused to give up hope. Passover came to mind, but it was too late now to paint the doors with sheep's blood. It didn't matter anyway. This time God would not be passing over anyone.

"Our Father, who art in Heaven, hallowed be thy Name. Thy Kingdom—"

He got no farther than that.

Although he was a great distance away, Sarius had gathered his awesome power into its singular state and sent it forth, just as he had done at the hospital when Emma's life had been given back to her. All movement within the earth's solar system came to an abrupt halt. The killer star too, instantly slowed its passage.

God Himself had warned the angel not to interfere, but Sarius felt he had no choice but to defy God. No matter what happened now, even if he were to discover a means to save this troubled planet, the angel knew his own fate was sealed.

0000 HRS

⁊

The star had stabilized a long time ago, with pressure and gravity coexisting in perfect, yet precarious, harmony. It was not a pearoid or a geoid like normal stars, but a brilliant white spearoid with a dead smooth surface and a core gravitational pull so great that not even the slightest blip could disturb its half-mile-deep crystalline crust. For this was the most rigid material in the universe, more than one million billion times stiffer than steel.

Omega was small, barely fifteen miles across, with a mass so heavy that a single cubic inch weighed just under two billion tons. Neutron stars achieve such intense compaction when normal electrons of iron are squeezed onto their nuclei and in the process convert their protons to neutrons. With the increase of pressure inside the nuclei, the neutrons soon begin to dominate everything.

Sarius had observed countless thousands of these miniature bodies scattered throughout the universe, but never one that tore though space at such great speed. Nor did he believe for one moment that Omega's deadly trajectory was merely the random outcome of a natural stellar collision.

This one had God's own hand on it.

Not only did the worried angel have to find a safe means to upset the star's delicate balance, but he had to address the more fundamental question of whether it would implode or explode. He could not simply exert the necessary force to redirect the star without being certain of the outcome of his actions. Cause and effect were very much the heart of the issue here.

213

Physicists on earth still believed it was compulsory for neutron stars over a certain mass to implode, but Sarius knew this depended on a number of factors. As he had earlier explained to Copeland, implosion would create a singularity, which in turn would instantly form a gravity tunnel through which Earth's entire solar system would quickly fall victim. On the other hand, should his meddling cause pressure to overcome gravity, the immense thermonuclear explosion from the resultant supernova would just as quickly extinguish all life forms within the solar system.

There are no schools for higher learning in heaven. Angels are created with instinctive knowledge and intelligence, much the same as a tiny bird is programmed with intuitive knowledge regarding location and direction. In the angelic realm such gifts are freely granted and sustained. So while Sarius knew full well how to alter time and matter, until now he'd had no reason to consider the quantum mechanical properties of bodies of extremely high density.

He was about to find out.

Angels, in their natural state, possess no mass. Sarius, therefore, was able to penetrate the star without danger of altering its balance and observe firsthand the agitated neutrons pushing and pulling against each other in a kind of claustrophobic panic. It was this degenerate force that he would have to deal with in order to find a solution.

The star was still speeding toward its target, albeit slower and slower so long as the time band remained in place. Sarius had no way of knowing how much longer the band would hold, and so he frantically ran through the combinations and permutations of defusing a neutron star, but nothing he could come up with suggested that a solution was even possible, and indeed God Himself had told the angel it was too late.

Only at this point, with defeat staring him in the face, did it occur to Sarius that he was taking the wrong tack altogether.

If the star were to implode, he reasoned, space-time curvature inside it would become enormous. Might there be, therefore, some means of using the implosion to create a hiatus, or even a reversal of time? The idea excited him. Yes, an entity would be formed that was even deadlier than the neutron star, but it would be powerless against a body that did not yet exist.

Sarius realized he was onto something. Implosion would naturally impact local solar time, but what form would the disruption take?

His great intelligence soon came to the fore, as new and innovative calculations were logically derived and juggled around to fit the problem at hand. He took a quantum leap forward when he remembered that space-time curvature and gravity have essentially the same properties, and are therefore interchangeable. With this in mind he began to explore the possibility of using the implosion to create an entirely separate dimension.

Yes . . . but . . . could the most powerful of all heavenly bodies, a gravity funnel, be contained within the boundaries of a single dimension?

He had to carefully review the properties of matter and antimatter to see if this were possible, concluding after some frenzied speculation that it was at least theoretically possible.

Due to the time band, Omega was slowing at a rate of three hundred miles per second every second. Precious little time remained for Sarius to put his plan into action.

But he hesitated.

He had to consider one last time whether saving this species was worth the price. Even if he succeeded, God might well choose another means to terminate the human experiment.

Then his sacrifice would be for nothing.

The loss of freedom for all eternity was a heavy toll to pay, but Sarius had to face up to the fact that he was but one of many millions of angels. His banishment would mean little. Who was there to miss him? He had no family or close friends. Brooks and Rachael were the closest he'd ever come to real family. Besides, he was usually away so much that his permanent absence would hardly be noticed.

Destruction of an entire species, on the other hand, even an experimental species, was a profound tragedy, although their Creator obviously did not see it that way.

His indecision lasted so long that the time band popped. A dimensional transfer allowed Sarius to view the panic inside the church and to observe with mixed emotions Kathleen Kelly's tiny form laid out at Brooks Hennessey's feet.

Father Flynn was doing his best to lead the congregation in prayer, but his efforts fell on deaf ears. Some of the objects began to rise from the altar as though a magician were directing their movements. Flowers were drawn from flower pots and dripped water over the fearful assembly.

The big flags on either side of the marble alcove had unfurled themselves and were pointing upward. Breathing was becoming labored.

Then came the worst sign of all: A tiny three-day-old baby boy rose from his parent's seat at the rear of the church and was out of reach before anyone could grab him. The child drifted slowly toward the altar while his mother screamed her head off.

Pandemonium reigned. In church, in New York City, across the continent, all over the world.

Along the street, shingles and roofing from older structures were being ripped away. Smaller buildings began to shake on their foundations. Huge clouds of dust being sucked up by Omega's awesome gravity field would soon have the city in darkness. The number of gunshots increased by the minute.

Why? the angel cried out. This was wrong. He knew it was wrong. So why was it happening?

Sarius focused the terrible anger he felt into a single beam of energy and thrust it into the heart of the star.

The neutron star did not implode. It split in two. Trillions of pent-up neutrons exploded at the same instant of time. All gravity dissipated. On earth everything that had been airborne came back down. The child was happily caught by a waiting father's arms. There was laughter, a few exclamations of joy, a kind of "I told you so" feeling on the part of Father Harry.

The raging thermonuclear monster took just over thirteen minutes to reach earth. Those outside the church saw it coming, and the sound that erupted from their throats was not even human.

Their cries lasted barely a second.

Brooks Hennessey pulled Rachael and Millie tight to his chest. His final thought was not one of fear for himself, but a feeling that Sarius was in trouble.

"Don't worry about me, Brooksie," the angel had told him.

The radiating fireball turned the blue planet into a puff of smoke. The force of the exploding neutron star was so great that six minutes later even the sun itself was reduced to its primary particles.

Everything Sarius had calculated was entirely correct. Except he did not think to allow for two key variables.

His first mistake resulted in rapidly advancing the annihilation of the human race. The second contributed to his own demise.

Sarius had not yet come to realize the most basic premise so well understood by those who inhabit the world of castoff angels: that anger is capable of doubling the energy output.

Nor did it occur to him that he himself might be vulnerable. After all, angels are eternal spirits created by an eternal God to enjoy His creations forever. They do not die, cannot die.

This holds true in all but the most extreme circumstances.

In order to disrupt the star's enormous gravity, it had been necessary for Sarius to convert his spirit energy into physical energy. When the chain reaction instantaneously achieved the speed of light, the angel's converted energy had no choice but to obey the laws of relativity and change into mass. One billionth of a second later, the mass vanished inside the fireball.

Sarius did not have to worry about repercussions from on High.

He was no more.

0000 HRS

❦

All children begin life with a guardian angel at their side who might remain with them until puberty and sometimes well into their teens and beyond. Indeed, it is not unusual for certain sensitive people, those who are able to listen to their intuition, to remain in touch with angels their entire lives. The angelic presence is not intended, as many would believe, to avert tragedy or even to offer a helping hand, although it is common enough for angels to lend assistance when danger threatens. But extracurricular activity is entirely up to the individual guardian.

Being fully multilocational allows a single guardian to look after, say, an extended family in India, a small condo unit in suburban Montreal, or an entire village in the Amazon. Plus, it has recently become standard policy for the two hundred million or so overworked guardians on active duty to constantly move around to wherever they are needed.

The massive logistics inherent in such an undertaking are overseen by Saraqael. But the appointed procurator of spirits had long been complaining that the new millennium was stretching his resources beyond their effective limits. His dire warning had subsequently brought into question the long-established tradition of using angels as the primary means to deflect Underworld influence.

It was Urial, the archangel who had been given command over the primary elements, who first suggested that the lower orders be put to work. This would, after all, more than triple the number of frontline troops. His proposal had naturally met with strong resistance on the part of Metatron and Saraqael. Even the three moderates, Remiel, Gabriel, and Raphael, could see this idea was fraught with folly.

But as has so often happened throughout the course of human history, it was the great archangel Michael who had the final word unto God concerning the fate of the human species. He agreed with Urial, but only on condition that a rigorous trial be set in place, a dynamic ordeal that would determine once and for all whether the lower orders have the right stuff.

Rather than give in, Metatron went on to paint a disturbing picture of the chaos that could erupt once millions of lower-order angels were let loose on earth. He held the strong opinion that these junior angels were not properly disposed to take on such a heavy burden of responsibility. Nevertheless, Michael's wisdom prevailed, and after many long sessions held in absolute secrecy, the parameters of the grand trial were agreed upon by all seven. With God's final blessing, it became fully operational.

Sarius had been selected for a number of reasons. He was typical of the Ophanim—if anything, he was even a bit more independent than the others; plus, he had twice asked to become a guardian.

And, of course, he was already there.

So it came to pass that a junior angel had been prompted at the instant of Kathleen Kelly's death to become more fully involved with the human species. This, too, was Michael's idea. After all, what better way to understand their nature than to merge with one of them?

One million years from now, if by some phenomenal run of good luck they might have been able to survive that long, humanity would also learn to master time. Along with other multidimensional functions, the ability to turn back the clock would be programmed in at birth. By then the human species would be well on its way to leaving their physical bodies behind, and time would have lost its ability to strike fear into the hearts of man.

But for now, in the closing months of this particular year of the new millennium, time was everything. And time, for the six point five billion souls crowded onto the third planet from the sun, had run out. It was too late for them, it was too late for their planet, it was too late for their solar system, already in a state of collapse.

One angel down, one star system down.

The inhabitants of the Kingdom were utterly dazed by the speed and finality of the great catastrophe. They did not understand why God had decided to do away with His favorite species on such short notice, especially after all the trouble He had gone through in the first place to rescue them.

MONDAY

0725 HRS

❧

The reason Brooks Hennessey found himself in church that morning was because he'd missed Sunday Mass. If he had missed Mass because he was sick or traveling or something like that, he would not have bothered. But the third commandment was sacred to him. The sixth commandment, the reason for his absence, he had learned to accommodate ages ago.

Brooks had spent the entire weekend with his new mistress, Annie. Annie was twenty-two, Brooks forty-four, but the age difference presented no problem, at least not in this early stage of their relationship. A passionate lover, the big man had no license to display his talents at home, which left him little choice but to seek consolation elsewhere. As for Rachael, she didn't seem to care one way or another what Brooks did. They still maintained a cordial relationship but hadn't shared the same bedroom for eight years.

So come Monday, Brooks was up at six sharp to make certain he caught early Mass before work. Brooks did not aspire to being a *good* Christian—his lifestyle prohibited such a lofty goal—but being brought up in an Irish Catholic family had superimposed a certain structure on his life. Going to church was part of it. Although, true enough, as a result of his affairs he could not receive Holy Communion, and it was this self-imposed separation from God that weighed so heavily upon him.

He raised his head to take another quick peek at the Gang of Five, as they were known in his younger years: five great frescos laid out in a semicircle behind the magnificent marble alcove that housed the crucified Christ. All the main players were there: Moses, David, Jesus, John the Baptist, and Paul. For some reason this morning Brooks felt as if those cold painted eyes were bearing down on him. He had the distinct impression that John the Baptist in particular was annoyed about something.

When the church door creaked open halfway through Mass to allow old Mrs. Kelly to enter, Brooks could hear her labored breathing as she made her way up the long church aisle, her cane tapping away on the tiled floor. Brooks was kneeling on the outside of the tenth row, immediately right of the center aisle.

The old lady struggled by him, then stopped and turned around to look him in the eye. The look startled Brooks. It was as if she could see right into his heart.

Suddenly the elderly parishioner was kneeling beside him, a peculiar grimace tilting all her wrinkles to one side.

When Father Harry set the chalice down again on the altar, eighty-two-year-old Kathleen Kelly leaned toward Brooks and whispered, "Got a story for you, Brooksie, a dandy."

Brooks heaved a deep inward sigh. It was not uncommon for parishioners to ask him to read their creative efforts. They figured since he ran the local paper he must be interested in the written word. Especially theirs.

After Mass he made a valiant attempt to step over her and get away, but the old woman grabbed hold of one big arm and would not let go.

Outside, on the church steps, Mrs. Kelly said, "Come on, I'll buy you a coffee."

"That's nice of you, my love, but I have to get to work."

"Work'll keep. Let's go."

❧

At the summit of Mauna Kea, six thousand miles to the southwest, at precisely 1:57 in the morning, Mari Yamakura, the female member of the Japanese astronomy team, was the only one watching the screen when it happened.

"Ayiiii!"

The others, including Copeland, had stepped outside the building for a quick look around the mountaintop. They all charged through the door at the same time, resulting in a momentary blockage. Copeland was not unduly concerned, thinking one of the resident mice had put in an appearance.

Sure enough, Mari Yamakura was backing away from the main computer desk with both hands jammed to her mouth. Copeland glanced at the assembly. No mouse, but the visuals CRT was awash in brilliant white light. The astronomer raced across the room and switched it off. The thing looked like it was about to self-destruct. Oddly enough, a quick readout of the various circuits on the adjoining text monitor indicated everything was functioning normally.

"This is weird. Never happened before that I know of."

"No, no!" said Mari, having regained her voice. "I am certain it is a stellar explosion. Please, Dr. Copeland, you must look and see."

Copeland smiled down at the young woman. If a collision or a supernova of that magnitude had occurred, it would have to be pretty damn close, or pretty damn big. Or both. He was prepared to humor her because loss of the visuals CRT meant the night's program was cancelled.

He flicked the monitor switch and waited for the screen to return to life. All six astronomers crowded around the four foot square tube to watch the extraordinary light flood across the surface. It stayed like that for thirty minutes or so, just an indefinable blob of white light.

Then it began to recede.

"Wow," whispered one of the visitors.

"I hope it was a known star," said another.

"That would be most joyful!" exclaimed a third, before the four males lapsed into their native tongue.

In receding, the shape of the image revealed itself as circular. Twenty minutes later, when the light began to change into different colors of the spectrum, Copeland felt a charge of electricity run through his veins. He swallowed a few times and lowered himself into his chair.

Here was a mystery. How could it have grown so large in so short a time? How long had it been going on? How could something this massive have escaped notice? Normal supernovas might last for days, even months. Still . . . this extraordinary event had all the markings of a supernova, and if so, then it was far and away larger than anything ever before observed.

He and the others could only gape in amazement as the stellar explosion continued to diminish. Copeland anxiously checked the data recorders to make certain the event was on tape.

He took a few deep breaths before rising from his chair. He was utterly speechless. One could study the heavens for an entire lifetime and never witness an ordinary star committing suicide, let alone something like this. In a few minutes he would call up his other colleagues on the hill and together they would conduct a thorough analysis of the characteristics of the explosion.

First there was a matter of protocol.

Copeland left the room and returned a few minutes later with a bottle of champagne and six glasses. Most observatories kept a bottle on hand for special occasions. By now the rush had worn off, and he was grinning exuberantly.

He popped the cork while the Japanese astronomers continued to talk at each other in rapid-fire bursts. After pouring the champagne, he held up his glass and said, "I propose a toast. To Mari, may she have long life and witness many more supernovas."

Her teammates, though more than a little jealous, were fully caught up in the excitement and all chimed in, "To Mari," then touched their glasses together. The young woman was quite taken back by this and could think of nothing else to do but offer each man a deep bow of gratitude.

Copeland caught her by the shoulders before she could bow to him. As she looked up into his eyes, he noticed for the first time that Mari was quite beautiful. "None of that for me. By the way, notwithstanding the possibility that someone else may have witnessed the explosion, you also have the right to name the event."

The young woman would not hear of it. Her head lowered again, Mari said shyly, "It would do me great honor, Dr. Copeland, if you were to name it."

Then a strange thought crossed Copeland's mind. Just came at him from out of nowhere. He wondered what it would be like to be married to another astronomer, someone who could share his passion for the heavens. This, he realized as he noted her bare ring finger, was the stuff dreams were made of.

Dreams!

It came back to him then, not all of it, but bits and pieces of the wild one he'd had the previous night. He was astonished at how real it had been at the time, and just as surprised that the whole thing had slipped his mind until now.

He took both of Mari's hands in his, looked deep into her eyes, and spoke one word. "Omega."

Brooks reluctantly allowed himself to be led across Fifth Avenue and half a block down the street to a small Italian bakery.

As soon as they were seated, Mrs. Kelly leaned across the table and proceeded to tell him about her dream. In it she had died, right there in church, in fact; but instead of moving on, she turned into an angel.

Trapped, the editor of the *Village Review* decided to make the best of it and ordered two chocolate cinnamon doughnuts with his coffee.

But with the telling his interest soon picked up, and a full hour later he had to admit this was wild stuff: angels and astronomers, magical golf games, he and Rachael getting together again, and the big kicker—the world being blown up by a killer star!

It was laughable, and he would have laughed, except for one small item: Mrs. Kelly had described the inside of his house in minute detail, yet he knew for a fact that she'd never been inside it.

When he realized the old woman had stopped, Brooks asked, "That's where it ends—with all of us in church?"

Mrs. Kelly was tired out from all the effort. She nodded, then took a noisy sip of tea before going on. "I don't mind telling you when I woke up, me old ticker was racing so hard I was afraid she might pop a valve. Scared the living daylights out of me, it did."

"No wonder. What do you think it all means?"

The sun was now striking the two front windows with full force and illuminating not only the shelves of exquisite goodies, but several rows of plaster saints. The Virgin Mary in particular was present in all colors and sizes.

With blue eyes squinting into the sudden brightness, the little old lady scratched a mole on her chin as she moved her narrow shoulders up and down. "Don't have the slightest, Brooksie. I was hoping you'd be able to figure it out. And that's not all—on the way over here I was accosted by the same three young hooligans who've been at me before, you know, cleaning my purse out, pushing me around. But this morning they no sooner laid a hand on me when someone must have put the fear of God in them. Slimy little scumbags began to scream like a troop of banshees and took off like the devil himself was after them. Very strange it all was because after it was over I began to get the most wonderful sensation, like everything was going to be fine. Why, right now I feel the best I've felt in years."

With a small chuckle she added, "You don't suppose my angel guardian finally got mad at seeing those guys hassle me? Wouldn't that be something?"

Brooks gave his head a good shake, trying to loosen up a memory or two. Guardian angel . . . there was something, vague but powerful, that seemed to fit in with Mrs. Kelly's unusual dream.

He glanced at his watch, groaned, then laid some bills on the table. Back on the sidewalk, Brooks placed one huge arm around her shoulders and turned back toward St. Andrew's, where his car was parked.

"Well my love, it's a dandy all right, like something out of a science fiction story. Why don't you write it all down? Maybe I'll even print it in the *Review*, some of it anyway."

Mrs. Kelly heard her name being called, turned around, and spotted her dearest friend bearing down on them at a good trot. "There's Millie, so I'll be off. You figure it out, let me know. Bye, Brooksie. Have a nice day."

"You too," said Brooks. Then his cell phone went off. "Yeah?"

"Brooks?"

"Rachael—that you? What's wrong? You at the club?"

"No. I didn't see you all weekend, and this morning you were gone before I got up. Why did you leave so early?"

As if she cared. "I went to Mass."

"On Monday? I need to talk to you."

His wife never *needed* to talk to him. "You're sick, Rachael, you gotta be."

"I feel fine, physically anyhow. But . . . I had a disturbing dream last night, about—"

Oh no! "The end of the world."

After a sharp intake of breath, his wife asked, "How could you possibly know that?"

"An old lady just told me."

"Not Kathleen Kelly?"

"The very same."

"Brooks, this is downright scary. She played the most important part—she was the angel!"

By now Brooks had wandered back up to the intersection at 59th. He turned around and saw that Kathleen Kelly and Mildred Manuel had linked arms and were strolling up toward Sunset Park. He had the cell phone jammed to his ear, talking away, scrambling to make sense of what was taking place. Both women experiencing the same dream told Brooks something out of the ordinary was going on. Not only that, but he had the uneasy feeling that he had just been made privy to some dark secret, but could not figure out what it might be.

He did not realize the light had already changed to red when he stepped off the curb.

The BMW convertible was on him before he could even look up. The woman driver screamed, but she knew there wasn't a chance of missing him.

Then a hand more powerful than anything Brooks had encountered in his life snapped him out of harm's way at the last instant of time. The driver and the few people nearby did not see where the skinny black guy had come from. It was as if he had just materialized out of thin air.

Safely back on the curb, the black guy said to Brooks in a stern tone of voice, "See here, my man, you just about got that fat ass splattered all over the street. Now you give me 'dat there thing. They're dangerous, you know."

Before Brooks could think about resisting, the guy had his phone and was talking away to Rachael. "Hey, Momma, how you doin'?"

"Who is this? What happened to my husband?"

"Man damn near had a BMW up his be-hind."

"Oh no! Is he all right?"

"Sure enough, just a bit shook up. Man's gonna need a whole lot of TLC to help him get over it, know what I mean?"

"Please put my husband back on."

Brooks snatched the phone back in time to catch Rachael's last words. "I'll be home in ten minutes, honey. Don't go away."

The black guy was in his mid-thirties, a sniff under six feet, a regular beanpole. A wide Afro framed an unattractive face pitted so bad it looked like the aftermath of an artillery barrage. His clothing was no screaming hell: a pair of faded jeans and scruffy old runners, a soiled blue T-shirt that read: *Simon Peter's Offshore Fishery. You catch 'em, he'll clean 'em.* But his dark brown eyes glowed with warmth and intelligence.

Brooks put out his hand. "Thanks. I probably owe you my life."

"No probably about it, Brooksie."

Since no more than five people on the face of the planet addressed him this way, Brooks said to the guy, "I know you?"

"Yes and no, but I wouldn't worry about it. You're going to get to know me a lot better."

Brooks didn't like the sound of that one bit. He could sense a shakedown in the making.

"Hey, you saved my life, so I'm prepared to pay for it. How much you got in mind?"

The black guy grinned as wide as he could, then placed a hand on Brooks's left shoulder. "That one was on the house, Brother Hennessey. Next one might cost you."

"I didn't catch your name."

"Sarius."

Sarius . . . the name in the dream—the name of the angel! Brooks tried to remain calm. "That your first name or last?"

"You decide. Don't matter much to me."

All this time the guy was watching Brooks with a bemused expression. "You mind me asking what you do for a living? Besides hauling dumbbells like me off the street?"

"It so happens, Brooksie, that I'm your guardian angel." Seeing the wide-eyed look, Sarius added, "Yeah, it was a surprise to me, too. Anyway, it looks like I arrived just in the nick of time."

Brooks didn't know whether to laugh or cry. It had all the makings of a scam, and yet . . . He let out a tentative chuckle. "I got me a real live black man for a guardian angel. Unreal!"

"You got a problem with black? Maybe you prefer green . . . "

Meanwhile, in a special place not far away, the head of all the angels was shocked, but not surprised, at what was taking place. Metatron had predicted this would happen and now tried to envision what the third millennium would look like a hundred years from now. In his opinion, millions of free spirits roaming the world, without any discipline to speak of, in any form they might choose, seemed to defeat the purpose of assigning guardians in the first place. The whole idea baffled him.

Closer still, the Master of the Universe was carefully reviewing this very issue. Being able to alter time as He saw fit had allowed Michael to set into motion a set of circumstances, extreme though they were, for a junior angel to be tested by fire. The ordeal was successful. Now the entire heavenly host could be called upon to serve as guardians.

God had known for some time that the more subtle approach was no longer effective. Modernism always impeded communication, and while a whispered suggestion here or a stern warning there still worked for some, it did not work for many. He was fully aware that the direct approach would make for a far different world, but if Sarius's behavior was any indication, one of the major spinoffs would see a lot more people having a lot more fun.

God did not regret His decision. After all, perhaps it was time the human species lightened up.

RODNEY CHRISTIAN POWER grew up in Grand Falls, Newfoundland, joined the Canadian Corps of Engineers at an early age, and entered the military survey school in Ottawa. Upon returning to civilian life, he became a professional land surveyor and planner, establishing his practice in Vernon, British Columbia. Rod's overseas experiences as an international consultant occasionally took him to isolated parts of the world and into dangerous circumstances. The seeds for *Shadow of Light* were planted while sorting out a NYPD communications problem in Brooklyn.

NOTE TO MY READERS: What did you think of this story? Several readers have asked if I intend to write a sequel. Should I? If you wish to forward your opinion, you can contact me at *rod@rodpower.com*.